READY TO
Wed

READY TO
Wed

CINDI MADSEN

Entangled Publishing, LLC
2614 South Timberline Road
Suite 109
Fort Collins, CO 80525

Visit our website at www.entangledpublishing.com.

Edited by Stacy Abrams
Cover design by Libby Murphy

Print ISBN 978-1-62266-258-6
Ebook ISBN 978-1-62266-259-3

Manufactured in the United States of America

First Edition July 2014

10   9   8   7   6   5   4   3   2   1

To Stacy Abrams, for believing in that first book and all the ones that came after.

Prologue

What I hadn't taken into account when Grant suggested the whole cruise-wedding combo was that while I was standing here in my white wedding dress, veil fluttering in the breeze, bouquet of fake blue roses in my hands, waiting for him to get his slow butt off the ship, all the other cruise-goers would be staring at me as they disembarked. I was used to being behind the scenes at weddings, ordering people around, making sure the ceremony went flawlessly. The spotlight wasn't for me, especially when most of the onlookers were wearing floral-print casual wear and staring at me like I was an area attraction instead of an anxious bride.

My nerves were dancing all over the place and my stomach had relocated to my throat. I hadn't realized how serious and final it was going to seem, these last moments before the I dos. Not that I wasn't ready—I totally was. I loved Grant with my heart and soul, and I'd been waiting for this day my whole life. The day when I married the man of my dreams. Originally the setting hadn't been Jamaica, but now that I could see the white sandy beaches and peer into the clear blue water, it was so perfect that goose bumps broke out across my skin.

Our wedding is going to be so beautiful.

And as soon as the preacher performed the marriage, we'd start our honeymoon, complete with stops to the Cayman Islands and Cozumel, Mexico. The first two days on the ship had been nothing short of amazing, and I knew the rest of the trip—when we were finally married—would be even more so.

Still, I couldn't help but wish Jillian were here. When Grant and I first started discussing the wedding cruise as a possibility, I'd asked my best friend about coming with us—I wanted her to be my bridesmaid. She said that as much as she'd love to be with me on my special day, she thought it'd be awkward to be the third wheel on a seven-day cruise. I saw her point, but right now, I was thinking it couldn't be more awkward than standing here all alone in a wedding dress.

I tapped the bouquet against my palm. Blue wouldn't have been my original color choice, but I was multitasking. The flowers used to be a centerpiece in my apartment, so they were my something old *and* something blue. When your baggage is limited and your dress takes up an entire suitcase, you take shortcuts where you can.

I glanced at my watch again. "What's taking him so long?" I muttered to myself. The preacher was going to be waiting on us. The photographer should be with the preacher, too. It was a package deal I'd negotiated over the phone. Not meeting the people in real life beforehand made me a bit twitchy, but everyone I'd spoken to had been super friendly, and even better, their reviews were stellar. Everything was going to go smoothly—I'd triple-checked my triple checks.

And yet I could feel my blood pressure steadily climbing, anxiety seeping in. I was entering bride freak-out mode, the one I referred to as Code Fuchsia, because that's a shit's-about-to-get-real color. If I didn't get it together, everything would quickly spiral out of control. I closed my eyes and pictured myself opposite me, what I'd say to a bride in this situation.

It only took a moment to find it, something I'd told countless brides who were waiting for their grooms. I'd give them a reassuring smile and say, "You know how guys are. Throw a few extra buttons on a shirt and it becomes impossible to put on." And it was true. I'd seen guy after guy stare at a tux like it was the Rubik's Cube of clothing. Girls had to deal with strapless bras and corseted backs and buttons and ribbons and tiny eyelets that would make you go blind if you stared at them for too long. But hand a cummerbund and a bow tie to a guy and he just blinked at them, mouth hanging open.

I took a deep breath of ocean-scented air and held it in until my heart rate returned to normal, and I was more Tangerine than Fuchsia. And even though the disembarking passengers still made me want to yell, "Why don't you take a picture? It'll last longer!" it also made me realize just how many people there were. Of course it was taking Grant forever. It's not like he'd shove old people and kids out of the way to get to me.

Maybe I should've just let him dress in cargo shorts and flip-flops like he'd wanted. But I'd gone along with the let's-get-married-on-a-cruise idea—let go of all my old wedding plans and embraced the impulsivity. I still wanted the fancy white dress and to see Grant in a tux, though. I had a right to ask for those things, didn't I?

Of course I did, although suddenly not letting him see me in the dress until we were outside seemed silly. Stupid tradition. It wasn't like it'd even count, because he'd still see me before the ceremony. I'd simply wanted it to be out in the sunshine, where the light would catch the intricate beading of the bodice, instead of a tiny, dark cabin where moving meant whacking a knee or elbow on something.

I shifted my weight from my right foot to my left, and the heel of my rhinestone-and-pearl-encrusted pump sank in the ground, most likely getting coated in dirt.

It'll all be okay once he gets here. Then these silly little details won't matter. In fact, they'd be a great story to tell our friends and family, and our future kids when they asked about our wedding day.

For fifteen minutes I did a pretty good job of convincing myself everything was awesome. Totally on track. Not a big deal in the grand scheme of things. I didn't let the doubtful voice in the back of my head take over.

But then the rush of people coming off the ship slowed to a trickle, only the occasional couple or family here and there.

My breaths came faster and faster, my entire body started shaking, and the world around me blurred. "He changed his mind," I whispered. "He doesn't want to marry me." As quietly as the words came out, they smothered the air around me and echoed in my head. *He doesn't want me.*

This wasn't happening.

Couldn't be happening.

I fought the urge to fall to the ground in my dress and cry. I told myself that there was still time. No reason to freak out. Grant loved me. He wouldn't do this to me.

I decided that I'd give him five more minutes.

Five more minutes until we had a very awkward boat ride home.

Part One

FANATIC FUCHSIA - SEVERE
(SEVERE RISK OF MELTDOWN, CRYING JAGS, AND/OR BRIDEZILLA-LIKE BEHAVIOR)

"Men are like puppies...you will get attached, bring them home, and they will shit all over everything you love."

—UNKNOWN

Chapter One

The swirly red letters on the front door of my office seemed to taunt me this morning. READY TO WED, they proclaimed—there were even matching vinyl hearts on either side. I wanted to punch through the glass, watch the words and hearts shatter to the ground. I might even welcome the pain that the shards would be sure to bring to my knuckles, simply to have something to detract from the hollow ache that had settled over my heart.

Maybe this was a bad idea.

I had to face my office sometime, though, and with a client coming in first thing tomorrow morning, that only left today to do it without an audience. I didn't want to end up crying at the sight of wedding paraphernalia during the consult. Brides had dibs on breakdowns in this office, and as I'd gotten to relive every day for the past two weeks, I definitely wasn't a bride.

I shoved my way inside, frowning at the cheery room that was so covered in depictions of romance that even Venus, goddess of love herself, would probably say, "Whoa, girl. Maybe it's time to stop hitting the ambrosia so hard." Simply being in my office used to make me feel enamored, but right now it was rubbing salt in an open wound.

I took a generous sip of my coffee, hoping more caffeine would help, walked over to my desk, and dropped the giant stack of mail on top. There were a lot of envelopes in varying shades of white, cream, and pink, no doubt family and friends sending their matrimonial well wishes.

I tore one open and slid out the contents. There was a gift card to Bed Bath & Beyond inside. The next one had a hundred-dollar bill, and the one after that, a donation made in Grant's and my name to save a seal. I was going to have to find a way to send it all back—well, not the save-a-seal gift. They'd have to bite the bullet on that one, because I wasn't going to un-help the seals. But the rest would need to be returned. Did they make a *thanks for the thought, but I'm still single* card?

Even worse, I knew this was only the tip of the congrats iceberg. Most of Grant's and my family and friends would've sent cards and gifts to the house, and they'd all need to be dealt with, too. My lungs felt like they were collapsing in on themselves. I shoved aside the rest of the cards, too depressed to deal right now. The *Las Vegas Beacon* was at the bottom of the stack. Because I'm obviously a masochist, I opened up to my column.

My wedding advice column, Get Ready to Wed, now made me feel like a bigger fraud than the six-foot-five drag queen who played Mariah Carey down at the Strat. Don't get me wrong, the guy could sing—even hit those glass-shattering high-pitched notes—but he was no Mariah.

I used to be the real deal. The wedding planner who made it all happen, regardless of the snags involved in pulling off a perfect wedding. When people used to ask me how I did it, I threw out terms like "attention to detail," "perfectionist," and all of those nicer-sounding descriptions, but I'm not afraid to admit it anymore. It's because I'm a control freak. I like making charts and lists and checking off one item at a time. When it's Go Time and everything falls into place exactly like I planned—because I've ensured it will— satisfaction pumps through my veins. I even like the challenge of a last-minute problem. Plus, making a couple's wedding dreams come true makes me feel like their fairy godmother—except I'm much younger and better dressed than your typical fairy godmother.

Vegas is synonymous with weddings, and believe it or not, some people who live here don't want to get married in any of the little chapels of right here and now. I'd made a name for myself by pulling off extravagant weddings without a hitch—at least the clients didn't know about all the hitches I frantically fixed behind the scenes. Which was how I'd landed an advice column in the local paper.

For my last one, I'd decided to go unconventional. I wanted to announce to the world—or the greater Las Vegas area, anyway— that I was about to marry the man I loved. Since we'd decided on a low-key wedding on a cruise ship, this was my way for everyone to share in the tingly awesomeness of an in-love couple tying the knot. I stared at the article now, and it definitely wasn't giving me any kind of tingly feelings.

In fact, I was relatively sure I might puke.

GET READY TO WED by Dakota Halifax
I'm Getting Married

The time has finally come for my very own wedding! My fiancé and I are going a little unconventional, which I know I sometimes frown upon (eighties-themed weddings—just say no). But to each their own, I guess. I'm going to go ahead and advise you to do whatever makes you happy. Not your mom, your sister, or your mother-in-law-to-be, but *you*. I suppose you might also want to consider your significant other's feelings as well. I've heard that grooms now have a say in weddings—when the hell did that happen? (Don't worry, in a future column I'll teach you how to talk them out of that misguided *Star Wars* theme they want.)

But back to my wedding, because this time, *I get to be the bride!* The decision to get married on a beach in Jamaica was rather unplanned and out of character for me, but as soon as my fiancé suggested it, I knew it'd be perfect for us. As someone whose life revolves around planning weddings, it's nice not to have to coordinate my own. Spontaneity can add an element of excitement, but to ensure it doesn't turn into a source of stress and ruin the fun, there are some things to remember. You're going to need a license, rings, and two people to witness your nuptials. There's no reason you can't throw in a bit of tradition, finding something borrowed, something new, and something blue. Be creative! It'll only add to the memories. Coordinate with people wherever you're going, be it a hotel, a church, or a Vegas chapel. Double-check credentials, too, especially if you're going to wed out of the country. Then you can relax and enjoy the lead-up to the nuptials, whether it's a couple hours, days, or weeks.

Special thanks to all the brides who've hired me to help them out on their special day. I now feel better prepared for anything that might come my way. But most importantly, I feel so lucky to have found a great guy. I can't wait to become Mrs. Grant Douglas! As for the rest of you, I'll be back to get you ready to wed in a few weeks.

Tears blurred my eyes as I read the last few lines. You'd think I'd be all cried out. I laid my head on the paper, let my hair fall over my eyes like a dark brown curtain that'd hopefully block out the day, and felt the wetness slide down my cheek. How was I supposed to come in tomorrow and act excited as I planned the next bride's wedding? How was I supposed to write wedding advice columns when I couldn't even pull off my own?

I'm a fraud. Although my checklist *had been* perfect. All those things I said a bride needed in that article were accounted for. I'd done everything I could to make sure the wedding went off without a hitch. As I'd so painfully learned, though, preparedness—or even experience—doesn't mean anything if the other person doesn't show up.

I heard the door open and slowly peeled myself off the paper. I thought maybe it was someone from UPS or FedEx, but the guy wasn't wearing a uniform or holding any packages. I didn't get many walk-ins. Especially not dude walk-ins. Several got dragged in eventually, but none had ever come in without his bride-to-be.

I so wasn't ready to be in open-for-business mode, but I sucked it up and offered the best smile I could. "Hi. How can I help you?"

He ducked his head to avoid the hanging light fixture as he stepped closer, which had me guessing he was at least a couple inches past the six-foot range. "D.J.?"

Wow. Right to the point. "Sure, I can help you find a DJ. I'll just need some information about what kind of music you want, where the event is going to be, and when it is." I gestured to the chair across from me. "If you have a seat, we can get started."

He tilted his head and studied me like I was an art exhibit instead of a person, two creases forming between his eyebrows. I couldn't help but notice how good-looking he was, with messy dark blond hair that was longer on top than the sides, a strong nose that a girl could never pull off but suited him, and cheekbones usually found on male models.

I bet he's getting married to a modelesque bride he won't stand up at the altar. I hate her already.

"You're not D.J.? I heard she owns this place, and you looked like you could be…"

No one had called me D.J. in years—not since high school. There was something familiar about this guy, like I'd seen his features before but not the exact way they were arranged.

"I'm D.J.—I usually go by Dakota these days—and this is my company. And you look very familiar, but I'm sorry, I can't place you."

He grinned, and something about it stirred memories that my mind couldn't quite catch hold of. "It's Brendan."

"Brendan West?" I stood, looking him over in a new light, seeing a hint of the boy I used to know. "No. Way."

His grin widened. "Yes way."

"No freakin' way!" I rounded my desk and hugged him, then felt a little awkward. Maybe a hug was too much? After all, it'd been about fifteen years.

But then he hugged me back, so tightly my feet left the ground. "I was almost sure it was you, even though"—he pulled away a few inches and peered at my face again—"you look so different. But the same."

"I know exactly what you mean." The thirteen-year-old boy I'd known hadn't had all the height, muscles, or a five o'clock shadow on his chin.

He wiped a finger across my cheekbone, which made me freeze in place, not sure how to respond to that oddly intimate gesture. Then he held it up, a dark smudge now on his fingertip. "At first I thought you had a black eye, which wouldn't have surprised me all that much, since I remember how rough you were when it came to sports."

A black eye? I leaned back so I could see in the mirror hanging on the wall. There was a fabulous mixture of tear-streaked mascara and newsprint across my cheekbone. I wiped at it, but it just smeared more. "Hazards of taking a nap on a newspaper." And crying, but I wasn't going to mention that. "So, what are you doing in Vegas? Don't tell me you're getting married."

"No," he said in a way that made it seem like marriage would never cross his mind. "I moved back about a month ago, actually. My mom got in touch with your dad, and once I found out you were still here, I knew I had to look you up and see what became of the girl who used to be my best friend."

I wished he'd chosen a different day, because I felt like a total mess. Not just felt like—I had black ink smudged on my face. I rubbed at it again. Before I could say anything, the office phone rang.

"Excuse me for just a minute," I said, then answered the phone.

"Dakota," Grant said, his voice stabbing me in my already-raw heart.

I gritted my teeth against the pain and the anger welling up in me. "How dare you call here."

"You won't answer on your cell, though, and we have to talk sometime. If you'll just—"

"Don't call here again, you hear me?" I slammed the phone down, holding it there as if that'd stop him from ever dialing me back.

Brendan raised an eyebrow, and I rubbed my fingers across my forehead. I knew Grant and I would have to talk eventually. I still needed to move the majority of my stuff out of his place, after all. But I wasn't ready, and I needed to find a storage unit and—

"Is someone bothering you?" I was surprised at the concern in Brendan's voice, and there was a bit of a protective vibe, too, if I wasn't mistaken. He and I had been glued to each other's sides from ages seven to thirteen, but that was a long time ago, and I didn't want to drag him into my drama now.

I flopped into my chair. "It's nothing I can't handle."

Brendan sat on the edge of my desk, facing me, and I couldn't get over how…big he was. So tall and filled-out and oozing confidence—not that he'd ever been short on that. "Look, security's my thing. I work at the new Aces Resort and Casino. I get to take people down all the time. It's kind of like I never finished playing Fugitive, only now I have much cooler high-tech gadgets."

Despite my bad mood, I couldn't help but smile. Fugitive. The game we used to play where there were two teams, the fugitives and the cops. It involved hiding and chasing, and sometimes—if you were lucky—tackling. When I was a kid, there was nothing like that adrenaline rush of taking someone down. Or getting away when someone tried to take me down. Brendan and I were always on the same team, and whether we were fugitives or cops, we always won. We were also always covered in dirt and scratches by the end of it, too, which was half the fun.

"You need cool gadgets to tackle people now?"

A boyish grin spread across his face. "Not need. Just like. Plus, I've got more so-called fugitives to watch out for." He nudged me. "So, do you need to talk to the police? What about a restraining order?"

I waved off his words. "It's nothing like that. It's just my ex, and it's complicated."

Brendan frowned. "Complicated."

I leaned back in my chair and sighed. "I take it you don't read my column in the paper?"

"You're a writer, too?"

"Not really. It's just a tiny column with wedding tips. My last one was different from the norm because... Well, you see..." My mouth went dry and my lungs didn't seem to be taking in air anymore. "I was supposed to get married a couple of weeks ago."

"Supposed to?"

Heat filled my cheeks, and it was too humiliating to say while he was staring at me like that. So I dropped my head in my hands. "He stood me up. At the altar. Only the altar was a beach in Jamaica, and we were on a cruise ship, which was basically like being held captive after that, and I'm just not ready to talk to him. So no restraining order required. Just...space, I guess."

"Sorry, D.J.," Brendan said. "I didn't know. If there's anything I can do..."

I pushed my hands through my hair. The fact was, it was time to go see Grant and figure out a more permanent living situation than crashing on Jillian's couch. Not to mention my dog was still at his house—yet another complication that made me angry and sad and too many emotions to pick one from the next.

"I'd love to catch up sometime," I said. "Next week I'll have this mess sorted out better, but honestly, I've got a lot going on right now." Like fighting the impulse to burst into tears again, which pissed me off. I'd never been much of a crier, and it was like all the years of holding back I'd done were gushing out of me now. Grant so didn't deserve to have so many tears shed over him.

Brendan nodded, pulled out a business card, and gave it to me. "Come by the casino or give me a call." He walked to the door, but turned around instead of pushing out of it. "I know you throw a killer right hook…" He rubbed his jaw as if he could still feel its effect, and then flashed me a smile. "But if you decide you need someone, you know where to find me."

"And if you decide you need my help at the casino, I could use an excuse to get rowdy. You'd be surprised how few weddings give me the chance to use my hook."

He laughed, and I waved good-bye. Joking with him left me cheered enough to fight back the tears. Funny enough, the last time I'd cried so much was probably when he'd moved away. Losing my best friend in junior high had seemed like the end of the world, and it'd taken a long time for his absence to stop sucking.

Technically, Brendan was my first fiancé. I smiled at that, thinking of all our plans when we were young, which were usually more about where we were riding our bikes, whose house we'd eat dinner at, or which sport to play. I wondered if I'd see him often now that he was back in Vegas, or if we'd try to hang out and it'd be weird. Then again, he was already trying to take care of me, something I'd always told him he didn't need to do, though that never stopped him.

But before I could even think about rekindling my friendship with Brendan, I needed to deal with the guy who'd broken my heart into a thousand little pieces.

Chapter Two

I pushed my way into Jillian's and sighed when it was clear she wasn't home yet. She was good at keeping my mind off the current mess that was my life, whether we were talking about the changes she was implementing in her catering business or just chilling watching movies. Without her there to distract me, I also noticed that my stuff was everywhere. There was the blanket-and-pillow stack off to the side of the couch for when it became my bed at night, and the two suitcases I'd taken on the cruise were crammed into one corner. I'd had to borrow an outfit for work today, and on the way home I'd bought a new one for tomorrow. Originally I thought I might try to face Grant tonight, but then I'd gotten an email about a sale at one of my favorite stores, and I'd needed new slacks anyway.

Okay, so I was delaying the inevitable. Putting off things wasn't my usual style, but this wasn't a to-do list item that could be easily crossed off with one of my bright-colored gel pens. It was my ex-fiancé and my life that was supposed to be.

Admittedly, it was getting to the ridiculous point. A suitcase filled with a barely worn wedding dress and another with shorts, tank tops, flip-flops, and bikinis wasn't quite meeting my needs anymore. I missed my clothes, and especially my shoe collection. Not to mention I was usually neat to the point of OCD-ness, and the lack of places to put my meager belongings and the fact that I might be driving Jillian insane with my mess dug at me. I needed to find a better solution, and soon.

Dad's place would be a hell of a commute, not to mention moving back in with him felt like a total fail on top of my other fails, and I wasn't sure I could do it. I also wasn't sure I'd have a choice before long. I headed to the kitchen and pulled the carton of rocky road ice cream out of the fridge. It'd always been my favorite flavor, but I'd never quite gotten the name before. Now I knew that when the road got rocky, it was always there for you. Of course it wasn't so nice in the added-poundage aspect.

Note to self: Start going to the gym again. Maybe join a volleyball or softball league. Something to keep me motivated.

I grabbed a spoon and headed to the couch, kicking aside the pair of shoes I'd left next to the coffee table yesterday. Apparently the lid to my ice cream hadn't completely sealed, and now the chocolaty goodness had a layer of ice crystals and was rock solid. I stabbed at it, trying to chip off a bite.

"Come"—another stab—"on." Were a couple bites of ice cream really so much to ask on a day like today? So much for it being there for me.

My phone rang, and I groaned when I saw it was my mom. I licked off the minuscule amount of ice cream that'd gotten onto my spoon and then answered.

"How are you doing?" she asked. I'd give her credit, she had the sympathetic tone down, but I didn't quite trust it. After all, last time we'd spoken she asked why I was even bothering to get married. Conversations with her were always tricky as it was, and I hadn't had the energy to attempt one since I'd texted to let her know the wedding hadn't happened.

I hugged the ice cream carton to me, hoping a tighter grip would help me dig a bite loose. "I've been better, but I'm hanging in there."

"I can only imagine, knowing how much you wrapped your entire life up in that guy. I said you needed to be careful. That a wedding wasn't a guarantee." Here went the I Told You So speech. The divorce from Dad had left her with the opinion that marriage was something best avoided, and she liked to remind me of her stance on a regular basis. Not seeing eye to eye with Mom was nothing new, though. What little time we did spend together during my childhood, she'd filled with encouraging me to act more ladylike, and when I'd gone into wedding planning—which I thought was pretty freaking ladylike—she'd asked why I didn't want to put my brains to better use. Still, she was my mom, and it was nice of her to check on me, even if her words often came out barbed.

"I loved him. I wasn't just marrying him for the fairy-tale wedding, you know."

"That was pretty obvious when you chose to do it during a cruise," Mom said. See? Definitely had a problem with saying things the nice way. Up until five years ago, we hadn't really had a relationship—I felt she'd worked hard to forget about me, so I tried to do the same. But when she'd come to me saying she regretted that we didn't know each other better, I'd decided I'd deal with some of the verbal jabs so we could be in each other's lives. How exactly I felt about that decision depended on the day. "You could come visit. Get away for a while."

Mom and her current boyfriend, Frank, lived on the outskirts of L.A. and were in the middle of a remodel project on the house they'd recently bought. For the first time in her life, she was setting down roots, which meant she actually cared about Frank—not that she'd admit it.

"I've got nonstop jobs lined up right now," I said. "And I need to find an apartment on top of everything else, so now's not really a good time."

Mom sighed. "Well, I offered earlier, when you did have time off, but you didn't return my calls. I hope you're not just sitting around alone, moping and eating chocolate."

I stared into my ice cream, which was not softening at all and starting to freeze my arms, so cold it burned. "Of course not." *Because I can't get the chocolate out, damn it!*

"Trust me, the best thing to do is move on and forget the past."

Her words caused pricks of pain in my chest, duller than they used to be thanks to years of telling myself that it didn't matter that she'd chosen to leave me behind for her career. Dad had done a good job of stepping up, even if my younger years were mostly a blur of high school football games, either the ones he coached or the games we'd travel to so we could scout out another team. And whenever it was Mom's turn to spend a week with me, I'd fly to whichever city she was in at the time and try to settle into a temporary place.

I wanted to say that not all of us could leave people behind without a care, but it would only cause a fight, one I always lost, so I simply said, "Thanks for checking in on me, Mom. I've got an appointment, though, so I'd better go."

She filled me in on a few remodeling details first, but eventually I managed to get off the phone. My appointment was with trashy TV, the kind that made me feel like I had my life together. Only I couldn't stop thinking of how, after a taxing conversation with my mother, Grant used to be there to wrap his arms around me and say, "Call my mom. She thinks you're amazing. In fact, I think she likes you more than me."

It wasn't true, but I'd been surprised at how well I got along with his mom. Evelyn was the motherly figure I told myself I didn't need, since I was already grown, but liked having around anyway.

I'd felt like part of his family after just a few months of our being together, and after we'd gotten engaged, Grant and I had even discussed having kids of our own someday. How'd they look, how we'd raise them. Our own little family, settled in one place. It was all I'd ever wanted, and then it was just gone, no warning. And now I was sitting alone, with not even my dog curled up next to me like he should be, begging for treats since I had mine.

"Ugh!" I jammed the spoon into the ice cream so hard that I actually made an inch of progress. But when I tried to scoop, the handle of the spoon wouldn't budge, so not real progress. Kind of like what I'd accomplished since being stood up at the altar. I'd basically put my entire life on pause, but two full weeks of feeling sorry for myself was enough. Time to type up a game plan and do what I did best—take control of the situation. In fact, I was getting kind of excited thinking about entering it into my task list and highlighting the sections in different colors. One color for fitness goals, another for my housing situation—one that'd allow my dog to live with me—and eventually, one for a new dating plan. That last goal would be long-term, of course. I wasn't in a hurry to jump into another relationship. My heart was obviously a crappy judge of character. And just so I wouldn't fail, I would even schedule in a couple of nights a month when I could watch sappy movies and allow myself to be a bit sad that my wedding hadn't happened.

Yeah. I've totally got this.

But first things first; this ice cream was going down. I took it into the kitchen and dug around in a few drawers, looking for something to cut through the impenetrable arctic-frost layer.

"Ooh," I said, pulling out a flambé thingy I'd seen Jillian use for a wedding that'd involved crème brûlée. I'd just fired it up, the flame blowing nice and hot, when Jillian walked in.

"Put the culinary torch down and no one gets hurt," she said.

"My ice cream's frozen."

Jillian dropped her purse on the table and walked into the

kitchen. Her curly dark hair was spilling out of the bun she kept it in when she was cooking, a breadth away from falling out completely, which meant it'd been a long, nonstop day. "That'll turn it into soup."

"Good, then I can forget about the stupid spoon and just drink it."

Jillian pursed her lips and held out her hand.

I slowly handed over the torch. "I know this looks sad, but it's okay. I realize I've reached the allotted amount of being heartbroken time, so tonight's the last night I'm allowed to be pathetic. I'm going to create a supercool work sheet, and I'll be back to normal in no time."

Jillian tossed her torch back in the drawer and closed it with her hip. "You can't plan how long it takes to heal from a heartbreak."

"You know I'm goal oriented. If I write it down, I'll make it happen, no matter what it takes."

"You need closure, babe. That's what it's going to take to even *start* the healing." Jillian took the ice cream carton to the sink, plugged the drain, and ran hot water into it until it was just to the brim. I probably should've thought of that, but the flame seemed faster and more destructive. Lately, that was more my style—yet another thing I needed to work on. "You're going to have to face him sometime. Get some answers, say your official good-bye, and hear why he stood you up, even if it ends up being total shit."

Jillian didn't believe in sugarcoating things. She told it like it was and got things done, which was why when she catered the weddings I planned, everything went that much better. But it also meant she wasn't the girl to go to if you were looking to hear what you wanted to hear.

My shoulders fell. "You're right. I know I need to see him and talk out a few things. But I've got to go into work tomorrow and act excited about planning a wedding."

Jillian wrinkled her nose. She'd never been much of a wedding fan—her claim was that they were good for business, bad for individuals. Silly me, I'd defended the idea of happily ever after. She pulled the carton of ice cream out of the sink and handed me a fresh spoon. The edges were soft at least, but after only one bite, it wasn't what I wanted anymore. I held it out to her and she waved it away. "No nuts, remember?"

"Right." I slid the ice cream out into the sink and tossed the carton in the recycling bin. "I think that'll be my new motto for guys."

Jillian laughed. I watched the ice cream slide down the drain, sure I'd regret dumping it later, but at least I was getting to work on my goals. I braced my hand on the counter. "Tell me I'll get through it. That it'll stop hurting eventually."

Jillian wrapped an arm around my shoulders. "You'll get through it. One day, you'll realize that you haven't thought about him in weeks, and then you'll be ready to find someone else. Someone better. You know I wouldn't say it if it weren't true."

I flashed her a smile and leaned into her. The sorrow was still there, hanging heavy, all my dreams popped and pressing against my chest. But I felt better than I had when I first walked into the apartment, and I realized, if nothing else, I had one of the best friends ever.

With my *I love weddings* attitude replaced with a *weddings blow* one, and the fact that I was about to take on the busiest wedding season I'd ever done, there was no doubt I was going to need her.

Chapter Three

"**W**eddings are awesome, weddings are awesome, weddings are awesome," I said as I paced my love-paraphernalia-filled office, waiting for my morning appointment. Binders filled with invitation choices and pictures of complicated cakes that'd take your breath away and send you into a sugar coma were stacked on my desk.

I picked up a black Sharpie, contemplating drawing mustaches on all of the framed blushing brides. The one beaming across the room at me deserved a few blackened teeth at least.

I tossed the marker away before I gave in to temptation and focused on a blank white spot on the office wall. "Love is beautiful. Not a load of crap that just leaves you heartbroken and rethinking your entire life. Nope, not at all." I thought after last night's talk with Jillian and taking the time to type up my goals before going to sleep, I'd feel better. Be ready for this. But now that I was faced with planning a huge ceremony for someone else, I started thinking of all the times I'd assured brides about their weddings. One of my most-used lines was, "I've done this long enough to recognize love when I see it, and I've seen the way he looks at you."

Did Grant ever look at me that way? Like he'd do anything to make me happy? I'd seen guys sit through tedious discussions on cakes, place settings, flowers, and decorations. Once, when we arrived at a venue and found the swans were missing, I'd even sent a groom sixty miles north to pick up a few. And he'd done it, because it was what his bride wanted. My groom hadn't even walked off a ship to explain he wasn't ready to marry me. The entire time we were trapped on that stupid boat, he'd stayed away from the room as much as possible, slipping in late and leaving early in the morning. At the time I'd been glad, but why did he keep calling me now, asking to let him explain instead of having just spit it out then?

Sure, when he had started with the excuses, I'd picked up the ice bucket and told him I didn't want to hear it or I'd launch the metal thing at his head. Still felt a bit bad about that, but really, he was lucky I didn't follow through—my aim is pretty good, and that bucket weighed a ton. Maybe I'd been blind from the start, though, unable to see what was missing when my groom-not-to-be looked at me. Because the life I'd always dreamed of was finally within my grasp, and I wanted it so badly I hadn't paid close enough attention to the most important thing. If my fiancé even loved me back.

The bell over the door chimed and I plastered a smile on my face. "Willa, hi!"

"Omigosh, I'm so glad you're back! I've been freaking out, worried every place will be all booked up."

Apparently fake smiles hurt more than real ones, because my cheeks were already burning. Or maybe my smile was out of shape from lack of use. "No need to freak out. Everything's on track."

Willa took the seat across from me. "And how was your wedding? Was it amazing? Should I forget this whole big ceremony and hop on a boat, too?"

My stomach took a nosedive. I'd assumed everyone would instinctually know I hadn't gotten married. I mean, the reception that was supposed to happen two days after our return had been canceled, which left me in the doghouse with several of my vendors, especially since they'd all helped throw together the party with very little prep time. So more fun times ahead for me. But Willa wasn't close enough to me to be invited—we'd barely started planning her wedding.

I picked up the Sharpie I'd tossed away earlier and rolled it between my fingers. "I, uh, didn't end up getting married."

Willa's face dropped. The only thing worse than feeling sorry for myself was having other people pity me.

"But the cruise was amazing! I mean, it was slightly hampered by the fact that I was trapped in a tiny room with a guy I wanted to toss overboard…"

Now my client's eyes bulged and her eyebrows arched so high they disappeared under her fringe bangs.

"Kidding, of course. I mean, things were awkward, but we're adults who still care about each other." Now that was laying it on a bit thick, but I couldn't seem to stop rambling, trying to make her see I was totally fine, no pity needed. "Jamaica's totally beautiful, too." *As long as you're not sitting on your butt in a wedding dress crying, and even then, the scenery is at least pretty.* "And you can get ice cream day or night on the ship, and same with pizza, so, score."

The more I explained, the more concerned Willa appeared. But if she wanted to go for a cruise wedding…well, I'd say hell no, don't do it. There was just too much that could go wrong.

"Anyway, for *your* wedding, I've narrowed it down to three locations." I twisted my large computer monitor toward her so she could see the pictures. She was from Alabama and wanted a big Southern wedding on "a plantation-type place," complete with big hats, parasols, and a never-ending supply of sweet tea.

Unfortunately, she wasn't dissuaded from the subject of my failed wedding as easily as I'd hoped. She grabbed one of my hands in both of hers, a poor-you expression written all over her features. "Oh, honey, that guy was obviously not the right one for you. You'll find your prince, don't you worry."

I'd never been great at faking optimism, so I charged on with the planning—at least that was a subject I knew I could handle, even if my follow-through sucked. "So, there's Splendor on the Green," I said, expanding the photos that showed other ceremonies that'd happened there. "And then there's a ranch out on the edge of town, and a country club that'd work. There aren't really plantations around Vegas, but these places have the lush green backgrounds and trees."

Willa leaned in close, tapping a French-manicured nail to her lips as she studied the options. "I don't know. I'd really like to see them in person."

I'd only met her once before, but I'd suspected Willa would be an In Person type. "Well, I made arrangements to see them today if we need to."

"Perfect!" She shot out of her seat.

At least she was enthusiastic enough for both of us. "We'll head there in a bit, but I thought you might want to look at save-the-date cards and invitations first." I handed her the binder, opening up to the section I thought she'd like.

I couldn't fault Willa for wanting to check out all of her options. It'd made me nervous not seeing beforehand where my ceremony was supposed to be performed. Even though I'd never made it to that spot on the beach, I'd sent a check for their troubles. The deposits I'd made for the food and the reception hall were nonrefundable, and I'd also paid my vendors for things they couldn't get rid of, like the flowers for the reception and the giant cake that was already halfway made before I could tell them to cancel the order. So my bank account looked like I'd gotten married and had a big party, even though it didn't happen.

Stop thinking about it. That was going to be my biggest challenge, the constant reminders of a wedding that never happened as I planned ceremonies for other couples. I simply needed to focus on my clients and their details. Not mine.

"This one! It's so perfect for us!" Willa lifted the book, pointing to the same embossed silver hearts invitation Grant and I had used for our reception. Cold filled my chest as I stared at it, remembering all that time I'd spent addressing and stuffing the matching envelopes, carefully tucking the silver ribbon inside so the bow wouldn't get smooshed. The excitement I'd felt that it was all going so smoothly, and how close I was to my happily ever after.

"Those are…" I forced the corners of my mouth into another fake smile. "Lovely." So lovely I'd known they were what I wanted for my wedding someday, even before Grant was in the picture. "And I'm here to help with the addressing and that kind of thing if you need it."

Challenge was an understatement. Clearly, not thinking about my failed nuptials was going to be the Everest of goals.

It was weird to pull up to a place that used to give me such comfort and happiness and feel nothing but apprehension and nausea. I hadn't lived at Grant's long—I was going to wait until after the wedding at first, but then it'd seemed wasteful to keep paying for my apartment when I was never there. So I'd hauled over all my earthly possessions a couple of months ago and settled in. Because silly me, when he asked me to marry him, I thought he'd meant it.

Just like I thought I was ready to see him again. I'd made it through today, and it seemed like a good idea to charge on to the next to-do list item. But now I fought the urge to reverse out of the driveway and flee to Jillian's.

She'd only tell me to suck it up and go back anyway.

Unless she's not home… I eyed my phone and then picked it up and opened my productivity app, where I'd input all my goals and to-do lists. Two items remained for today.

Get clothes from Grant's, and closure from him.

Gym.

I'd rather hit the gym first, but then I'd be sweaty for this confrontation, not to mention my workout clothes were here. *Maybe getting closure is a little ambitious for one afternoon, though.*

I edited it to say "and start to get closure," then inhaled a deep breath. Now that I was feeling in control, my goals right there in front of me, I was ready to deal.

Anyway, I thought so, but then I got to the front door. I had a key, but it wasn't my house, and Grant and I were over. Then again, ringing the doorbell seemed odd when most everything I owned was inside. A bark made the decision for me. I unlocked the door and dropped to my knees as Cupid bounded for me. I threw my arms around his neck and pressed my face into his soft black hair.

"Hey, boy! I missed you so much!"

Cupid licked my cheek, which I took to mean he missed me, too. Ironically enough, he was the reason I'd met Grant in the first place. I'd just gotten the little Labrador retriever and was still trying out a few monikers when I'd taken him to the park to get some exercise. A group of cute guys were tossing around a Frisbee nearby, and my little puppy, doing what he was meant to do, chased after the yellow disk. He tried to get it in his mouth, but it was big compared to him, and he was having trouble carrying it. Grant smiled down at him, then squatted and patted his head.

I was pretty much a goner at that moment, between the killer dimpled smile and the fact that he was being nice to my dog.

Then my puppy lifted his leg and peed on the guy's shoe. I turned three shades of red and apologized profusely, but Grant took it all in stride, and by some miracle, asked if he could call me some-time. If that's not a meant-to-be love story, I don't know what is.

So I'd called my little doggie Cupid that night, and the name stuck. He was much better trained now, too. When he wanted to be, and with the right motivation, anyway. But he was just one more part of my life that was wound so tightly with Grant's that it was hard to separate who I even was without him.

"Dakota?" Grant came from the back of the house, and I remained crouched by my dog, despite the burning in my thighs. It felt safer. And honestly, I was tempted to ask Cupid to pee on him again. "I was starting to think you'd never talk to me."

"I'm here for some of my things. And as soon as I find a place that takes dogs, I'll be back for Cupid." I risked a glance at Grant's face—the one I'd fallen in love with all those months ago but which caused my chest to constrict now. "You can take care of him for me until I find one, right?"

"As long as you need me to," Grant said softly. His naturally wavy dark hair was slightly longer than normal, and he hadn't shaved in a while—he must not have gone in to work yet. As usual, he wore a fitted polo shirt. When he'd picked me up for our first date, I'd thought he might be too preppy for me. I'd grown to love that about him, though, how he always dressed nice and acted like a proper gentleman. So opposite of most of my former boyfriends.

I stood before my thighs decided to lock in place. I couldn't get over how weird it was to see Grant now that everything had changed. I'd expected to feel more anger and less heart-tugging.

"How many times do you need me to say I'm sorry?" he asked with a sigh, as if the question exhausted him.

That extinguished the heart-tugging. I clenched my fists at my sides. "You jilted me at the altar, Grant. You left me standing in a wedding dress on a foreign shore while everyone stared at the poor lonely bride. Then the first thing I had to do when I got home was cancel the reception, which was extra awkward considering I'd used all the vendors I usually work with. Sorry doesn't quite cut it."

When I'd finally found him the night we were supposed to get married, he'd told me that he just wasn't ready. There was a pathetic "sorry" thrown in, too, but I'd been too utterly crushed to really process any of it. "You didn't even explain. Didn't tell me why."

"I tried, but you threatened to throw an ice bucket at my head."

Oh. Right. That was when the She-Hulk had taken over my body and red was all I could see. But now everything ached, inside and out, from my muscles to my heart, and I needed to get the answer and move on with my life. "Then tell me now. What happened? And if you didn't want to marry me, why did you propose in the first place?"

"I did want to marry you." He reached his hand toward my shoulder and I took a large step back, bumping against the door. Cupid moved in front of me, creating a barrier, though he seemed confused as to what was happening. His black muzzle moved back and forth from me to Grant. "It was just all happening so fast, and I needed more time."

I jabbed a finger at him. "*You're* the one who suggested the cruise. You said the planning was too stressful and that you'd rather just have it done so we could start our life together."

"That was before."

"Before what?"

Grant ran a hand through his hair. "An ex-girlfriend came to visit me the week before our wedding—"

"You...cheated on me?" Icy fingers gripped my heart and lungs, squeezing tighter and tighter. I'd suspected the possibility of someone else, but I hadn't wanted to believe it.

"No!" Grant's blue eyes flew wide. "I'd never do that to you, Dakota, I swear."

"I never thought you'd do a lot of things to me, but here we are." I clenched my jaw, hoping it'd keep me from bursting into tears. "You canceled our wedding for an ex-girlfriend?"

Cupid whimpered, and I reached down and patted his head. His hair under my fingers comforted me, even as waves of pain radiated through my chest.

"She has a two-year-old son, and she told me he was mine."

Grant moved forward, too fast for me to react, and then his hands were on my shoulders, his body so close I could feel the heat coming off him and smell his familiar cologne. "I asked for a paternity test and decided I'd wait to tell you until I was sure—I didn't want to ruin everything. But as I was getting ready to go meet you that morning in Jamaica, I thought about the fact that I probably had a son, and everything was happening too fast, and I panicked."

"You could've at least had the decency to come tell me in person instead of leaving me standing outside the ship like that. Do you have any idea how painful it was? How painful it still is?" My voice cracked, and I hated that I'd let him see my sorrow.

"I'm so sorry, and I'll make it up to you, I swear. Please just give me another chance." His fingers tightened on my shoulders. "The paternity results came back, and he's definitely my son."

The world around me blurred, my pulse pounding through my head, so loud it was all I could hear. He had a son. With someone else. It was supposed to be us, a happy family, kids that looked like him and me. My dream, and now some other woman had it instead.

"Dakota, I have no idea how to be a father, and I need you."

I wanted to wrap my arms around him and tell him it'd all be okay, the same way I used to when he'd come home from a hard day. We used to call ourselves a team. Say it was us against the world, and we could take on anything together.

I swallowed past the lump in my throat and pulled back. "I don't know. I…" The logical side of me said it was important for him to be in his son's life. That he could be a good dad if he tried. But there was still jealousy and anger and suspicion about his ex. I didn't know where any of it left me, or if it was anything I could simply be okay with, especially when he'd chosen to tell me now instead of when so much pain could've been avoided.

Holding back tears was now taking an epic amount of control. They lodged in my eyes, burning with the need to be let out, but I dug my nails into my palms, refocusing the pain there. "I need some time to process. And I need to pack up my things." I made the mistake of looking at him again. Vulnerability swam in his eyes, and I could see the stress hanging on him. Maybe he'd been hurting as badly as I'd been these past few weeks, but was that for me? Or because of his current situation? "Could you go? While I pack up my stuff? I just can't…I can't do this right now."

He exhaled and hung his head. "Sure. The place is yours for tonight. I'll stay at my parents' so you can take your time. But just pack up what you need, and leave the rest here so you don't have to deal with putting everything into storage. At least let me do that much."

I bit my lip, trying to distract myself from the barrage of emotions swirling through me. "Fine."

"We'll talk later, though?"

I reluctantly nodded.

"I know I screwed up, but it's not because I don't love you," he said, and the thickness in his voice made it hard to keep from crumpling to the floor and giving in to the grief tearing at my insides. He dropped a kiss on my cheek and brushed past me, leaving me in the house alone.

Tears broke free and slipped down my face. I didn't bother holding them back anymore or even wiping them away. As soon as my body stopped trembling, I packed a couple boxes of clothes and other items I'd need over the next few weeks. With Grant gone, I was tempted to sleep over in the comfortable bed instead of spending another night on Jillian's couch. But looking at it was enough for me to start thinking of all the nights I'd spent cuddled up next to Grant, and that was a slippery slope with more heartache written all over it. So I texted to let him know I wouldn't be staying overnight and asking him to come back and take care of Cupid.

I hated saying good-bye to my furball, and I made sure to spoil him with extra treats so he'd remember whom he loved more. By the time I was driving away, the only thing that was clear was that I was more confused than ever.

Chapter Four

The circuit training class was step one of my get-in-shape plan, but after hauling a couple of loads from Grant's yesterday, and an especially restless night on Jillian's couch, my muscles ached. I dragged myself up to Jillian's third-floor apartment—I wanted to catch the elevator, but one of my goals was taking the stairs instead. Stupid goals that I couldn't not follow through with. When I got inside, I rubbed at the knot forming in my back. What was that all about?

That class was supposed to make me feel strong and empowered, not weak. And definitely not old.

At least the form on my hook is still solid, even if my swing's a little weaker than it used to be. As I'd thrown it during the kickboxing circuit, I'd thought of Brendan mentioning it, and the way he'd rubbed his jaw afterward. When I was younger, I had a huge competitive streak, and I'd loved that Brendan didn't just let me win because I was a girl, almost as much as I hated losing because I was smaller. Once in a while I'd surprised him, though, like that day he'd first learned what messing with me could earn him.

Admittedly, the competitive streak was still there, but now it was channeled into meeting goals and pulling off perfect events despite what life threw at me. Of course, being able to move was also important to my job, and with how stiff I was getting already, that might be a problem. Luckily my appointments today were all in the afternoon, so I decided a soak in the apartment hot tub might work some magic on my cramping limbs and help me feel ready for the day. Especially since first up was cake tasting for the Phelps/Watson wedding, a couple so lovey-dovey that even in my former obsessed-with-love state, I thought they were overly mushy. I could only imagine the havoc they'd wreak on my current confused-if-I-even-believed-in-love condition.

At least the class at the gym had helped me focus on completing the moves and trying to get more oxygen to my lungs instead of everything Grant had said last night. But now it was running through my mind again, the way it had on a constant loop as I'd tried to sleep. Over the past couple of weeks, I'd imagined a lot of scenarios and excuses he might give—horrible ones about not loving me or another woman—so I'd been relieved when he'd given one that was actually decent-ish.

But now he wanted me to just forgive and forget, with a side of help-me-meet-my-kid. Clearly there were still a lot of questions that needed answering. Like why hadn't he confided in me instead of shutting down? Why hadn't he said something pre-wedding, regardless of knowing whether it was true?

Then, the one that stopped me from giving up on Grant altogether: What if this was my shot at love and I threw it away because I was angry? I knew there were ups and downs in every relationship. The hard part was figuring out if it was salvageable, despite the downs, differences, and past mistakes. If only I had a crystal ball, it'd be a much easier decision.

When I came out of the bathroom wearing my red bikini, towel slung over my shoulder, Jillian was at the dining table, steaming mug of coffee in hand as she studied her laptop screen. "How are you feeling about things this morning?" she asked, the same tight-lipped expression on her face as she'd had last night when I relayed the bomb Grant dropped about being a baby daddy. There was no doubt which side of the debate she was on.

"I know you think it's stupid to even consider giving him another chance, but you didn't see his face. He didn't know about the kid for two whole years, and it *is* life-changing."

"So is being too much of a wuss to tell the person you claim to love that you're not going to show up for your wedding. That was life-changing for both of you."

"You're right. And I'm not saying I can ever fully forgive him, or that I even am giving him another chance for sure. I'm just saying I can see why he might freak out. He said he needs me, and the fact of the matter is, my feelings for him didn't just turn off because he didn't show up on that beach." Until I'd said it, I didn't realize how true it was. Figuring out what it all meant in the grand scheme of things was the real challenge.

Jillian's blue eyes lifted to me, and there was concern with an edge of pity. "I know, D, which is what worries me. I don't want you to get hurt again. That boy screws up one more time, and I'm seriously gonna show him the definition of balls julienne." Since I'd seen her wield a knife, that visual was way too graphic.

"I'm glad you have my back—so much so that I'm going to need brain bleach to get that image out of my head—but like I said, I'm still not sure what I'm going to do. Right now my plans involve soaking in a hot tub and making it through one more day of wedding planning." I tilted my head toward the door. "Wanna come with?"

Jillian waved me off. "I've got to get all these invoices done. Have fun. Meet a hot guy." She flashed me a quick smile that said she was teasing but wouldn't mind if it happened.

"I'll see what I can do," I said with a laugh, and headed

outside—taking the stairs again.

An older gentleman and a woman about my age were already in the hot tub. They both looked at me, and I sorta felt like changing my mind. But it might seem rude, I'd come all the way down, and my back was still aching. So I sank into the water, frowning at the lukewarm temperature.

I glanced at the timer dial on the wall. "Need me to turn on the jets?"

"They are on," the man said.

Okay, so the water was lukewarm and the jets nonexistent. Grant didn't have a pool or hot tub, but he did have a ginormous tub with high-powered jets and an extra-large water heater that lasted for hours. Speaking of baths, it felt like I was taking one with this woman and her dad. In swimsuits. Double awkward.

But as the woman chatted about the weather, I thought that at least they were friendly. And it was nice for the daughter to keep checking on her father, asking about his sore back—apparently I had the same issue as a man in his sixties. Stellar.

When the woman leaned over, kissed the guy on the lips, and asked if he was ready to get out—adding a "babe" to the end of her question—I realized they weren't father and daughter, but a couple. I managed to wave good-bye, wondering about how that worked in the bedroom, then wishing my thoughts hadn't ventured down that disturbing path. Maybe that was what I needed—a groom too old to run.

I snort-laughed at myself, because I was sexy like that. My phone rang, and I glanced at it, perched on my towel out of reach. With a wedding this Sunday, I didn't dare ignore it. Hell hath no fury like a bride in an emergency ignored.

With a sigh, I hauled myself out of the pathetic excuse for a hot tub and stared at my phone's display. *Grant.* I so wasn't ready to deal. But I always worried it had something to do with Cupid, and I was a sucker for my dog. And okay, maybe just a sucker all around. Ever since I'd seen him last night, I craved seeing him again, while thinking I shouldn't want to.

"You answered," he said, and I could hear the relief in his voice.

"Is Cupid okay?"

"He's good. He misses you, though. I do, too. The house is way too empty without you here."

My throat tightened. My yo-yoing emotions were driving me crazy. One hour I missed him, the next I wished we'd never met. I'd been ready to graffiti the bridal pictures in my office yesterday, and now a pang of longing for the chance of still being Grant's bride went through my chest. But I thought of Jillian telling me to be careful, and my sense of self-preservation kicked in. "This isn't exactly giving me space, Grant."

"And that's what you want? I thought maybe after you had some time to think about what I said yesterday… Honestly, I hoped that you'd want to set up a time to talk some more."

I gripped my phone tighter. It'd be so easy to throw on some clothes, drive over to his place, and fall into his arms. I missed the way we used to sleep, me tucked against his side, his arm draped over my waist. I missed the dimpled smile he flashed as we'd get ready for our workdays together—he knew not to start a conversation until after coffee. I longed for the kisses hello when we arrived back home. It wasn't as simple as breaking up with an ex. It was losing the life I planned and the guy who knew me better than almost anyone else.

But I again wondered if I could really ever get over how he'd left me alone in a wedding dress, waiting and waiting. If I could move past the awful days following.

"Dakota?"

"I don't know," I said, which was at least honest. "I've got several appointments over the next few days and I've got a wedding on Sunday. I need to get through those things before I can even start processing your news about having a son."

"Okay. When you're ready to talk, you know where to find me. Good luck with the wedding."

I couldn't help flinching. After pulling off close to fifty weddings over the past three years, I no longer got nervous about them. I simply checked my lists and took problems head-on. But my failure to wed made me question if I'd ever pull off another event again. Which was stupid.

Right?

As I told Grant good-bye, a new couple entered the hot tub, the guy and girl much closer to the same age than the previous one. They started kissing, not super graphic or anything, but a press of the lips here and there as they spoke, whispering and laughing, that glow of love radiating from them. I'd never been one of those little girls obsessed with fairy tales or romance when I was younger. I was much more interested in sports—I guess part of me always thought I needed to keep my coach father happy so he wouldn't be upset he'd been stuck with me.

Then, I really wasn't sure quite when it'd happened, but suddenly I started looking at boys for more than if I wanted them on my team because they were good at sports, and more how they filled out their clothes and if they had cute smiles they'd flash at me when I made a great catch. That was when the butterflies started, and after a few boyfriends who taught me how nice hand-holding and kissing could be, I finally got what the fuss about love was.

My job wasn't so much about being obsessed with love as the ability to organize and orchestrate every minute detail. But I'd always get a happy buzz when betrothed couples came in so obviously in love. When I'd been on that cruise ship, though, the pain of being stood up at the altar so raw it felt like I'd lost every part of who I was, I'd looked around at all the other couples and thought love, love, everywhere, and not a drop for me. Then I'd stared at them, so much bitterness pumping through me that I was sure I'd never be happy again.

Right now I was surreptitiously checking out the kissing couple, trying to gauge where my love-o-meter was hitting, from loathing to empathy butterflies. It didn't give me a happy buzz, but I didn't want to scoop up water, toss it on them, and tell them to get a room. So I supposed it was progress.

Somewhere around progress I'd turned into a creeper—or so the couple thought, judging from the way they were both looking at me. Yes, I'd been staring at them, but in my defense, it was more like *through* them.

Well, my love-o-meter toward them was dipping, that was for sure. "Those jets suck, huh?" I asked, attempting a solidarity smile.

Apparently talking was not the way to go, since the guy pulled the girl closer, as if he needed to block her from me.

Now that I was feeling super cool, I decided to take my sore, pathetic self back up to Jillian's. She was still typing away, papers stacked all around her. When I saw my suitcases crammed in the corner, along with the two huge boxes I'd brought yesterday, I wondered if it wouldn't be better to give in and stay at Grant's—he at least had extra bedrooms, and I could sleep with Cupid curled up at the foot of my bed.

Bad idea. Then he'll think we're cool, and we're most definitely not cool.

I wasn't going to let myself be one of those girls who got pushed around and just went with whatever her significant other said—I'd had those brides, too. No, Grant needed to *earn* another chance, not expect one.

"I forgot to tell you I have another dinner to cater tonight," Jillian said. "This entire week is crazy, but Sunday after the wedding we'll celebrate."

Yeah, by crashing and thanking our lucky stars we were done, the way we always did after a wedding. I nodded, though, so she knew I was on board, and went to get ready for the cake tasting, telling myself despite the overly sugary PDA from my couple, I'd get cake. Then tonight, I'd have to resist buying another gallon of ice cream and sitting in front of the TV while eating straight from the carton. The quiet late nights were the worst, the times I missed Grant the most.

Maybe I should call Brendan. Or even swing by and see him at work. I hadn't been to the new Aces Casino yet—I steered clear of the Strip most of the time, actually. But it'd be something different, and it'd be fun to talk to him again. Originally I'd told myself I'd wait to finish catching up with him until I'd gotten my life together, but with all the complications, that was going to take longer than I thought it would. And regardless of what I decided about Grant, I definitely needed all the friends I could get.

What if I start crying or have another breakdown in front of him, though? That'll be so embarrassing.

I told myself that I didn't need anyone else. That I'd be just fine on my own.

But I had a feeling it might be a while until I actually believed it.

Chapter Five

*A*partment hunting wasn't going so well. Vegas was such a clash of extremes, which fit the city's vibe and definitely made for an interesting mix of characters, but it made finding a place to live more of a challenge. My options were ritzy, you-can't-afford-groceries-if-you-live-here, or carry-a-weapon-'cause-you'll-need-one. There were a few more in the Goldilocks just-right range, but they meant driving across the busiest part of town at rush hour, when people were flocking to the Strip and trying to get to whichever spectacular show they'd booked or one of the many all-you-can-eat-and-drink buffets. With all the driving I did anyway, the thought of being stuck in that traffic made me want to cry.

In between office appointments, I sent emails to a few apartment complexes to ask for more information and see if they had openings, and then called my dad back, since he'd left a message. When I told him I hadn't found a place yet, he said, "I can clean out your room if you need me to. You know I'd be happy to have you."

"Yeah, but like I said before, the drive would be killer, and you wouldn't be so happy to have Cupid."

"I could take allergy pills. And if he stayed outside most of the time…"

While Cupid enjoyed a good run, chasing butterflies and lizards, or a game of fetch, he was also spoiled and enjoyed long naps in cool air-conditioning and sleeping at the foot of my bed. Not to mention Dad's yard was tiny and, ever since the city went bonkers about the pollen of olive trees, banned any future planting, and asked residents to keep old ones trimmed to practically nothing, it had almost no shade. "Really, I'm close to finding a new place," I lied, closing out of my apartment search window and opening up my calendar. "How're the boys looking this year? You had camp this morning, right?"

I entered a couple of appointments and added notes on my to-do list as he told me about the defensive line, how the past few years training his quarterback were paying off, and how they were working on a zone blitz but it wasn't going so well yet. Summers didn't mean time off from football as far as Dad was concerned. There were constant training camps, and with the season nearing, he'd torture the boys with two-a-day practices.

"By the way, I forgot to ask, did Brendan West find you? His mom called, and apparently he's moved back to Vegas."

"Yeah, I saw him for a minute the other day. We're gonna catch up sometime." Last night I'd decided I needed to learn how to be alone—I tended to bounce from one relationship right into the next, and I'd never been single for long. But that didn't mean I couldn't look up an old friend, right? The goal was to not *have* to have someone, not turn into a hermit. So as soon as I got off the phone with Dad, I pulled out Brendan's card.

I was halfway through dialing his number when the door to my office swung open. At first all I could see was a dark figure against the blinding sunlight. Then the door closed, my eyes adjusted, and I gasped.

"I know!" Valentina, one of my favorite, and usually calmest, brides-to-be half cried, half shouted, her green eyes bulging. "Marcus likes blondes, and he always jokes about how he fell for me instead, so last night I got this idea that'd it'd be cool to surprise him and go blond, and then…" She lifted a frayed orangey strand of hair. "Then this happened! We're taking pictures for our invitations tomorrow! And they're putting them in the paper— Oh shit! They're going to be everywhere, and I'll be looking like this!"

I could feel my mouth hanging open and forced myself to shut it. Not only was her hair a coppery-orange color, it was chopped off at crazy angles. She looked more like a punk rocker than a bride. Actually, punk rockers would probably find that an offensive comparison, and it seemed most of them went out of their way to look weird. I carefully rearranged my features in a no-problem expression that I hoped also masked my thoughts.

"Who…did this to you?"

"A woman at the mall—Celia from Classy Cuts. I was walking by, there was a special going, and like I said, I wanted to surprise Marcus. I was trying to be spontaneous." Valentina's chin quivered and she burst into tears. I made a mental note to warn brides away from that salon and picked up the phone. Page two of the packet I handed all my clients when they first signed up with me advised against doing anything drastic to their looks before their wedding. It seemed like I needed to add an addendum to apply the same before engagement photos, or pretty much anything in the six months leading up to the wedding.

Valentina Maddox's wedding wasn't just the event of her lifetime, but one that pretty much the entire city was involved in or invited to. The *Beacon* had covered her and Marcus Beecham's engagement, calling them Vegas royalty—they were the children of two of the biggest casino owners, families that'd been here since Vegas was just a blip in the desert. Every step of their engagement and wedding would be covered and analyzed. With all the coverage, planning her wedding would really get my name out there, and hopefully take Ready to Wed to the next level and ensure I had plenty of business for the foreseeable future. Granted it all went smoothly, of course. Good thing I worked well under pressure.

"Give me a minute, and we'll figure out how to fix it, okay? Nothing to worry about," I said, though holy crap, I wasn't sure this was a problem I could actually fix. I called Fusion Locks and asked the receptionist to tell Raquel it was Dakota Halifax and it was an emergency.

Valentina sniffed and wiped at the tears running down her cheeks. I could tell by the red rims around her eyes, she'd been crying for a while. Usually she was the girl cracking jokes and bouncing in her seat as we discussed wedding details, so seeing her in such despair sent a pang of empathy through me. *I've gotta do whatever it takes to get the happy girl back.*

When Raquel came on the line, I told her I had a hair emergency. "I know you're super busy, but she's got engagement photos scheduled for tomorrow, and her cut and color went… well, wrong, to say the least. You're the only person I know who might be able to fix it." Valentina's deflated expression caused me to amend this to, "Who *will* be able to fix it. I know you can do it."

Raquel was quiet for a moment, and I could hear her flipping through pages—the appointment book, I guessed. "Hmm. I'm supposed to be going to lunch in fifteen, but tell you what. You bring me food, I'll scarf it down and squeeze her in."

"Thanks. I totally owe you." Not only did Raquel take care of my hair, I referred people to her like mad, and it looked like it'd pay off for Valentina. It didn't hurt that Raquel was as much a sucker for a fabulous wedding hairdo as I was. Used to be. Whatever. The important thing was she was a miracle hair worker. I hung up the phone and gave Valentina a reassuring smile. "You're in luck. We've got to go now, but we're going to get you fixed up. It'll be fine. You'll see."

And if not, there's always the possibility of working a cute hat into the pictures. She could totally pull off a fedora if it came down to it. Or maybe even a veil, but that might be weird pre-wedding. Then again, celebrities sometimes posed in wedding dresses before they got married. If an actress could do it on the cover of *People,* surely it was a viable emergency option for a Vegas princess.

Valentina followed me in her car while I picked up a sub sandwich and then buzzed over to the salon. The scent of dye, perm chemicals, and perfumed hair products filled the air, along with the buzz of chatter, blow-dryers, and music from a Top 40 station.

"Dakota!" Raquel came forward and threw her arms around me. The girl was a burst of energy packaged in a tiny Puerto Rican body, her bronzed skin and shiny dark hair giving her the type of exotic beauty that made guys stop and stare. Her favorite word was "fab," like she couldn't bother with the entire thing, even though she talked twice as fast as anyone I knew.

Sympathy filled her features as she pulled back. "How are you doin'?"

Raquel had been invited to the reception, which meant she knew about the whole it-not-happening thing. Why did I have to tell everyone I knew that I was getting married? Now I felt like I had to go around the city and discuss its demise. Stupid celebratory column made things a hundred times worse than it would've been, too. "I'm good."

One of her eyebrows quirked up, making it clear she wasn't buying it. Then her gaze went to Valentina. "Oh my," she said, her other eyebrow arching, and Valentina burst into tears again. "No worries, hon. We'll have you looking fab in no time." She flashed me a wide-eyed look—which I hoped meant it was one of those *Mission: Impossible* missions that was actually possible, but maybe filled with hair carnage—and then led us back to her station.

Just over an hour later, Valentina was crying again. Only the tears had morphed to happy ones. Raquel had done a super-extreme deep conditioning treatment filled with seaweed and snail serum—whatever that was. Then she'd dyed Valentina's hair back to its natural dark color, cut it into a choppy bob with long pieces in front, and given her a thick fringe bang. Valentina now looked even better than she had pre–devastating haircut, and her signature smile was back on her face.

The bill was eye-popping—conditioner from the sea is pricey, apparently—but the bride-to-be didn't even bat an eye when she plunked down her credit card. She just kept hugging Raquel and me and saying, "Thank you," over and over.

I was exhausted from just witnessing the transformation. As soon as I'd assured Valentina everything else was on track for her wedding plans and waved good-bye, I sagged against the reception desk.

Raquel put her hand on my arm. "I've got my last appointment of the day next, and after that I'm gonna give you fab caramel highlights, a little heavier on the bottom so it's like a softer, more natural ombré kind of thing."

"Oh, it's okay."

"Nuh-uh. Whenever a girl goes through a breakup, it's time for a shake-up. Trust me, you'll thank me later."

I was going to argue, but I did need a pick-me-up, and my hair might as well benefit from it. Luckily, I'd brought my laptop with me—it was about time to get started on my next article. Judging from today's disaster, it was time to remind people the ins and outs of hair. The nice thing about Valentina was I knew she wouldn't mind or get overly sensitive about my using her situation as a warning to help other brides—not that I'd ever mention names, but I did have the occasional client think I was slamming her in my column. It was a tricky line sometimes.

By the time I had the rough draft typed up, Raquel was ready for me. Once she had me in her chair, the plastic cape secured around my neck, she started talking a hundred miles a minute.

"I don't know what in the hell Grant was thinking. He'll never find anyone as good as you. I mean, I know I never met him, but obviously he's an idiot."

"I guess he just wasn't ready." I thought about telling her about his newfound son. After all, I needed to vent about it to someone who hadn't already formed an unchangeable opinion the way Jillian had.

But then Raquel spun me in the other direction, taking up her chatter again as she swiped color on the ends of my hair with her brush. "Yep, definitely an idiot. I mean, obviously not as bad as that Joe guy you dated who lost all his money in blackjack and then moved himself into your place without you asking him to."

"Yeah, kicking him out after we broke up was a nightmare." I shook my head. "I tell you way too much." Which probably meant I shouldn't tell her about Grant's kid. But there was something about being in a salon chair that made you want to spill every detail of your life. It was like therapy, but with fewer tissues and leather couches and more chemicals and shiny hair. So I told her about how Grant found out he was a daddy.

Raquel spun me to face her. "Whoa. He never knew?"

"Apparently not. Her timing couldn't have been worse. So he claimed he panicked, which I get, I do. But he would've married me still if he really loved me, right?"

She pulled up another strand of my hair and covered it with purple goop. "I don't know. Kids are a big deal. I can't imagine finding out two years later. Probably because I packed the kid around for nine months. The surprise I got was how much crying and pooping there was."

A picture of the daughter Raquel had at eighteen was tucked into the corner of her mirror. She'd had a shotgun wedding, followed by a divorce at nineteen—I knew because we'd already planned her next wedding, even though she hadn't found the guy yet. Her daughter was now almost ready to go to school.

I bit my lip. "So should I give him a second chance, then?"

"He wants one?"

"He claims he does, anyway. And I'm mad, but I love him, too. Then again, he hurt me worse than anyone ever has. Which is why I keep going back and forth."

Raquel pushed away the cart with the hair dye and foil wraps. "You'll have to decide that, chica, but with your body and this fab hair, you're going to have guys *drooling* over you. Might as well enjoy it for a while before deciding if you want to re-settle down."

Since she was so enthusiastic about it, I didn't bother telling her that the only men I was around these days were about to marry my clients. I'd been out of the dating scene—any scene, really— for a long time. And I thought I wanted that. But if Grant wasn't sure, how could I be sure? Maybe there was another guy out there waiting, one who'd be better for me.

Or maybe I needed to stick with my plan to forget about guys and just focus on myself. My in-shape plan and an apartment of my own where I could be with the only guy I needed—my dog. So what if he also drank out of the toilet?

The thing that killed me was that I didn't used to be one of those girls who needed a guy. I knew how to take care of myself, and I prided myself on being able to fix my own problems, no help needed. What happened to that girl? And how could I get her back, because this caring and crying was really starting to blow chunks.

After Raquel had washed out my hair, trimmed up the ends, and styled it, I stared at myself in the mirror. She was right. I'd needed a shake-up.

I needed to remember who I was before Grant and the wedding had eclipsed everything else.

Chapter Six

GET READY TO WED by Dakota Halifax
Hair-Raising Tales

Perfect hair isn't essential to your big day, but why would you want anything less than your best? So here are some hair dos and don'ts. Avoid specials from unknown stylists. Sure, they *might* be great, but is discount hair what you really want? You don't want to be looking at those wedding photos for the rest of your life, wishing you'd gone with the sure bet instead.

Choose a style that's still true to you. You need to be comfortable, and the hairdo needs to last through a ceremony and a reception that might include dancing, and then there's the weather. I know, it's hard to predict the weather, unless you happen to be psychic. How's this for psychic? If it rains, your hair will get ruined. Have a covered area as a backup.

Make sure your hair, accessories, and style of dress go together. They should all complement, not fight one another. Avoid all drastic changes, especially before the big day, but also before having engagement photos taken. Remember, dyeing and perming are also hard on your hair, so even if you're only looking for highlights and volume, you might end up with more of an I-just-got-electrocuted look. The good news is most problems are fixable as long as you're willing to lose a little length or pay for hair extensions, and you can always find a bigger veil. My number one tip is to find a hairdresser who knows what he or she is doing. Always do a practice run, and do all cutting and coloring two weeks in advance. You'd hate for an oops to happen, but you'd hate even more if you didn't have time to fix it.

I'd like to give a shout-out to Fusion Locks, my favorite place for all hair needs. Book an appointment and book it early. Trust me, you won't be disappointed.

*W*ith my heeled feet propped up on my desk, I finished reading through my article one last time before hitting send. At some point, I was probably going to have to address the subject of my failed nuptials, but how would that get people ready to wed? Right now, hair was much more important. Admittedly, I'd admired my new do each time I'd passed the mirror. And deciding to get back to who I used to be helped me look at the smiling bridal pictures in my office without wanting to maim them.

In fact, I was doing so well I decided to change the color of my "get over my bitterness toward love" to-do list item from Fuchsia to Tangerine. No anger, but I wasn't quite at Wary Canary yet. I'd get there, though.

My cell rang, and since it was Jillian, I picked it up. "Have you seen Phoebe's social column today?" she asked.

"No. Why?" I swung my feet to the ground and sorted through my pile of mail, searching for my copy of the *Beacon*. "Did I miss someone famous?" Most of the time, the column was filled with what celebrities were performing where, or who was seen at what nightclub. I didn't know why anyone would want to read it, but apparently Phoebe's column was popular.

While I'd come a long way from the days when I couldn't be friends with girls, Phoebe Pratt, gossip columnist, was an exception. She considered herself the social butterfly of Las Vegas, and unfortunately, she did seem to know everyone, which meant she attended a lot of my clients' weddings. She always had something negative to say about the weddings, too, and she liked to tell me how she would've done it better. I'd heard from one of the other columnists that she'd pitched an idea that got turned down in favor of Get Ready to Wed, which had her hating me from the get-go.

There was also an incident where she threw herself at Grant. So needless to say, I avoided her as much as possible—it wasn't too difficult, considering I didn't have to go into the newspaper office very often.

"Just don't read it," Jillian said. "But if you do, I'm totally down for jumping the woman in whichever nightclub she's trolling tonight."

The pages of my paper stuck together, and I thought I probably should've just pulled up the *Beacon* on my computer instead. But I was prideful enough to have it delivered to my office so I could see my articles in print, so I might as well use it. I scanned to Phoebe's column—she was forever trying to get me to give her dirt on my clients, especially the more well-known ones, like when I did the governor's daughter's wedding. I'd told Phoebe that I didn't want to be involved, and told her I wouldn't comment due to planner/client confidentiality.

"Seriously don't read it," Jillian said as I skimmed the beginning that covered a young starlet drinking in a nightclub.

My name stood out, and I blinked, thinking I must be seeing things. *I* shouldn't be mentioned in the social column—I wasn't even social.

A few weeks ago, well-known wedding planner and fellow newspaper staff member Dakota Halifax wrote about her upcoming nuptials with all the excitement of a blushing bride. It turns out that her best-laid plans didn't prevent her from being stood up at her own wedding. The exact details are unknown. Her friends haven't responded to my calls, and her now-ex-fiancé claimed he didn't want to talk about the disastrous day. I finally squeezed the following response out of him. "I love Dakota and I always will." So, was it a case of cold feet, or is our wedding planner off her game?

My breaths came faster and faster with each sentence, and angry heat traveled through my veins. No more Canary. As far as anger levels went, I was pushing into the Fuchsia zone for sure. I crumpled the paper in my hands. "I'm going to kill her."

"Like I said, you need an accomplice, I'm here for you."

"How could they even print this? How would they know that I was stood up? Did she call you?"

The hesitation on the other end was answer enough. "I ignored the call and the message asking me to call her back. I thought she'd leave it alone—that she was just curious. I never thought she'd print anything about it."

"This is *so* embarrassing. It makes me sound desperate." Right now, I felt desperate. Desperate to corner Phoebe Pratt and make her eat her words—literally. I was going to jam my paper down her throat. "I'm going down to the office. If I need bail money, I'll call you. I suggest Barry from Barry Bonds." I'd had to deal with him before when bachelor parties got a little out of control. He was faster than most, and easy to deal with, which was always important when brides were screeching at levels that could shatter glass. Plus, he used a play on a sports star's name, and that made me oddly happy.

"I know it sucks," Jillian said. "But I called to check in and help you talk crap about Phoebe if needed, not send you on a rage spree. Besides, it's Friday afternoon, and everyone will be leaving for the weekend, with her already off to some social event."

I exhaled. "Fine. I'll have to hunt her down Monday, because there's no way I'm searching through every club this weekend." I did wonder if she'd actually answer her phone if I called. She probably would, and she'd be all smug, and then I'd be angrier, and I wanted to have the confrontation face-to-face.

"I've got a bat mitzvah to cater tonight. Not sure how late it'll go, but I'm hoping to have everything cleaned up and be home by nine. You'll be cool till then, right?"

"Yep. I got a new office supply magazine today." I ran my hand down its glossy surface, the thought of all the pretty organizational tools inside helping calm the throbbing pulse beating behind my temples. "And I'm an independent woman now, remember?"

"Right. At least until you get arrested for assault on a socialite wannabe."

"All good things have to end sometime," I said with a laugh, then wished her luck at tonight's job and hung up. This was why we were good for each other. Whenever one of us got angry, the other one knew just what to say to make it all okay, while still acknowledging the suckiness of the situation.

My door chimed, and Brendan stepped inside. His height and the fact that he was so built compared to the scrawny boy I used to know struck me again. Today he had on a navy button-down and a black tie, and his hair was smoothed into place, a total business look that was part intimidation and part yum.

Okay, I did not *just think of Brendan West, the guy I used to climb trees with and have sleepovers with, where* The Sandlot *and*

The Mighty Ducks *were the main forms of entertainment, as* yum.

"Hey," he said, his boyish grin taking the edge off the serious look.

Yep, yum. He's definitely yum.

As he came closer, I noticed he smelled nice, too. Something crisp yet earthy. "I know you said your life is crazy now, but I was driving by your office, saw the light on, and thought I'd take a chance and see if you had plans."

"Sad pathetic plans involving takeout and kicking back on the couch that also currently doubles as my bed." I lifted the thick magazine I'd just been admiring. "But I do have my office supply porno mag, so not totally pathetic."

Amusement crinkled the corners of Brendan's eyes as he glanced at it. "Kinky."

I laughed and slid the magazine into my bag. "What did you have in mind?"

"I swear this is the best Italian in the city," I said.

"I lova good Italian joint," Brendan said in the worst Italian accent I'd ever heard.

I shook my head but couldn't help laughing. "You're still a total ham."

"You know what they say. If it ain't broke…" He reached in front of me and opened the door to the restaurant. As I passed, he picked up a strand of my hair. "This is different than it was the other day. Looks good."

"Thanks. I just had it done, actually. I can't believe you noticed." Grant often complimented how I looked, but he didn't notice haircuts or new outfits or jewelry. Which was fine, but it was nice that someone appreciated Raquel's handiwork besides me.

"Well, my job is all about the details."

"Just like the devil," I said, and Brendan's eyebrows drew

together. "You know. The devil is in the details."

One side of his mouth kicked up. "Yes, just like the devil, then. My mom's so proud."

I laughed again, relieved things between us were so easy so quickly. I couldn't handle any more complicated relationships.

"Dakota, Dakota, Dakota." Antonia, the woman who ran the restaurant with her husband and sometimes catered my smaller weddings, came forward, shaking her head as she looked at me, which wasn't the reaction I usually got when I came in to pick up dinner. "I read about it in the paper today. Your failed wedding." She picked up my hand and patted it. "Are you okay? I read Enrico the article, and he says, 'What kind of a guy would stand up that sweet girl?'"

She stared at me like she actually expected an answer, then her eyebrows lowered as she looked at Brendan. "That's not him, right? I remember him being shorter. Darker hair."

Heat crept up my neck and into my cheeks, and I was back to feeling like I should hunt Phoebe down and throttle her again. Leave it to her to make my humiliating situation mortifying. "This is a friend of mine. We're just here for dinner."

"Oh. Well, I have a nephew who's single. He works in the kitchen. Maybe I introduce you sometime?"

Instead of brushing her off, or even attempting to explain that the last thing I was in the mood for was a setup, I said, "Hey, if he can make lasagna, I'm sold."

A huge smile stretched across her lips, and I wasn't sure she got that I was kidding. "You want to eat here tonight, or you picking up to go?"

I'd been thinking here, but now that everyone was going to be asking about my failed wedding, I eyed the door, wanting an escape.

Brendan put his hand on my elbow. "Wanna go to my place? Kick back and relax?"

All our years apart, and he could still read my thoughts. "Sounds perfect." Brendan and I ordered, and then we stood in the lobby to wait for our food. I glanced at him, and he gave me a tight smile, not the easy one he'd been flashing earlier.

"I don't want pity." It came out harsher than I meant it to, but I needed to not have him looking at me like that. I'd gotten too much of it lately, and after the mention in the column that reeked of desperation, I couldn't take any more. Especially not from the guy who'd made it all disappear for a few magical minutes. I wanted the careless vibe back.

He held up his hands. "No pity. A girl who marries for lasagna obviously has her priorities straight. In fact, I'd call it admirable."

I clamped my mouth shut, fighting a smile. He thought he was too funny for his own good. I failed at not smiling, so I shoved him for good measure.

"You're as violent as I remember," he said with a laugh.

"And don't you forget it."

He grinned at me, and I was again reminded of all our time together growing up. The football, baseball, and soccer games. Running through the desert and hiding under poky bushes to keep the nearby "cops" on four-wheelers from catching us. And it all started in second grade, the day he threw a stick at my head and I stormed over and punched him—I didn't want to be the girl who got pushed around. I was already the new kid who moved in halfway through the year, not to mention I was dealing with my parents' divorce. I wasn't about to add wimp to the list.

As Brendan had rubbed his jaw, he'd said he was sorry about the stick, claiming he didn't realize I was a girl—which almost made me punch him again. In his defense, that was the year I'd had my hair cut super short—not sure what I was thinking, but let's just say it was the opposite of flattering, although very little maintenance, which used to be my main concern.

But after that day, Brendan and I started playing together, and I ended up being the only girl in a group of guys. The games changed over the years, but it was almost always something physical, with the occasional video game thrown in. The other guys were fine, but Brendan and I really clicked. On my ninth birthday, he even proposed with a Life Saver.

"What?" he asked, narrowing his eyes at me as if he suspected I was up to no good.

"I was just thinking about you and me as kids. It still trips me out to look at you and see the guy I knew, yet totally different."

"You look different, too." His gaze ran down me, lingering on my red suede Mary Jane heels. "For one, I never expected you to be so girly."

"Sorry to disappoint."

He wrapped an arm around my shoulders. "I'm not disappointed. It's just, well, you lived in jeans, baggy T-shirts, and jerseys. You could throw a curveball that'd make any guy jealous."

"Stop or you'll make me blush," I said, swiping a hand through the air, and got rewarded with a big grin.

"And now here you are wearing a skirt and heels and planning weddings. How did that happen?"

"It's more of a control thing than the dresses, cakes, and fancy decorations, even though I've learned to love those things, too. During my last few years of high school, my girlie side kicked in and I found that I actually like getting dressed up. And that I could dress like a girl and still play sports—I was on the soccer team, since the football team seemed reluctant to have me. What with my dad being the coach, I probably could've pushed for it, but at that time, I wanted to have something separate from Dad—but something he'd still be proud of."

"I'm sure he was."

"He came to all of my games. One even overlapped with football, and he let the assistant coach take over for that game. I still kind of can't believe it." Movement in the back of the restaurant caught my attention. Antonia was talking to a tall, scrawny guy who looked like he'd just gotten out of high school. She pointed at me, and I had the feeling he was the nephew she suddenly wanted to set me up with.

I ducked behind Brendan, using him to hide me, though it was too late anyway.

"What are y— Oh." Brendan chuckled. "He looks like just your type, D.J. Probably barely made it out of jailbait age."

I gripped the back of his shirt. "You're so not helpful." I tipped onto my toes so I could peek over Brendan's shoulder and see if Antonia was still pointing at me. Not sure what hiding was going to accomplish, but it seemed like the thing to do.

Antonia came up front—alone, thankfully—and handed us bags of food that smelled of garlic and marinara and made my stomach rumble in anticipation. I did my best to hide the fact that I'd been using Brendan as a shield. Though I did notice he was a rather sturdy one.

We took the food and got back into Brendan's truck. As he drove, he bobbed his head to the music, humming along with the radio, and I relaxed back in the passenger seat, glad to have someone to chill with on a Friday night.

"So, how do you like being back?" I asked. "And what exactly do you do at the casino?"

"So far so good—some of my best memories are here." He glanced at me and warmth flooded my chest. Then he looked back out at the road, the streetlights outlining his profile and the way he draped his arm over the steering wheel. "I take care of security for our high rollers and make sure no one steals from the casino. And if they do, I make sure I grab them before they get away. There's a lot of carding for underage gambling and taking care of people who get drunk and disorderly, too. And a lot of behind-the-scenes stuff that I can't really talk about." He said it lightly, but I could tell he was higher-level, and that he took his job seriously.

"You go with your James Bond self."

The headlights from a car coming the opposite way flashed across his curved lips. "You never finished telling me how you got into planning weddings. You were too busy hiding."

"Well, if I knew you were practically a spy, I would've asked for a cooler avoidance technique." I readjusted the seat belt and twisted my back against the door. "It all started when a teammate's mom got married, and I went to the wedding. I was awed by all the flowers, decorations, and waiters serving fancy meals. Everyone looked so happy, too. I started wondering how it'd all come together. It looked like a challenge, and I wanted to know if I could pull off something like that. So I looked into planning, and since organization has always been my thing, it just fit. And I like that no matter how many weddings I do, they're always different. Problems inevitably arise, and I get a rush when I take care of them and manage to pull off another wedding."

Except for mine. I totally failed at that, no awesome adrenaline rush included. I quickly shook off that unwanted thought and shrugged. "Plus, I get to boss people around."

"You always did like to do that," Brendan teased, and I smacked his arm.

He turned into a newer subdivision and pulled into the garage of a tan two-story house with Spanish roof tiles and a tall palm tree in the front yard. Within a few minutes, we were seated at the table in the kitchen, digging into dinner. As our conversation hit a lull, my mind started spinning. At first it was focused on how nice it was to be with Brendan again, laughing and joking the same way we used to, but then I was thinking about how different he and Grant were. Not just in looks, but Brendan's decorations were sparse and there were piles of clutter here and there that, okay, I kind of wanted to sort and put away. Even though he was fairly neat already, Grant hired a maid to come in and clean, and his decorations were pieces he'd picked up in high-end galleries. He'd minored in art, so he knew the history behind each painting, too.

I had a feeling Brendan's pictures had a history that went something like, they came with the house. Not that I was really into art or cared about that kind of thing. I just tended to look at a person's style, vehicle, etcetera, and see if I could guess what his or her personality was like. When it came to brides and grooms, I was about 75 percent right.

"You like it?" Brendan pointed at the picture hanging on the wall that I'd been studying.

"Where'd you get it?"

"Came with the house."

A smug zip went through my core.

"I'm going to decorate eventually," he said. "I'm thinking movie posters."

"In the kitchen?"

"Why not?"

I shrugged, because I couldn't think of any reason besides it wasn't usually done, and that didn't seem like a good enough one. "I suppose you'll have sports stars and 49ers posters plastered on your walls, too, just like you did when you were a kid."

"Yeah, my bedroom—the only room I've decorated so far—still has some. But now they're framed, because I'm way more mature and fancy." He nudged my knee with his hand. "Don't act like you're not gonna be impressed by my signed and framed Steve Young jersey."

"No way. You have a signed jersey?"

He nodded, a crease forming in his cheek as he grinned. "Not so smug about mocking my decorating choices now, are you?" He stood and held out his hand. "Come on, I'll show you."

I slapped my hand in his and let him pull me up. The living room had a giant television on one wall and a large sofa with recliners and cupholders facing it—all function. I spotted a PlayStation in the entertainment center, too, so he clearly still liked his games.

It'd been years since I played. I wasn't bad, but I never could sit there for hours on end like Brendan and the rest of the guys, and I was always trying to get them outside instead, hellacious Vegas heat be damned.

Brendan pushed open the door of his bedroom. Like the kitchen, there were piles—clothes strung here and there, and the top of his dresser was a mess. But there on the wall were a couple of 49ers posters, one for the Colorado Avalanche, and a Steve Young poster. All were nicely framed. Then there was the scarlet jersey in the middle, Steve Young's name scribbled across the white number eight.

"Not only is it signed, I was *there* when he signed it. Got it the year he retired."

Brendan and I used to always watch the games together, and we agreed the 49ers quarterback was the best, hands down. Dad was there, too, yelling at the players and then giving a simple nod when they did something good, the same way he did on the field with his own players.

"Well, I'm definitely impressed, and it's totally awesome you got to be there. Still not what I'd decorate my bedroom with, but it'd definitely go in the den or entertainment room"—I flashed him a smile—"along with your maturely framed posters."

My email chime went off. I only had an alert for clients, because I assured them I was available when they needed me. They had my cell, too, but some brides preferred emails, and I preferred those brides. "Excuse me. I've got a wedding Sunday, so just gotta check if it's urgent, or something I can add to my to-do list for later."

It wasn't Erika, this weekend's bride, but one with a wedding scheduled this winter. *I regret to inform you that I've chosen to go a different way...* I scanned through the rest, my muscles tensing. From some of the phrasing about not being sure I was equipped to handle her wedding, I was sure she'd read Phoebe's column. The woman had come in a couple weeks ago, pleading with me to take over because she was so overwhelmed. I'd already gotten her location booked and started on her invitations. All that work wasted, and I'd only have a puny deposit to show for it. So on top of having limited funds already, my clients were going to start dropping like poisoned-by-Phoebe flies. Because a guy I had no control over chose to not marry me. If anything, they should question my choice in fiancé, not my ability to plan a wedding.

"Everything okay?" Brendan asked.

I turned my phone to silent and put it away. "Peachy." With a side of Temperamental Tangerine.

He gave me a look that he wasn't buying it.

"I could use a drink. Guess we should've picked up some wine to go with dinner."

"Well, you're in luck, because I have a couple of bottles waiting for an occasion like this."

Once we were in the kitchen, Brendan poured two glasses of wine. I took a few generous sips, but I was still thinking about that email. Surely I wouldn't start losing clients over something so stupid. I'd finally gotten my business up and running the way I'd always wanted it to. If I did go back to Grant, though, I wondered if people would view that as a success because it all worked out, or as a failure because I went back to a guy who'd stood me up. Not that I'd make huge life decisions based on what others thought.

Things are complicated, far more than one paragraph in a paper can cover with a couple of condescending lines.

I swirled my wine in my glass and glanced at Brendan. "What would you do if you found out you had a kid you never knew about?"

Brendan froze, his glass barely touching his lips, and then slowly lowered it. "Uh, I don't know. Why?"

"I mean, would it freak you out?"

"Hell yeah." He tilted his head, looking like he expected more explanation, but I wasn't ready to drag out all my dirty laundry—

or more accurately Grant's—for him to see. As comfortable as I was with Brendan, I wanted to keep everything happening with Grant separate right now. Each aspect of my life in its own space, just like I was dreaming of doing to that pile of mail scattered on Brendan's counter. Apples and oranges were just scattered on the counter, too, no nice bowl to hold them.

I took another drink of wine, draining my glass, and then stared out the patio doors. "Cupid would love to run around that yard." I glanced at Brendan. "Cupid's my dog. My last apartment had one tiny strip of grass for the entire complex, and it was hard for him to be cooped up all the time."

Brendan joined me at the patio door. "What kind of dog?"

"Black Lab. He's with my ex now, until I get my own place." So much for avoiding talk of Grant. Our merged lives made it so damn inescapable.

"That sucks. You can't have him where you are?"

I shook my head. "Like I said, I'm sleeping on a couch right now, so there's very little room, not to mention Jillian's complex doesn't take big dogs."

"Well, if you want to keep him here, you can. I've got plenty of space, and I run in the mornings…"

I bet you do, I thought as I checked out his physique. For the second time tonight. Then I felt weird, because this was Brendan. But, like, Brendan 2.0.

"…take him with me," Brendan continued. "Then you can visit anytime. Really, it'd be nice for me."

"Are you serious?"

"Yeah. I'd give you a key so you could come by whenever to see him."

"You're offering me a key to your house? Just like that? What if I come in and trash the place while you're gone?" More likely I'd find myself cleaning and organizing, but there was no way he could know that.

The beginning of a smile tipped the corners of his mouth. "Are you going to come in and trash the place?"

I shook my head.

"My instincts said as much. I know in some ways we just met, but it doesn't seem like that much has changed. Except for the clothes and job, and…" He looked me up and down as if he was assessing the differences, and I fought the urge to squirm. Was he thinking of me the way I'd just thought about him, or had I had too much wine? "Okay, maybe a lot of things." He leaned against the doorframe and shrugged. "But not who we are. I know you better than you think, D.J. Halifax. After all, how many times did we sleep over at each other's houses growing up?"

"Every weekend we could get our parents to agree to. Until you proposed, and my dad totally freaked out."

Brendan's eyes lit up—the same brown eyes that used to say so much with just a look. *Go long. Sneak out of the bushes on three. We'll ditch these guys in a few.* "That's right. After that, I was banished from slumber parties."

"I tried to explain to him that we were the kind of engaged where there was no kissing, but I think it was the first time he realized I might actually kiss a boy someday." An image from my ninth birthday popped into my head. Brendan and me sitting up in the olive tree in my backyard. He asked me if I'd marry him when we were "old, like twenty or something," and I told him sure, but that in order to be properly engaged, I'd need a ring—I'd been quite proud of my knowledge of the subject. Brendan took a grape Life Saver out of the roll he'd had in his pocket and tried to shove it on my finger. Since the hole was too small, he sucked on the candy, checking it every few minutes until it fit. And that was how I'd become engaged at nine, only to have my dad promptly remove the sticky, dirt-coated "ring" as soon as I informed him of my betrothal, and tell Brendan that he was no longer allowed in my room and couldn't sleep over anymore. Over the next four years Brendan had sneaked back to my room now and then, when my dad was at practice. He and I had never kissed, though, and I found my gaze drifting to his lips now.

Then I came to my senses. That was just a weird, random thought, brought on by the fact that this was the first good night I'd had since…well, pretty much since my wedding fell through. Did it mean I should give up a perfectly good offer that'd allow me to see my dog whenever I wanted without having to also see my ex? Honestly, it seemed like the perfect solution until I could find a more permanent one.

"Are you sure having my dog here wouldn't be too much trouble? He's fully trained and pretty low maintenance. I mean, he sheds a bit, but he also licks up anything that's spilled, so I consider it a wash."

"No trouble at all. I get a furry companion to hang out with, and it means seeing you more, too. Sounds like a win all around."

A lightness filled my chest. Usually I liked my plans followed to the letter, and this had definitely come from left field, but I had a feeling this slight detour was going to make my life easier.

"Come on," Brendan said. "Let's go watch a movie or play video games. I've got the new *007*, and with the updated graphics, I bet you won't be constantly stuck in a corner."

"Ugh, I swear the wall always closed in on me when I took a turn. Then I just got dizzy as the bricks spun around until someone came from behind, shot me, and my screen went red."

Brendan laughed, picked up the wine bottle, and gestured me toward the living room. As I followed, I thought not only was this new arrangement with Brendan and Cupid going to make my life easier, but it was also going to make it a lot more fun.

Part Two

TEMPERAMENTAL TANGERINE - HIGH

(HIGH RISK OF TEARS, PANIC, RAPID BREATHING, AND THE URGE TO BOLT OR PASS OUT)

"The prudence of the best heads is often defeated by the tenderness of the best hearts."

—HENRY FIELDING

Chapter Seven

"Where the hell are my doves?" I asked into my Bluetooth earpiece, though it probably looked like I was talking to myself. I wished I was talking to a real live person, but all I'd gotten was a generic voicemail greeting. The first couple of messages I'd left were nicer: *Hey, can I get an ETA on the doves* type messages, but by number four, my patience was gone.

Jillian stepped out of the large tent where the reception was going to be held. Her staff was bustling around, setting up the catering tables and food warmers. "Any luck?" she asked.

"He's still not answering. I'd better go check on the bride. If you see a guy with a big truck full of birds, give me a call." I strode toward the set-up aisle and chairs, twisting one of the floral-draped columns a few inches to the right on my way.

Ten months of work all coming together, all except for the damn doves. The wedding ring had been forgotten, but I'd already sent the groom's father to get it, and he was due back in five. Erika had a minor meltdown about the zit that showed up on her chin this morning, but after cold tea bag compresses, a toothpaste plaster spot treatment, Visine, and the magic of good concealer and powder, her face looked flawless, if a bit heavier on the makeup than usual. Last I'd seen her, her mood was more on the bubbly than stressed side. But the magical moment the groom was told he could kiss the bride as doves were released wasn't going to happen if my birds, along with their wrangler, didn't get here soon. And knowing Erika like I now did, there'd be tears if her oft dreamed-of moment fell through.

The whole dove thing was surprisingly popular. I'd never understood wanting the risk of extra crap at your wedding. While a bird pooping on you was supposed to be lucky, no one would be thinking, *Yay, so glad this happened!* as they scrubbed the luck from their hair or skin. Not to mention the unappealing effect on wedding photos.

At least they hired Louie. If anyone does get crapped on, he'll Photoshop it out. That is, if the doves ever get their feathered butts here.

I lifted my phone, silently urging it to ring. When it didn't, I slid it into my bra, so I'd be sure to feel it vibrate, even if I didn't hear it, and headed to see if the wedding party were dressed and ready to take their places. Animals were seriously going to be the death of me. A few months ago, I had to deal with horses. My bride had one that, as she put it, simply had to be in the wedding or her family wouldn't be complete. Five minutes into pictures, the horse decided the flowers looked delicious, bit into the bride's bouquet, and ran, red tulips hanging from its mouth. Without fully thinking things through, I sprinted after the stupid beast, heels and all, no idea what I'd do if I actually caught up with it.

A groomsman came to my aid and we managed to corner the horse. He grabbed the bridle, and I pried the mangled red tulip bouquet out of its mouth. After taking flowers from the bridesmaids and centerpieces, I managed to come up with a presentable bouquet for the rest of the sans-horse photos.

By being resourceful with whatever I had to work with, I could make do in most cases. Unfortunately, I didn't know how to fake doves. Maybe I'd arm some of the younger kids with slingshots and see if they could at least scare up some regular birds. Nothing says romance like pigeons and crows.

"Hey," a deep male voice said as soon as I stepped inside the blessedly cool office that housed the dressing rooms. One of the groomsmen walked up and put a hand on my shoulder—he was the one who didn't show up for rehearsal last night, so he was already on my blacklist. "You're the wedding planner, right?" He smirked as his eyes ran me up and down, and I had a feeling a lot of women had fallen prey to that cocky smile. I'd seen his type before—they thought they'd score with all the single chicks at the wedding because they'd be oh so desperate to be with someone. "I'm Clark. The groom's best man." He ran his fingers down my arm. "Save me a dance, why don't ya?"

Not only was I not impressed, I didn't have time to deal with his lame pickup lines. "Clark?"

He quirked one eyebrow, obviously thinking he was a regular Casanova. "Yeah, baby?"

I leaned in close, until my lips were a few inches from his ear. "Your zipper is down. You might want to fix that before the ceremony." I removed his hand from my arm, shot him a tight smile, and went to check on the female half of the wedding party.

On my way down the hall, I realized that dating again would mean dealing with guys like Clark. Was I supposed to swoon at comments like that? No, I'd never be able to do that, but I didn't even remember how to flirt anymore. *Guess I'll have to add a few extra goals to that section of my life plan if I end up deciding to date.*

I was just about to knock on the door to the bridal room when my boobs vibrated. I pushed the answer button on my earpiece. "Hello?"

"It's me," the gruff voice informed me.

"Me who?"

"It's Ed. I've got the doves here and ready to go."

I blew out my breath. Halle-frickin-lujah. With another canceled client—got that special voicemail message late last night—and Phoebe determined to make me look incompetent, I felt more pressure than I ever had to make sure this wedding went off without a hitch. "Set up right behind the altar, behind the draped columns. I'll be around in a few to talk timing." As soon as I hung up, my phone buzzed again.

"The dove guy's here," Jillian said. "Dude, the birds are totally crapping as he's pulling them out. It's a good thing the food's in the tent."

"Amen, sister. I just talked to the guy, but if he heads anywhere but the staging area behind the altar, point him the right way, will you? I've got to check on the bride, and the ceremony's due to start in ten. Reception should be about forty."

"Everything's on schedule for the food," Jillian said, "and I'll keep an eye on the bird man." She was as much of a perfectionist as I was, thank goodness. When she catered, I knew that not only was the food taken care of, but that she'd also help me out on the little things, which was why I strongly recommended her to all my clients.

I knocked and entered the bridal room. Erika was in her Krikor Jabotian gown, surrounded by her bridesmaids, a blur of white and cream contrasted with coral and lime. This wedding was one of my bigger budget events, although the Maddox/Beecham wedding made it look small in comparison. After losing a few clients, I needed every event to go smoothly, but Valentina's was always weighing on my mind, thanks to the added news coverage that could make or break me.

As long as it went off without a hitch, I'd be okay, and I'd kill myself to make sure it would. But with it still being several months away, that thought wasn't comforting enough for me to think I could afford to rent the beautiful, prime location two-bedroom condo I'd found online last night. My salary was always unpredictable, huge influxes followed by tiny paychecks, and I just couldn't commit to spreading my finances that thin right now.

"Dakota!" Erika shouted when she saw me. "Can you believe the big day is finally here?"

Every bride I'd ever had asked me the same question, or a variation of it, right before the ceremony. I'd asked it to my reflection the morning I was supposed to get married.

I'd been doing so well all day, focused on tasks and problems—totally back in my element. But it was that question that punched me in the gut. Suddenly all the tiny details stood out. How each of the floral pieces on her bodice had been laid on just so, giving the gown an antique yet modern look. How the layers of her voluminous cream skirt were puffed to perfection. The flawless makeup, the golden curls pinned with pearl bobby pins. The happiness and hope radiating off her.

This was different from witnessing happy couples during planning meetings. This was the magic day. A love story ending, yet only beginning. And for the first time since I'd been planning weddings, I didn't feel the hope and happiness. Not for her, not for me. I didn't feel bitterness, either, thank goodness—I sincerely wanted her wedding to be perfect. Mostly, I just felt empty. Lost. Which made no sense. I had a fab new hairdo. I had a color-coded life plan. Despite losing a few clients, I had enough to keep me plenty busy.

So why did I still feel like a failure? I told myself to stop it, but my emotions weren't listening. But like with the flirty groomsman, I didn't have time for whatever crisis I was having. I forced the corners of my mouth into a smile. "I can't believe it! And you look amazing, but no surprise there." I looked over the bridesmaids. "You all look amazing."

Lime and coral together was a bold color choice, much like risking dove poop and the couture gown that might overwhelm the wrong person. But Erika was a risky bride, and I admired her for it.

"Is there anything you need?" It was a dangerous question, often answered with last-minute, impossible requests, but it came out of my mouth every time. I couldn't help it—even when I was going through a personal crisis, apparently.

"I was wondering if we could get a couple of bottled waters. They sent up the cheap stuff, and I simply can't drink it."

"I double-checked they'd serve only the Fiji kind at the reception, and I can definitely get you a bottle, but you might want to stop liquids soon. Not to the point of dehydration, obviously, but you don't know how many times brides have gotten partway through the ceremony, needed the bathroom, and have to spend the ceremony wiggling around." So it had only happened once that I knew of. I needed to get down to the dove man and not have to worry about certain brands of bottled water.

"You think of everything," Erika said, hugging me. "I'm so glad I have you."

Now I felt even worse for not getting all hopeful and sentimental. What if every wedding I did from here on out left me this hollow?

No, I'll get my groove back. I have to. I noticed one bridesmaid squirming around in the corner, a panicked look on her face. "Do you have tissues handy in case you cry?" I asked Erika.

"I'll get them," the maid of honor said, and Erika's attention turned to her, which gave me enough time to go check on the wide-eyed bridesmaid.

"Is everything okay?" I whispered to the short redhead. For some reason, her name wouldn't come to me—with all the weddings and after a couple weeks away from the job, there was too much other information crammed in there. Okay, I had a system. She was the shortest. Her name started with Sh. *Shauna?* Not quite right. *Sharon?*

Yes, it was definitely Sharon. Between her hair and the lime dress, she looked even more perfectly color coordinated with the wedding.

"I'm afraid that I…well, look for yourself." She turned around, and I thought it was going to be a zipper problem—wax took care of that, and I had a sewing kit in my bag, so I was sure it wouldn't be a big deal.

Only then she lifted her shoe, and I noticed the heel dangling. "I went to step and it just snapped."

"No worries."

"And then when I fell forward, my skirt caught." She twisted to show me the rip in the fabric.

Shit. "We got this." I just wasn't sure how I was going to get to the dove guy in time. I glanced at my watch. Five minutes till Go Time.

I took out superglue, reattached the heel, and handed it to Sharon. "Hold it tight. Be careful not to get it on your skin." She nodded, her expression all-business, which was much better than a flighty bridesmaid. I threaded the needle and stitched up the tear as fast as humanly possible. I was just finishing when Erika turned to see what was going on.

Sharon tested the shoe and relief filled her features. "I think it'll hold," she whispered.

"Walk lightly if you can, and when you stand up front, weight on the solid shoe, 'kay?" I straightened, readjusted Erika's veil on the way out of the room, and then hauled butt to the bird man.

"*I* now pronounce you husband and wife," the preacher said. "You may now kiss the bride."

I snapped my fingers and Ed looked dazedly over at me. He mouthed, *Now?* and I nodded. He lifted the cage, and the bride and groom kissed as doves flew overhead and the audience cheered.

I sagged against a column. One of the guests glanced at the

sky, her eyebrows scrunched up as she patted her head. I suspected bird crap, but she wasn't in the bridal party, so I was still considering it a win. My minute rest was up, so I headed into the food tent.

Jillian was all set, her waitstaff ready to go the second she gave the order. "The dove thing turn out okay?" she asked.

I nodded. "It's a freaking miracle."

"Considering your creature curse, I'd say so." Jillian leaned in and whispered, "So no need to fry up a few birds?"

I laughed. "Not today." The first time Jillian and I worked together was my first solo wedding. I was pretty sure that was when the whole animal curse started. I'd arrived to find goldfish belly up in more than half of the centerpieces. Jillian helped me scoop them out, joking that we'd just add them to the menu. I knew right then we were destined to be friends. For the record, the fish got flushed, the empty bowls filled with floating roses I scalped from the floral arrangements.

"And how are you feeling?"

That was the other thing about Jillian. She could tell that I was off and knew to check in, but never made me feel like it was because of pity. "I survived."

At this point, I was going to count that as a win.

Chapter Eight

It was like my car just headed to Grant's place, the way it had done after countless weddings, a mind of its own. I wanted to chalk it up to being tired and not weak-willed, but as I walked up the steps, I didn't really give a damn what I called it. I used my key to get in and kicked off my heels.

Grant looked up from his spot on the couch. He stood and started over to me, but Cupid was faster. I leaned down and hugged my dog, then straightened. Grant had shaved and gotten a haircut since I'd seen him last. For a moment, we simply stared at each other, then he pulled me into his arms and hugged me tight.

I sank into his warmth, his embrace. When his lips covered mine, I stiffened. But then his fingers were traveling over my body and I was lost in his familiar touch and taste. When he pulled me tighter against him, though, my sense of self-preservation kicked in.

"Wait." It came out shaky, more air than sound, but Grant froze in place. My stomach rolled and my heart clenched and everything was wrong all over again. I pulled away, needing the distance yet despising it. The words "This was a mistake" were on the tip of my tongue, but it didn't quite feel like a mistake. Slippery. Dangerous. Those were better words. I was gambling with my heart, and after what the guy standing across from me had already put it through, it seemed like one of those times where both of us lost and the house won. Whoever the bastard who owned the house was.

"How was the wedding?" Grant asked.

"Only one lady got bird crap in her hair, but she was just a guest, and I don't think she realized it."

The dimple in his cheek stood out when he grinned. Why'd he have to be so sexy? "It wasn't too hard to be there after…?"

"It was hard."

"I'm so sorry, Dakota. If I could do it again—"

"Don't," I said, holding up a hand. I believed he was sorry. I just didn't know if it was enough. I did know I didn't want to have this same conversation every single time I saw him from now until…whenever I figured out my life. "I'm guessing you saw the social column in the paper?"

He let out a heavy sigh and nodded.

"You could've warned me it was coming."

"I didn't know Phoebe was going to print anything. I told her I didn't want to talk about it, especially with her. Why? What did she tell you?"

"*She* didn't tell me anything. Jillian called and told me it was in the paper, and I got to read it myself. Why'd you say anything to her in the first place? You know how she is."

He shrugged. "She kept pushing, so I just told her that I loved you and always would."

I fought the urge to turn and bang my head on the wall. Wasn't this why I'd come? To see if I could even feel love anymore? Now anger was mixing in, not so much at him, but at the situation. "Have you met your son yet?"

"No. Amy wanted to get him used to the idea of me first, and we're working on an arrangement. There are child support payments to set up, and I feel a little overwhelmed with it all, to tell the truth. I'm supposed to meet him this week, though." He looked at me with wide eyes, genuine nervousness in his features, and I knew if I continued to stand and stare at him there would be more kissing and then less clothing, and then steps I knew I wasn't ready for.

"I'm taking Cupid with me tonight," I blurted out, more so I wouldn't chicken out than anything. "I've got a friend who owns a house, and he'll keep him while—"

"He?" The muscles in his neck stood out. I should've known better than to mention another guy. Grant had always been a touch on the jealous side. I'd even learned to edit stories about groomsmen because they often got him all riled up. "Who is this friend?"

"You've never met him. He's a guy I used to know when I was younger. Look, that doesn't matter right n—"

"It matters to me." Grant grabbed my hand. "I don't like the thought of you doing anything with another guy. Just keep Cupid here. I'll take good care of him until you decide to move back in."

He said it like it was so final, like it was an outcome he was sure of and I didn't really have a say.

"We'll just go back to how things were before all the wedding crap got in the way," he added. Wedding crap? Did he even *know* me? My car made a mistake coming here—fine, maybe I had something to do with it, too. But I had to be stronger from now on. I *would* be. Time to amp up my goals and get back to my independent self.

Step one: Take Cupid to his new home.

Step two: Find an apartment that fit my budget.

Step three: Figure out what the hell to do about my ex-fiancé, who'd switched to trying puppy-dog eyes on me to get his way. Actually, that was more like step four or five. I'd sort it out later when I was at Brendan's, where I could relax, get Cupid acclimated, and actually think clearly.

I pulled my hand free. "Everything's changed, Grant. I can't just go back to the way things were." Confusion and irritation battled it out for control on his features. I didn't want this to turn into a fight, so I tried to explain. "It's like you offered me chocolate cake and I took a bite and it was amazing, but now you're shoving broccoli in my face, telling me to settle for it."

"No, it's more cake. We can still have what we did. If you're set on marriage, we can" — he swallowed, his Adam's apple bobbing up and down — "we can go down to city hall. Is that what you want? A marriage certificate to prove I love you?"

Clearly that wasn't what *he* wanted, and I wasn't about to stand across from a guy and say "I do" when he didn't think of it as the best day of his life, too. "Now you're offering me chocolate-covered broccoli. I'll take a bite and discover it's a lie."

Grant scrubbed a hand over his face. "Can we abandon this metaphor?"

"Fine. You want me with you now because you have a son and I'm good at dealing with problems and making things work, despite the challenges. I need you to want me because you can't imagine not having me in your life. Because marrying me is something you can't wait to do so I'm always yours and you're always mine."

"But I *can't* imagine not having you in my life. Hell, I've lived it the past few weeks and it sucks."

Now I wished I felt hollow and numb the way I did at the wedding, because it'd be better than the pain radiating through my chest. "It's different than sucking or not." I blew out a frustrated breath. "You need to learn what it means to be a dad and how that's going to impact your life. I need to figure out who I am independent of you. And once we both work out those things, we can see if we want to give our relationship another shot."

Grant sighed, but slowly nodded.

"Come on, Cupid," I said, patting my leg. I grabbed his leash and his favorite mangled squeaky ball, and opened the door. Cupid ran to my car and danced around in front of the passenger side. I glanced back at Grant. "Good luck with your son. Call me and tell me how it goes, okay?" That seemed like good neutral territory. Friends who cared about each other and such.

By the time Grant's house was in my rearview mirror, Cupid already had his head out the window, his tongue dragging behind him. I reached over and ran my hand down his coat. Right now, I felt a bit like sticking my head out and feeling the wind in my hair, too. We were together again, were actually making progress on goals—anyway, I was. Though I was pretty sure Cupid would make a goal of spending more time with me if he could.

I thought of today's wedding, and how wrong it'd felt compared to others I'd planned. I had to believe that eventually I could put on one and get a tingly, hopeful, happy buzz.

That I could find my faith in love.

Maybe then I'd know exactly how I felt about Grant.

And hopefully by then, the rest of the city would have forgotten all about the time I got stood up at the altar.

Using my brand-new key seemed like busting into Brendan's personal space, but when I called to see if he was home so I could bring Cupid by, he told me to let myself in. Brendan was on the couch, his tie undone, along with a couple of buttons. There was something sexy about it, all businesslike yet casual.

Okay, I needed to stop thinking about my new-slash-old friend as sexy, especially if this arrangement was going to work. I needed a friend I could relax and be myself with, not a buddy to leer at. He glanced up from the TV, and even though I'd been trying to tame my thoughts, I still felt like I'd been caught doing something I shouldn't. "How'd the wedding go?"

"Crazy, but good. I'm exhausted." I set the bowl and bag of

dog food I'd picked up on my way over on the floor, and gestured to my dog. "Cupid, Brendan. Brendan, Cupid."

"Sorry about the name, dude," Brendan said, holding his hand in front of my dog's snout before petting him.

I shot him a dirty look. "Hey. His name rocks."

"Right. Very tough. Who's a tough boy?" Brendan scratched behind Cupid's ears and his tail thunked against the coffee table.

"Cupid is a god. He had arrows," I added when Brendan failed to look impressed. "And I'll have him shoot you in the ass if you don't shut it."

"Again with the violence," Brendan said, shaking his head.

There. Now that was more like us. Just like that, life felt a little more bearable. Cupid's nails tapped on the hardwood floor as he explored the room.

Right as I was about to sit, Brendan stood, sliding his tie off and tossing it onto the couch. "I was about to cook up a burger. You want one?"

My stomach growled in response. With how hollow the wedding had made me feel, I hadn't bothered eating, and it wasn't until he mentioned food that I realized just how hungry I was. "Yes, please. Need help?"

"I wouldn't turn it down."

The thought of one more step in my heels made me wanna cry, so I kicked them off before following him into the kitchen. Pots and pans clanged together as Brendan riffled through his cupboards. I'd realized he was tall, but without my shoes I felt like a total shrimp next to him. While he got to work on the patties, I opened the fridge and took out an onion, lettuce, and tomato. It took me a couple tries to find his cutting board—there really was no rhyme or reason to where things went—and then I sliced the veggies as the scent of meat filled the air.

"Open these?" Brendan held up a can of baked beans. "The can opener's right behind you." He tossed the beans to me.

Within a few minutes I had them open and cooking in a pot on the stove. Brendan was putting condiments on the buns. "No mustard for you, right?"

I wrinkled my nose. He loved the stuff and I hated it. He used to chase me around with a glob on his finger, telling me he was going to force me to eat it. Thanks to him, I'd once had to wash it out of my hair. "No mustard."

We settled onto the couch, plates on our laps, and Brendan turned on ESPN. As we kicked back and ate, the stress of the day melted away. My adorable lazy dog snoring at my feet added another layer of comfort. Obviously he already felt at home.

I glanced at Brendan, now fully engrossed in sports highlights. His careless, go-with-the-flow attitude was so the opposite of what I was used to. I found myself soaking in his strong profile, his Adam's apple, and the sliver of skin exposed by the open buttons on his shirt. There was no reason to pretend he wasn't sexy, just like there was nothing wrong with realizing he was. The important thing was that we were friends who had history, and we'd managed to bridge all those years apart with a couple of easy nights.

I leaned back on the cushions and kicked up my feet on the coffee table.

Suddenly, my life didn't feel like such a mess anymore.

Chapter Nine

The newspaper office always smelled stuffy, like all the years of stories were trapped inside with the people frantically writing them.

Item one on today's to-do list was confronting Phoebe Pratt. The rage I'd felt toward her Friday night had mostly abated, but I wanted to make it clear my life wasn't up for gossip in the paper, and I needed to talk to Tess about my column anyway—it was item two, actually. Each task I needed to accomplish today was typed into my phone, color-coded and waiting for a simple tap to cross it off. God bless technology.

"Just the girl I wanted to see," Phoebe Pratt said, stepping into my path. Her dark hair was up in a loose bun, and she wore her usual cat-eye glasses with crystals.

"I was looking for you, too, actually." Now that the woman was in front of me, her red lips stretched into a spiteful smile, the heat was instantly back in my veins. What happened to respect for colleagues? Or at least a little girl solidarity?

She lifted her blinged-out iPhone between us, and I noticed the recording app on her screen. "So, Dakota Halifax, do you think people will still want to hire you when your own wedding didn't go as planned?"

I glared at her, my fingers curling into fists. Did she seriously just ask me that? After she'd already cost me business?

"How do you plan on preventing the same thing from happening to your clients? Isn't that what they hire you for?" Her thin eyebrows arched above the frames of her glasses.

"Well," I said through clenched teeth. "I'd say that not everything, no matter how well organized, goes according to plan. For example, I didn't plan on punching you this morning, but here I am, ready to do just that."

Her jaw dropped and then she yelled, "Dakota just threatened me! I have it on tape."

Heads swiveled in our direction and a couple of people popped out of their cubicles. I rolled my eyes and shoved her phone away from me. "My personal life isn't available for your column, Phoebe. You crossed a line."

"Look, it's nothing personal. Valentina Maddox's wedding is set to get national attention, and I'm going to cover it better than anyone else out there. And for some reason, people in the city are actually interested in you because of it. I've gotten emails wanting to know more, and you're a public figure. Deal with it."

"Listen to me, you wannabe attention whore—"

"Let's calm down here," George from Classifieds said, putting his hand on my shoulder. "There's no need for violence."

"Maybe not need, but want...?" I narrowed my eyes on Phoebe. "No, it's actually need."

"Keep talking." Phoebe waved her phone at me. "I've got it all recorded."

I lurched for the phone, and I would've had it, too, but George held me back. Irritation burned through me at how out-of-control this situation was getting. Now I was the bad guy? Fine. She could have her recording of me saying I was going to punch her. As much as I wanted to follow through on the threat, lucky for her, I'd learned to deal with things differently since second grade. I'd just steer clear of her, and then go over her head to Tess.

Speaking of my boss at the paper, Tess had come out of her office and was looking from Phoebe to me, and then at the guy holding me back like I was some kind of rabid dog.

"She threatened me," Phoebe said. "I'm putting it in my column. Wedding planner has meltdown after her failed nuptials."

I glared and stepped forward, quickly enough that George couldn't catch me. Phoebe shrieked and threw her hands up, which was almost as satisfying as taking a swing at her. "One last warning. Leave me out of your column."

"Dakota! In my office. Now." Tess was usually so soft-spoken that her I-mean-business voice stopped me cold.

"I want to file a complaint," Phoebe called as I turned my back to her. "If she were anyone else, security would've been called by now."

Since I'd already acted with the maturity of a little kid, I held back the urge to stick my tongue out at her as I stormed into Tess's office.

"How could you let her print a story about my failed wedding in her column?" I asked.

Tess rounded her desk and sat in her chair. "Was what she wrote false?"

A sharp twinge went through my chest. "Not exactly. But it's my private life."

"And how are you doing with that?" Tess looked at me with the poor-you expression I'd gotten a lot since my *I dos* turned into *I don't even bother to show up*.

"I'm fine."

"You're threatening a coworker."

"It's Phoebe. Don't tell me you haven't wanted to take a swing at her before."

Tess steepled her hands on her desk and sighed. "Your articles are good, Dakota, and people like them. But I can't give you preferential treatment simply because you did my wedding. I consider you a friend, but I can't have you threatening my reporters."

I hung my head like Cupid did when he got scolded for chewing up the furniture. "I understand."

"So now you've got two options. You resign, or you take an anger management course."

"Anger management? Are you kidding me?" I yelled, then managed to restrain the anger, which was slightly ironic considering. And proof that I could contain my temper, if you asked me.

Tess glared down her nose at me, which I took to mean a big hell no to the kidding.

My column wasn't a huge moneymaker, but I enjoyed it, and after draining my bank account for the event everyone wanted to remind me didn't happen, plus those clients I'd already lost, I needed all the extra cash I could get.

"You know how Phoebe is; she'll complain till someone listens, whether it's the police or her readers. This way I can say it's being taken care of."

Well, this day sure had gone up in flames quickly. I wondered whether, if I'd moved looking at apartments to my top spot instead of placing it third, I would've missed Phoebe. Or at least had enough coffee in my system to better deal with her egging me on like that. But since there was no use crying over spilled social columnists, I figured I'd take the stupid course and move on with my new life. But my anger level was definitely high—like past Fuchsia and into Raging Ruby, a color I didn't even use. That's how serious this was. "Does she have to take obnoxious management classes?"

Tess's eyebrows simply rose higher.

"Fine," I said. "I'll do it."

"Great. I'll email you the details." Tess spun around in her chair, opened her filing cabinet, and pulled out a copy of the *Beacon* from two months ago. "And maybe you need to reread your column in this edition. There were some good tips in there."

As I made my way out of the office, I got the walk-of-shame feeling. Only the vibe was less I-just-had-sex and more I-just-had-my-ass-chewed—and not in a good way.

"This is all you have open?" I asked, glancing around the newly carpeted apartment. The scent of fresh paint filled the air.

"Right now, everything else I have is leased," the manager of Sunrise Apartments said. She crossed over to the blinds and pulled them open, displaying a view of the crystal-blue pool that looked so inviting I wanted to dive in and let the cool water wash over me. "I already showed this place three times today, too. It'll go fast."

I had no doubt. It was a dream place with granite countertops in the kitchen, a spacious bedroom, and a walk-in closet so huge you could get lost in it. The second we'd stepped inside, I'd been tempted to yell I'd take it. "Do you think you might have a one-bedroom come up soon?"

"I doubt it. I've already got a wait list for people looking for one-bedrooms, if you'd like to add your name to it."

A wait list. So months, most likely, and even then the rent for a one-bedroom was high. The knot in my back throbbed at the thought of another night on Jillian's couch. She'd been so great, not saying anything about the squished quarters, but I was starting to feel like I was abusing her hospitality. I knew she was as much of a neat freak as I was, and the fact that my belongings were everywhere was starting to give me hives. I could move at least some of it to Dad's, but it didn't solve the main problem. My stuff needed a place to go. *I* needed a place to go.

This apartment would definitely solve that problem, but it created another. I'd grown accustomed to eating, and I wasn't ready to give it up. Between the rent for this two-bedroom apartment and at my office, though, that seemed like the decision I'd be making. And if I were going to pay that much every month, I wanted it to be going toward buying a place.

"I know one of our residents just lost a roommate and has an ad listed for someone to move into the other bedroom and split rent," the manager said. "I could give you the contact info if that's something you'd be interested in."

Being independent sorta implied going solo, but I supposed if I could go solo in my own room, it was still progress. Then when things stabilized, I could find a more permanent solution, possibly even a condo or a small house. Six months from now I'd be back on my feet, I'd hopefully see the influx of business from putting on Valentina's wedding, and I'd know better what I could or couldn't afford.

Until then, a roommate might be the perfect solution.

After the manager gave me the phone number and left for her office, I called, figuring I might as well try seeing it while I was here.

"Hello?"

The voice was male. I'd assumed it'd be female, but I supposed plenty of girls moved in with guys they didn't know. I just wasn't sure I was one of them. Then again, there was that beggars-can't-be-choosers aspect to consider. Within a few minutes, I was in front of the guy's apartment door so he could show me around.

There was a bong on the table, so I was already feeling pretty confident about the match. The empty pizza boxes as tall as the furniture were just an added bonus. The bedroom he showed me was at least empty, but I wouldn't go so far as to call it clean.

The guy stared at me with his bloodshot eyes as I checked out the dark spots on the carpet. This place was obviously a step down from the last one—give or take a hundred steps. Everything needed deep cleaning, with an extra side of industrial-strength cleaner.

"How old are you?" I asked.

He blinked slowly at me. "Twenty-two. I'm taking a break from college right now, but I've got a job at a pizza place. I can bring home free pizza. Just one of the many perks if you move in."

How the hell did he afford rent working at a pizza place? And was that supposed to be his way of hitting on me, or was he offering to share his bong? He said everything so monotone it was hard to tell. "And how do you feel about dogs?"

"I'm cool with them, but I'm not gonna walk after one with, like, a bag. I don't clean shit up."

Understatement, I thought, but managed to keep it in my head. See? I had self-control. "Okay, well I have your information, so…"

"No offense, lady, but I'm not sure I'd want you as a room-mate."

It was a toss-up as to whether the *lady* or the *not wanting me as a roommate* was worse. Not that I was ready to move in, but now I felt old and rejected. It wasn't even noon, and I'd already hit the max level of suckiness I could deal with. Screw the rest of my to-do list, along with the guy standing across from me.

This day could go to hell for all I cared.

Chapter Ten

GET READY TO WED by Dakota Halifax
Keeping Your Cool

There are several tips to keeping your cool on your big day. The first, and most important in my book, is organization. A well-organized event, no matter how many unforeseen disasters occur, goes better than unplanned madness. If you can't afford someone like me, divide the tasks up among your most trusted friends and family. Whatever happens, remember to keep it all in perspective, take deep breaths, and tackle one thing at a time.

Now, as for the actual heat: If you're getting married in the middle of summer, make sure to ask about air-conditioning when you book the chapel or reception hall. Keep hydrated. Every bride likes a dramatic exit, but the ambulance is never a good way to go.

I've seen a lot of meltdowns over the years, but if you know what's coming in advance, it can help avoid disaster. If your fiancé doesn't understand the importance of place settings, cake toppers, or flowers, don't blow up. Not all grooms get it, and some simply don't know how to express exactly what they want. There are also some who don't care about wedding details at all, which doesn't mean they don't care about you. Some have very strong ideas of what they want, and they might not match the image you've had in your head since you were a little girl. You can find a happy medium no matter what side of the spectrum you and your significant other land on, and there are people who will notice and appreciate all the planning and effort you put into the event. When your mother, your mother-in-law, one of your bridesmaids, or anyone else tries to take over, inhale a deep breath, count to ten, and then calmly remind them that it's your wedding. Things don't always work the way you want them to. Getting angry doesn't fix it, so again, deep breaths and a little perspective about what—and who—is really important. You're stressed, and that's cool, but then you lose your temper and yell at the friends, family, and workers who are trying to make your big day awesome, and that's not cool. Smile and remember that you're getting married. And after that, there's cake and presents. Oh, and happily ever after living with your groom, of course. That's the whole point of the awesome day after all, isn't it?

I think that Tess meant for me to read about taking deep breaths, compromising, and how getting angry didn't fix anything, but my eyes kept focusing on the last few lines. Surely she'd forgotten that part of it—the part promising cake and presents and a freaking groom. I tossed the *Las Vegas Beacon* on Brendan's coffee table, dropped my head in my hands, and tried the deep breathing thing.

The fact that I had to take anger management classes hit me all over again, making it seem like a weight had been placed on my shoulders. Lately I had been feeling angrier than usual, but really? I'd be in there with people who got into bar fights and such, and I hadn't even gotten to throw a punch. Seemed unfair to say the least.

Cupid came over and dropped his head onto my lap as if he knew I needed him. After the whole apartment debacle, I'd found myself at Brendan's door. Last night I'd been so comfortable, and while I'd still hesitated to let myself in, eventually I decided it was better than having a breakdown somewhere public enough that Phoebe would somehow find out and put it in print.

My phone rang and I glanced at the display. I answered when I saw it was Valentina, crossing my fingers that she wasn't having another hair emergency. Then again, maybe focusing on solving someone else's problems would make me feel better.

"Hey, I was hoping I could email you my engagement photos so you could help me pick which one I should go with."

"I'd be happy to." I pulled my laptop out of my bag. The wifi was secured with a password—should've known Brendan would be into security in every aspect of his life. The chime on my phone went off, letting me know I'd gotten her email. I tried to look at her photos, but I hated to give an opinion on them when I couldn't see them on a bigger screen.

After a moment of going back and forth, I asked Valentina if I could call her back in a few minutes. Then I texted Brendan, explaining I was at his place to check on Cupid and was hoping to sneak in a little work but needed his wifi password. My phone chimed within a couple of seconds.

Brendan: I'm starting to think you're a spy.

For the first time in hours, I actually smiled.

Me: Damn, my secret is out. Considering I can't even break into your internet, I'm not a very good one, though. This leaves me no choice but to use my impressive physical strength. I know a hundred ways to kill a guy simply by looking at him, so we can do this the hard way or the easy way.

Brendan: I have no doubt that's true. I know I should just give in now, what with the impressive strength and all, but I prefer a challenge.

Me: Of course you do. How about an exchange? Chinese food for the password, and I won't have to kill you. Tonight, anyway. No promises after.

Brendan: Deal.

As soon as I logged on, I pulled up all the pictures and looked through every one. They were beautiful, and her hair was perfection, thanks to Raquel's magic with the scissors and hair dye. There was only one thing missing, and I kept waiting for it to show up.

Beautiful scenery that contrasted with the couple's outfits— check. Airbrushing that made them look flawless but not inhuman—check. Cute poses with hand-holding, intense gazing, and kissing—check. But a hollow hole opened up inside me, just like at Erika's wedding. While I'd never admit to having favorite brides, of course I did. This was Valentina. Fun, easygoing, and super nice despite her social status Valentina. The girl I'd bonded over Thai food with on our very first appointment because we'd both played soccer in high school and could quote *Bend It Like Beckham* ad nauseum. It should be different with her. But as I stared at the images on my screen, I got the same feeling I'd get looking at a nice painting at a museum. Totally detached, no desire to squeal and think about how that couple was one step closer to committing their lives to each other.

I amped myself up for the call before dialing Valentina's number and forced as much enthusiasm into my voice as I could. Regardless of my inability to get excited, my ability to see a picture and know if it'd work well with the invitations she'd picked was at least there. We chose one for the paper, one for the wedding invitations, and I suggested printing and framing a few to hang up at the reception.

When she wanted to talk about other wedding details, I told her I had another appointment to get to and that she should set up an office appointment for next week, hoping by then I'd be back to normal and be the wedding planner she deserved.

Once I hung up, sitting still become impossible—I could practically feel the to-do list on my phone glaring at me, reminding me how much I'd left incomplete for the day. All of the rest of the items were wedding-related, though.

I looked around the room. Compared to Stoner Boy's apartment, the place was clean, but it could still use some straightening. Brendan wouldn't be home for hours, the last place I wanted to go was my office, and if I headed to Jillian's I'd only have the fact that I had no space of my own shoved in my face, along with another side of guilt over her having to deal with it and me. So I lined up Brendan's remotes, took his mail to join the other pile on the counter, and put it all in a neat stack. Then I found a bowl for his fruit. Once I got started, I couldn't stop myself.

Right now, cleaning up was the only thing I could control, so I was going to control the hell out of it.

I woke up to the sound of a key sliding into the door, and it took me a moment to realize I was on the couch at Brendan's.

It was the best rest I'd gotten in weeks, too—the cushions more embraced me than conspired to toss me off. Cupid lifted his head when Brendan came in, but then dropped it back onto the arm of the chair he'd claimed—they were already buds, but apparently not enough to interrupt his nap to greet him.

Brendan tugged his tie loose and unbuttoned the top few buttons of his shirt as if a second longer might cut off his supply of oxygen, and glanced around. "Did you…clean my place?"

When I was in the middle of "being in control," I wasn't thinking that I might also be crossing a line. I slowly sat up. "I had a bad day, and then I just started organizing and scrubbing, and one thing led to another, and…"

Oh my gosh, I'm a total weirdo! So many times, I'd marveled at Brendan, the kid I knew all grown up, but as he arched his eyebrows and rubbed his fingers across his stubbled jaw, all I could think about was that he was a hot guy I'd shown my crazy side to. I'd gone through his mail and cupboards and scrubbed his counters to a sheen you could see your reflection in. No doubt he was rethinking this whole arrangement and wondering where the girl he used to toss around a football with went.

"I'm sorry. This haze that blocks my common sense settles over me when I start organizing or cleaning—it's a sickness, really. Most of the time I try to ease people into it, but I haven't gotten my hands on any lemon cleaner in a while, and you had the good stuff under your sink." My attempted joke didn't come out quite like I wanted it to, especially since his eyes were now on mine and my throat went totally dry. "If you want your key back, I totally understand."

"Are you kidding me?" Brendan stepped forward and skimmed his fingers over my shoulder. My lungs forgot how to work for a moment. "If you're going to clean, I'm never letting you leave."

The elephant-size panic sitting on my chest eased. "I ordered Chinese, as promised—I was too hungry to wait. But there's a ton in the fridge, all clearly labeled so you don't have to guess which one is which."

"Thanks." He squeezed my shoulder and I wasn't sure if the flutter that went through my tummy was exactly friendship-esque, but I didn't want to overanalyze and ruin the moment. He tossed his suit coat and tie on the arm of the couch, and I got a whiff of his cologne. *Man, he smells good.*

On his way to the kitchen, Brendan reached down and petted Cupid. I heard the beeps from the microwave, and a couple of minutes later he came back in holding a steaming white-and-red box. "You even cleaned out the fridge."

"Just did a little wiping down and rearranging," I said, shrugging like it was no big deal. Seriously, what had gotten into me? It'd worked so well, had shut everything else out for a while. Enough I'd even taken a nap, something I hadn't done in months.

Brendan sat on the couch and leaned back. "It must've been a really bad day. What happened?"

I sighed. "It all started with getting into a bit of a disagreement with a coworker at the paper. Everything just barreled downhill after that."

"Define 'bit,'" Brendan said around a chunk of Szechuan beef.

I hesitated to even say it out loud, wincing again at the stupidity of the situation. "While there was no physical violence, I did say I wanted to punch her, so now I have to take an anger management class."

Brendan laughed, and I frowned at him.

"It's not funny. Apparently she can print whatever she wants in her column, and I not only have to take it but also have to go learn how to control my anger—like I'm some kind of ticking time bomb!"

I could tell Brendan was trying not to laugh again.

I ran my fingers down the seam on my pants. "The stupid thing is, I do feel angry lately. Little things get to me more. It's not like I need classes, or that I'd take a swing at someone, but…" I picked at a stray black thread. "Well, that's not true, because not even an hour later, I was ready to hit a twenty-two-year-old stoner who made it clear he doesn't want me as a roommate. What does it say about me that I'm in the same place as him? Or let's be honest, that he's got it more together than I do?" I picked at that damn thread again and again, even though it refused to break free. "My life's a total mess."

Brendan took my hand, curling his long fingers over the top of it.

It made me feel like a girl, the way I never wanted to when I was younger, but suddenly didn't seem like such a bad thing now. But I refused to cry. "I don't even *like* weddings anymore." My voice shook—not a tear, though, let the record show. Then before I knew it, I'd laid out everything about meeting Grant, from standing on the beach on my wedding day, feeling completely off at my job now, to Grant having a kid and not knowing what to do about it.

Brendan wasn't fighting a smile anymore—he actually looked like he was at a total loss, a sort of wide-eyed deer-in-crazy-bridezilla-headlights.

"I'm not that little girl you used to know anymore—the one who was tough and didn't need anyone. I started falling in love so easily somewhere along the way. I'd never let the guy know I did, but I'd fall hard, and when things didn't work out, I'd hide myself away and close myself off. Tell myself to never care about a guy again. But then I would, and the cycle would repeat. But with Grant I thought I'd found someone different—thought it was going to be okay this time. But here I am, acting crazy now that we're not together, and I can't decide if that means I'm supposed to give him another chance, or if I'll never be me again, or what."

Brendan's mouth opened and closed a couple of times.

"See. Total mess." I threw my head back, sank against the couch cushions, and wished for the power of invisibility. This never would've happened if I hadn't given up my apartment to move in with Grant. I could be having my breakdown alone, where no one would find out I wasn't as tough as I appeared to be.

Brendan's warm fingertips touched my face, wiping away liquid on my cheek, which meant I'd lost the battle to not cry. And that only made me want to cry more. "No, you're not the girl you used to be," he said, and I opened my eyes to see his face near mine. "You've built your own business, you've opened yourself up, and you've gotten hurt. But it's better than not engaging, trust me. You think I didn't see how much you hid, even back then? How you flinched every time anyone mentioned your mom? Or how you'd send me home before you cracked and showed any emotion, telling me you wanted to be alone?"

My throat tightened. I thought I'd done such a good job of showing everyone those things didn't hurt me. How had he seen? How could he remember that long ago?

"You care about people, D.J. You always have. That's why I tried to protect you, even though you fought so damn hard against it. And like it or not, I'm not leaving you alone anymore to deal with it yourself, so get used to it."

I wasn't sure how I'd gotten so lucky to have him move back when I needed someone the most—someone who really saw me. But the fact that he was here and not backing away made my heart expand and press against my rib cage. I leaned forward and hugged him, dropping my head on his chest.

And for the first time since I could remember, instead of feeling like a failure because I couldn't hold back my tears, it felt like just the release I needed.

Chapter Eleven

Brendan handed me a cup of coffee over the bar in his kitchen. The early morning light filtered in between the blinds on the patio door, sending stripes of way-too-bright golden sunshine across the tile and into my eyes. Slamming back beers while playing video games until 2:00 a.m. probably hadn't been the wisest decision, but it'd proved to be the perfect way to turn a bad day into a pleasantly fuzzy one. Of course the drinking meant no driving, and even though Brendan tried to be all chivalrous and let the emotional drunk girl sleep in his bed while he took the couch, I eventually out-stubborned him. My back didn't even ache the way it usually did when I woke up. His couch was definitely a keeper.

"Creamer?" I asked as I wrapped my hands around the warm mug.

Brendan pulled the plain, boring kind out of his fridge. Not my usual hazelnut preference, but anything that helped facilitate getting the caffeine into my system would do.

After my breakdown, I thought I'd be embarrassed, but mostly I just felt like I could finally move on to the next stage of my life — the real way instead of the on-paper way. "Thanks again for last night."

"Anytime." Brendan settled on a stool across from me. "Actually, I was thinking…" He peered into his coffee and I froze with mine halfway to my lips, unsure if I was going to like whatever came next. "You know, I do have two empty bedrooms. I was planning on getting a spare bed for one of them already. If you want, you could live here."

Mornings weren't my strong point, and it took my brain a moment to connect his words and get what he was saying. "Live here? With you?"

One corner of his mouth twisted up. "I thought I might be a better option than a stoner pizza guy, but I could see how it'd be a tough choice."

"What you've got to ask yourself is if you'd really be willing to live with someone who'd been rejected by that dude. I'd guess his bar ain't near as high as he was, and I didn't even reach it."

Brendan casually shrugged. "I've always been a sucker for the guys no one else cheers for."

"As a fellow Niners fan, I'm pretty sure I'd have to say the same." I smiled at him and seriously considered the idea. Brendan was the kind of person who just jumped without looking. I liked lists and risk analysis charts and to know there was a soft landing ahead. What if moving in ruined the easy vibe we'd settled into? Being around him chased away the darkness always tugging at me, and I needed that in my life.

"I just figure we get along, I've got plenty of room, and it'd be better than you moving in with a stranger who might be a complete weirdo."

"Yes, it's far better to know my roommate's a partial weirdo from the get-go."

He laughed, the deep sound echoing through me. "Exactly."

As a fan of plans, I was surprised by how much I enjoyed our impromptu, completely unstructured hangouts. Living together would just be the extreme version of that, right? All the fun, all the time? The more I thought about it, the better the idea sounded. "I've already got a bed, so no need for you to buy one. I'd pay rent of course, and pitch in on everything. And—"

"Ooh, there's an 'and.'"

"Be nice," I said, shooting him a mock scowl.

"That's not gonna be easy. I—"

I slapped a hand over his mouth. "I was saying be nice about my 'and.' I know I had a mini-breakdown last night, but I can take care of myself. I don't want you to do this if I'm just a pity project. You don't need to take care of me."

He raised an eyebrow, and I slowly dropped my hand from his mouth. "That was a big 'and.'" He nodded, not quite able to pull off the serious expression he was taunting me with. "No pity. Got it."

He tipped back the last of his coffee, set his mug in the sink, and leveled the tie draped around his neck, sliding the fat end down to match the skinny end.

Was that really it? Didn't he need to know more? "As you saw yesterday, I'm a bit OCD about cleaning and organizing. Do you mind me touching your stuff?"

He paused mid-tying his tie, and the grin that curved his lips seemed to be in on a secret I wasn't. "Have at it."

Was his voice rougher than usual? My cheeks were suddenly hotter than they were supposed to be.

Brendan pulled his tie straight and began looping it over again.

"Here." Since my dad had to dress up on game day—something he grumbled endlessly about—I'd learned to tie ties. Being in the wedding biz, I'd gotten quite good at every kind of knot there was, and even bow ties stood no chance against me. I readjusted the silky fabric, and with a couple swift crosses and tugs, had it perfectly in place.

Brendan smoothed his hand down it. "Thanks. This one's a bit short, so it always gives me trouble."

There it was again. The deep voice. *Calm down, hormones. It's just his usual voice.* Obviously my lack of sleep was getting to me. I needed more coffee. I picked up my cup and took a gulp large enough to take out my taste buds for a while.

As Brendan walked by me, he dragged his hand across the small of my back, and I started second-guessing my decision to live with him, considering I was becoming all too aware of every glance and touch.

But then he asked, "So, roomie? When would you like to move in?" and I found myself diving right in without looking for the landing.

White dresses filled the space around me, a sea of tulle, lace, and satin, each begging to be taken off the rack and held up to see if it was the one. I'd done the dance with several brides, and had even had that moment myself. You justify how expensive the gown is by telling yourself you get married only once—ah, the optimistic, love-deluded thought. Mine hadn't even been worn long enough to count, and I never wanted to put it on again. Nothing said bad luck like your something old being the dress you already failed to get married in. Really, I should sell it and at least get a bit of monetary compensation to help ease the pain.

Still, it stung less and less by the day, which gave me hope that someday soon I'd look at wedding-related items and get an inkling of that love-deluded optimism. I just couldn't see myself continuing to do what I did for years and years without it.

"Almost ready," my client said from inside the dressing room. "This zipper is giving me a bit of trouble."

"If you need my help, let me know." There were plenty of brides who didn't involve me in the finding of The Dress, simply showing it to me after they'd picked it out. Occasionally they'd ask what I thought of certain styles, what I thought would flatter them, or what was in style right now. But Molly insisted I be at the shop to give my opinion. After all, as she put it, I knew who wore what when it came to the biggest weddings, and she simply couldn't have the same dress anyone else had already worn. Her girlfriends sat in the chairs facing the dressing room, flipping through a book with bridesmaids' dresses inside.

"Got it!" The door swung open and Molly came out in a strapless mermaid-style gown. Her skin mushroomed over the tight bodice, and I was scared we were one wrong move away from a wardrobe malfunction. Even though she was a skinny girl, the seams looked like they were about to pop.

"What do you think? I'll probably wear my hair up." She gathered her dark hair in a twist, and when she lifted her arm, it only emphasized that the dress was a good two sizes too small. The zipper in the back wasn't even all the way up—so much for "got it!"

I glanced at the bridesmaids to see if they'd be helping me break the news about the wrong fit. From the way they were blinking and avoiding looking too closely, I had the feeling they agreed but wouldn't be voicing it.

"Um." I hesitated, working out how to word it delicately. "You're a very skinny girl, but I don't think that size is showing off your best features. You're going to need to move during your wedding, so you might be more comfortable in a…" Hell, they hired me for my opinion, so I went ahead and blurted it out. "Larger size."

"Well, it doesn't fit *now*," she said as if I was being the ridiculous one. "But I'm going to lose two sizes by my wedding. If I buy one that fits now, I might not be motivated enough to lose all the weight. Two sizes in four months, right, Kayla?"

The maid of honor looked up and flashed her a thumbs-up signal. "We got this, girl. I'm gonna order mine smaller, too. Then we'll have no choice but to make it work."

Okay, Kayla just went from not-helpful to enemy-of-the-bridal-state. "Look, I've done a lot of weddings, and that has never once worked out well for a bride. First of all, you're tiny already. Your fiancé loves you for who you are, and who you are now. I doubt seeing your ribs will make him love you more. Buy the dress in your current size, and if you do lose weight and it's a little loose, you can have it altered. You can always make it smaller, but there's no making it bigger."

"But if I—"

"Nope."

Her mouth opened and closed like a fish struggling for air.

"You make one wrong move in that and you're flashing everyone at the ceremony. Do you want to Janet Jackson your grandparents?" Seriously, didn't any of my brides read my column? I'd done a whole article on this kind of thing.

"No," Molly said, her lips pressed into a pout.

"Why'd you hire me?" I asked.

"Because you're the expert," she replied, and while I could've done with a little more enthusiasm, at least she knew where I was going. "Fine." She glanced at the salesgirl, who'd reappeared at the wave of my hand.

"Can we try that in two sizes up?" When the salesgirl went to find it, I turned back to Molly. "I'm here to make your wedding perfect. It's my top priority, and I'm not going to let you down."

A few minutes later, Molly came out in the proper size, the fit perfect and the zipper all the way up.

Her bridesmaids gasped and Kayla shot to her feet. "That's it! It looks amazing!"

I fluffed the bottom layers. "I haven't had many brides doing the mermaid dress lately, but I hear it's making a comeback, so you'll be unique *and* in style." So I hadn't actually heard it, but surely somewhere, someone was making it the newest trend—styles tended to cycle every few years, but really it was about finding the right gown for the bride's body shape that also fit her personality. I straightened and took her in again. "It's totally stunning on you."

"It's the one, I'm sure of it." Tears bordered Molly's eyes. "Oh my gosh, I'm getting married!" She hugged me so enthusiastically I nearly tipped over—hazard of the biz and something I'd gotten accustomed to, although I obviously needed to amp up my game. Molly's bridal party got in on the group hug. I was better than I had been at Erika's wedding, or even the other consults I'd had, but I still didn't feel the tingly hope thing. The shortage of air on the other hand, I felt that. If I didn't know better, I'd think I was becoming allergic to weddings.

Chapter Twelve

I was studying the fabric swatches, place settings, dried flowers, and napkins laid out on the dining room table when Brendan came over and refilled my coffee without my having to ask. He even set the hazelnut creamer I'd bought next to my mug. Despite my best attempts to convert him, he'd insisted on sticking with his plain creamer.

We'd fallen into a nice, comfortable pattern over this past week. I'd moved in, we both worked long hours, and then our evenings were mostly filled with watching TV, heavy on the ESPN.

Brendan looked over my shoulder and I caught a whiff of his aftershave. "I didn't know orange, purple, and blue went together, but it looks pretty good."

"That's because it's rust, amethyst, and cerulean. With a hint of jade thrown in." I moved the jade and amethyst place setting over the cerulean fabric that'd make up the tablecloths at Valentina's wedding to make sure it worked.

Brendan cast me a suspicious sideways glance. "Now you're just making up colors."

"Pretty sure I know every color there is now. The first few

months I had a couple of brides surprise me—one requested cement. With dusty plum and blueberry. It was one of my favorite color palettes, actually."

"Cement? What's wrong with gray? It's the same thing."

"Not romantic enough, duh." I smiled and nudged him with my elbow.

"Silly me. Nothing's as romantic as the color you used to trip on and leave half of your skin and blood behind."

I laughed. "Okay, you got me there. How's pewter? Romantic enough for you?"

"I'm swooning just thinking about it." He took a sip of his coffee and then lifted the *Beacon* out from under the pile of my fabric swatches, my "Keeping Your Cool" article folded up. "Is this yours?"

"Yeah. I meant to throw it in the recycling." I reached for it, but Brendan kept it away and his eyes scanned down the page, his lips moving slightly as he read. The corner of his mouth twitched here and there. I'd never watched anyone read my articles before—it made my pulse skitter and my face get hot. And everything I'd ever written suddenly felt stupid and unimportant.

"Hmm. Interesting stuff. Guess I'll have to start reading it more."

"Planning to tie the knot soon, are you?"

He made a sort of strangled choking noise in the back of his throat. I raised an eyebrow and he set his coffee mug on the counter, where he often left it instead of walking it to the sink.

"I saw that," I said. "There's a story behind that noise."

"Don't know what you're talking about." Brendan tried to walk past me, and I put my hand on his chest to stop him. "B.S."

He cracked a smile. Since I used to go by D.J.—short for Dakota Jane—I'd taken to calling Brendan Scott B.S. whenever he exaggerated. Which used to be a lot, especially when we were in grade school.

"That's a story for another time." He tapped me on the head with the newspaper. When my jaw dropped, his smile widened. "Don't give me that mad glare, or I'll have to report to your anger management officer."

I gave him a gentle shove, but he caught my arms, his reflexes crazy fast. Then I was noticing the way his long fingers wrapped around my elbows, and my heart rate quickened. He leaned in, and for a moment, I thought he might kiss me good-bye.

For a moment, I thought I might want him to.

But he reached behind me for his keys, his body bumping into mine, one hand still wrapped around my elbow. "Let's go to a movie tonight. There's that new zombie one that just came out."

Did he seriously not realize our bodies were touching? Was he completely unaffected by it? Not that I wanted him to be affected. I licked my suddenly dry lips. "The one with all the brain-eating," I said, though I didn't know which movie he was talking about. It all came to brain-eating eventually in zombie movies, right?

"That's the one. I've got tomorrow off, so I can stay out late. Please tell me you still like your movies bloody and violent."

His warmth was seeping into me, his voice comforting in the way I told myself was because he knew my movie preferences, and hello, we *were* friends. "The gorier the better, I always say." That much was true. I'd grown up watching movies with Dad that he probably shouldn't have let me watch. Even after I started planning weddings—or maybe because I did deal with love so much—I liked to escape with what a lot of girls told me were "guy movies."

"Awesome. Tonight, then." I swore there was a flash of something in his brown eyes, but I couldn't tell what exactly. Excitement? More?

My imagination was running away with me. That had to be it. Needing a distraction, I shoved my fabric samples into my bag. "I didn't realize how late it'd gotten. I've got an appointment to get to." Now that I did notice the time, it wasn't even a lie. Valentina was coming by my office first thing to look at the fabric, make a few other decisions regarding flowers and the cake, and so we could order individualized party favors. Traffic was often slow this time of day, and I liked to get to my office with enough of a head start to set up before my clients arrived.

My binder was too huge to go in with the fabric and my laptop, so I put the bag over my shoulder, stuck the lid on my to-go mug of coffee, and attempted to balance my binder and keys in the other hand.

"Need help?" Brendan asked.

I hugged the binder to me, shifting the bag, since it was trying to swing forward and throw off the balance I was struggling to maintain in my heels. "I've got it. I'm an independent woman now. Self-sufficient and everything."

"It's okay to have help now and then, you know."

"I'll remember that if I ever need it," I said. "Have a good day, and I'll see you later for the movie." The door took me two tries and I nearly dumped the binder and my coffee, but I finally got it open. Locking it was going to be tricky, but before I could dig out my keys, I heard Brendan engage the dead bolt from the other side.

I just have to make it to the car, I thought as my arms started to burn—I really needed to figure out a way to bring less crap home every night. Two trips would probably make it easier, but it seemed like a waste of time when I could easily suffer through a few minutes.

When I rounded to the driver's side door of my car, the rim of my tire was on the ground, the black rubber underneath it completely flat. *Are you kidding me? Can't I get a break, like, ever?*

This *so* wasn't on my to-do list. I tossed my bag and binder in the car and headed to the trunk. Brendan was pulling out of the garage, but he parked in the driveway and got out of his truck, heading over to me.

I set the spare tire on the ground and then reached for the jack, making a shooing motion with my free hand. "I got this. I don't want you to be late to work because of me."

Brendan eyed me, his lips pressing into a skeptical line.

"I'm serious. I don't need help. And I can call Valentina and push our appointment back. No big deal." Actually, it threw off my entire well-planned day, but that was life. Especially mine lately.

"Didn't we just talk about how it's okay to need help?"

"We did, and I said I'd ask for help if I ever need it. Which I don't. My daddy taught me how to change a tire." I positioned the jack under the car and pumped it until the flat tire was hovering above the ground. Luckily I was wearing slacks today, although the heels weren't doing me any favors. I glanced up at Brendan. "Go already."

Brendan crossed his arms. "Not gonna happen."

"So you're just going to stand there and watch?"

"Unless you're going to let me help?"

Yes, it would be easier to have him do it, but the point of my new life plan was to get back to the girl who didn't get hurt because she counted on herself, and she knew how to take care of things *without* help. I'd already moved in with him. I refused to rely on him any more than I already had to. "That's a negatory, good buddy."

Brendan laughed, and as frustrated as I was about his hovering, the noise made me smile. I gave the lug wrench a good twist, but *holy crap* the lug nuts were on tight. I could feel Brendan's stare, so I cranked harder. Finally the nut came lose—pretty sure I only popped one eye blood vessel, too, so score! The second came undone after a few muttered swear words, and a struggle that left sweat forming across my forehead. By the third one, my arms were burning. Jeez! Had they welded the damn things on? I was sure those screw guns were quick and all, but they made being a modern girl who didn't need help more difficult than it needed to be.

Brendan readjusted his weight from his right to his left foot, not even bothering to fight the amusement playing across his features. "Ready for some help?"

"No."

I stepped onto the wrench, gripped the side of my car, and jumped. The thing didn't even budge. I jumped again. Nothing. My options were go inside and get sneakers so I could properly jump up and down, or let Brendan help. My pride objected to the latter option, but I was pretty sure it was leaking out of me by the second as it was.

Brendan held out a hand.

I reluctantly took it and stepped to the ground. "It's the heels."

"That's why I rarely wear them. They're a bitch when chasing down bad guys, too." He rolled up his sleeves, crouched next to the flat tire, and gripped the wrench. The muscles in his forearms stood out as he slowly turned it. "These really are on tight."

"See. I told you," I said, reverting back to my nine-year-old self, apparently.

"I'm impressed you got two off." He held up a hand as I started to open my mouth. "It's a genuine compliment; just take it instead of arguing with me."

I clamped my lips shut, watching as he continued to work the last two nuts free and then secured the spare tire in place. Admittedly, he was faster than I could ever be. Well, the kind of silent admitting, because I wasn't going to say it out loud. Not to mention, watching the show wasn't exactly hard on the eyes. Was there anything sexier than the muscles in a guy's forearms?

He stood, and it took me several seconds to realize he was handing me the wrench. My fingers wrapped around the metal. It was warm from the sun, but not nearly as warm as the heat starting to wind its way through my core.

Manly displays of strength must have some hypnotic power that made girls stupid—another point for taking care of things myself. Apparently it was the only way to avoid having dirty thoughts about my roommate that had nothing to do with the fact that he was actually dirty.

Oh holy crap, look at those black-smudged hands. I thought of them trailing across my body, putting black streaks over my skin. It was so thc opposite of what I usually wanted. I shook off that thought and shoved the tools back in my trunk. My feelings for him were slowly morphing into something that left me feeling off-center, and it had panic rising up and squeezing my chest. "Here." I thrust the package of wet wipes I kept for wedding-related dirt emergencies at him and then cleaned my own hands.

"Don't stress yourself out over your appointment, okay? It'll still be there whcn you get there."

Plenty of people had told me I was too uptight about my schedule, but the way he did it actually calmed my racing pulse instead of made it beat faster.

"See you later, Deej." He climbed into his vehicle, and I got into mine. He let me go ahead of him, ever the gentleman. I used to get mad at him for things like that back in the day, because I didn't want the other guys to look at me as a weak girl. I supposed there wasn't anyone else around right now, and it was nice, though not helping on the independent woman front.

As soon as we split off in different directions, I called Jillian. "I think I've got a problem."

Chapter Thirteen

$\mathcal{J}$illian was on a tight deadline with an event tomorrow, so I met her at the local organic market to chat and shop. Not having her to talk to as much, especially late at night, was the one thing I missed about crashing with her.

"So are you plotting Phoebe's demise and hit a snag you need me to help work out, or did a caterer pull out of one of your weddings?" she asked as she picked up a basket and headed toward the produce section. "I'm pretty booked, but if I can squeeze it in, you know I'll—"

"Actually, I'm having another kind of problem. I'm totally lusting after my new roommate."

Jillian whipped around so fast I nearly barreled into her. "You're lusting after the guy you just picked up and moved in with, even though you only knew him when you were a kid?"

To say Jillian had doubted my judgment about moving in with Brendan was putting it mildly—especially since she'd yet to meet him thanks to all of our busy schedules. When she helped haul boxes into the house, though, even she admitted it was better than our previous cramped living situation. And okay, maybe I could've found a way for them to meet if I'd tried harder, but I hadn't wanted her to find any problems with Brendan when being around him was doing wonders for my sanity. Before I'd started, you know, going insane thinking about his forearms and his dirty hands on me, that is.

I twisted a strand of hair around my finger, wrapping it up until the lighter caramel color was covered with the darker part. "It was better than moving in with a stranger, and it's not like I *meant* for it to happen. Although he is a good-looking guy, so I should've probably seen it coming. I thought the fact that we used to know each other so well would keep these kinds of feelings from developing. But he's been so great about everything, and I mentioned the super good-looking thing, right?"

"So the problem is he's attractive and you need rebound sex."

"No! I mean yes to the attractive…" I waited for the elderly woman to pick out a clump of tomatoes and then leaned in close to Jillian, keeping my voice low. "No to the rebound sex." I exhaled, trying to organize my thoughts. "The problem is I shouldn't be thinking about him like that."

"But if you're really going for the whole independent woman thing, sex without strings is the part I'd suggest embracing. It's one of the only benefits in a sea of crappiness, honestly."

Jillian was one of the few women I knew who could pull that off without getting attached. It didn't mean she wasn't picky, just that she chose hot, smart guys and viewed them as temporary fun, no false expectations. "One, you know how easily I fall for guys, and two, Brendan's my oldest friend. Even though we've spent years apart, he knows things about me that most people don't. Things I haven't even told Grant."

"Like…?" Jillian frowned at the bundle of cilantro she'd picked up and then tossed it down in favor of another one.

"Like stuff with my mom. I mean, Grant knows that she and I have a strained relationship, but I never told him how abandoned

I felt when she picked her job over me. I didn't really tell Brendan, either, but he knew. And he can read me no matter how hard I try to hide my emotions, which is annoying and comforting at the same time." I picked up an apple and tossed it in the air, just to have something to focus on besides my confession. "Right now my life's a mess, and he's making it all seem okay anyway. But I need to not think about if he's going to kiss me, and definitely not about doing anything more that would make things weird between us." I set the apple back on the stack, careful to not knock any over.

"And what about Grant? Is he still asking for a second chance?"

"We've been on a bit of a break, but he called earlier. I sent him to voicemail, and he only said to call him. But in theory, he's still on the table."

"Well, I think he lost his chance." Jillian's eyebrows drew low over her eyes as she tapped her fingers on the shopping basket. "But I see what you mean with Brendan. You do live with the guy already, so that makes things complicated with a high possibility of messy."

This was why I'd come to Jillian. No-nonsense, tell-it-like-it-is advice.

"I think you need a fling," she said, and I reconsidered the no-nonsense part. "Someone super sexy who you barely know. It'll get your mind off how hot your roommate is, and might also help you figure out if you even want to get back what you used to have with Grant. Maybe you'll find you like playing the field again."

"Doubtful. It's just going to feel like a huge step backward after being almost married. A fling is a drive-through wedding, and you know how I feel about those." I tried my best to not sound judgmental—she could do what she wanted, but I knew myself too well to pretend I could pull off no-strings-attached sex.

"They're a big no-no. But a drive-through wedding's promising forever in the fastest way possible, and this is promising fun for a little while."

"It's different, though. I don't want some random dude, and the guy I suddenly find myself attracted to—although honestly, I thought he was hot the first day he came into my office, before I knew who he was..." I pictured the way he always had his tie draped over his unbuttoned shirt at the end of the day, and the way the smile brought out the cleft in his chin. Then there was the memory of his body bumping into mine as he reached for his keys and the whole tire-changing incident.

Jillian waved her hand in front of my face. "Yes...?"

"I just got Brendan back in my life, and there's something about being around him that makes it easy for me to relax, and you know how hard that is for me to do. The last thing I want to do is mess that up, especially right now when work is such a challenge and I'm about to have to start that stupid anger management course. I've gotta keep my head on straight. I barely got out of a serious relationship, he's simply being nice to me because we're friends, and here I am ready to throw myself at him. I never was any good at being on the rebound. I make stupid choices." Like the guy Raquel had mentioned during my hair appointment. "I go for the McDonald's of rebounds—tastes delicious going down, regret it for a week. Then I still find myself heading back for more."

Jillian wrinkled her nose—she loathed all fast food, and when she could make everything taste a hundred times better when she cooked it herself, why go cheap?

"Of course, that's unfair to Brendan, because I'm sure he's not a McDonald's kind of—" I shook my head. "You know what, I'm not even gonna finish that. Like all my analogies, it's gotten way too abstract, and now I want french fries."

"You really do have it bad."

"Not bad. I came to you at the first sign of temptation. That means fixable, right?"

Jillian tossed a couple of red and orange bell peppers into her basket.

"Jill?"

One of her dark eyebrows shot up. "You want me to tell you the truth, or what you want to hear?"

Silly me, I was kind of hoping for both.

A cute college-age guy with shaggy hair was working the cash register, and he greeted Jillian and me with a huge smile. Jillian kept tilting her head toward him, eyebrows raised, lacking enough subtlety he no doubt realized she was trying to get me to hit on him. Obviously she hadn't been listening to the no-fling thing.

I left her to pay and waited for her at the front of the store.

No bad rebound, no needing a guy, no deciding to pay Grant a visit because at least I knew him, and no messing up my friendship with Brendan. So there was only one option really. I was going to chant *drive-through wedding* over and over in my head for the foreseeable future, to remind myself what I was *not* looking for.

GET READY TO WED by Dakota Halifax
Drive-Through Weddings

I was staring at my computer screen, trying to decide what words of advice to give the great city of Las Vegas this week. Let's face it, you guys have already got the whole party-hearty-rock-and-roll thing down. What's left? I was hungry, so I ignored my blank screen and decided I needed a food break. I went through a local burger joint's drive-through and it hit me.

Drive-through weddings are called that for a reason. Do you ever get halfway down the road after going through the drive-through at a restaurant only to discover you didn't get exactly what you ordered? (I specifically said *no onions!* And where's the ketchup I asked for?) Well, take a few minutes and think about your special day. Do you want to get married only to find out the guy performing your ceremony was also arrested for some horrifying reason? (Oh, the things I could tell you I've seen preachers dressed as Elvis do. Trust me, sometimes you'd rather not see hunka, hunka burnin' love go down. Actually, change that "sometimes" and make it "always.") Maybe you find out your union isn't even legal—it still totally counts, in case you were wondering. A promise is a promise, and your drunk-in-Vegas excuse won't hold up in court any better than you did after one of those drinks so large you needed a handle to lug it around the casino. You love your significant other, and this wasn't just a drunken mistake, was it? Of course it wasn't! Most any chapel can get you in and out quickly, and I'm not opposed to being married by any of the fabulous bejeweled and jumpsuited preachers out there if that's what you want. (Just don't go wandering into the chapel bathroom when they think everyone's cleared out—trust me on that.) After all, being able to get married on a whim to the one you love is just another thing that makes our fine city awesome.

But please, please get out of the car and take a few minutes to pledge your love to each other. Preferably wearing pants, something that can also be missing during a drive-through wedding, but isn't nearly as amusing a story for your children as you think it'll be. Take a few minutes and look around at the decorations—be they cheesy cardboard cupids, fuzzy dice, and flashing casino lights, or chandeliers, elegant draped fabrics, and a rose-petal-strewn aisle—and soak in the moment of standing at an altar and exchanging vows with the man or woman of your dreams. You'll thank me one day.

Chapter Fourteen

$\int$ ust because Brendan and I were only friends and I wasn't going to do anything to compromise that didn't mean I couldn't look nice for our not-date. I hadn't been to anything besides a wedding in a long time, and that was when I was also working my butt off, so it hardly counted. Even when Grant and I were engaged, we were mostly homebodies. I couldn't remember the last time I'd seen a movie on the big screen.

So that's why I put on my distressed jeans, fitted white top with the sheer lacey overlay, and five-inch hot-pink peep-toe heels with lips that matched. Not because I was looking for a fling with my *buddy ol' pal* roommate, but because it was nice to dress up and remember that I could pull myself together pretty nicely when it came down to it.

Man, these shoes pinch the toes. They'd always been on the tight side, but hey, beauty's pain, right? How many times had I told my brides to suck it up and deal with the uncomfortableness for a few hours—I said it nicer than that of course, but it was the same basic principle. I'd be sitting through the movie anyway.

Thanks to the email I'd gotten a few minutes after arriving

back home—the one detailing how and where to complete my anger management course—I knew this was going to be my last night out for a while, too. Besides logging hours for it and all my upcoming consults and weddings, I was going to hardly have time for pesky things like sleep and eating. Being gone all the time should help keep my lust feelings in check, though, so there was my silver lining. Magical, I know.

My heels clacked against the hardwood floors until I hit the large rug in the living room. Cupid ran up to me and flopped on my feet, which meant *stop everything and pet me if you ever want to move again.* I obliged, scratching him under the chin like he liked.

Footsteps sounded behind me and I stood and turned around.

"Whoa," Brendan said, running his gaze over me. My heart skipped a couple of what-a-nice-friend-I-have beats. But speaking of whoa, he was dressed in jeans and a vintage T-shirt that showed off his toned chest and arms. He looked good when he dressed up for work, but there was something about the dressed-down look that was making me silently repeat *drive-through wedding* and *McDonald's burger* again and again.

"You're all dolled up," he said.

"You're all dolled down," I said. Like a genius with words, I am. "I mean, you look nice out of a suit. Casual. Not that the suit's not a good look for you." *Omigosh, stop talking.* "Uh, ready?"

He nodded and put his hand on my back. I might've leaned into it slightly, my body reacting before my brain, but I made sure to straighten right away.

Once we were in his truck, everything went back to normal— easy, fun, joking and talking without me thinking about kissing him. Until I had that thought and accidentally homed in on his lips.

Focus, Dakota. "So, we never finished this morning's conversation. Either you're violently opposed to engagement, or you had a disaster with a girl."

"Disaster*s*," Brendan said. "But the last one was pretty set on marriage. She started dropping hints six months in. I liked her, but I wasn't even close to thinking about settling down. Then she decided to start asking when we were going to get married. She told me she expected a ring for her birthday."

"I've had a couple grooms like you. Dragged there by sheer force of the girl. It never goes well, even if the guy does go through with the wedding." I glanced out the window. I wondered if that was how Grant had felt. Though he was the one who first brought it up. Living together. Marriage. Starting a family someday. And then he'd proposed, surprising me one night with the question and the ring. But maybe he thought it was what I wanted, and at the time, it was. I ran my fingers along the armrest of the door. "So what happened when she didn't get a ring for her birthday?"

"Before we even got to that point, I told her I wasn't looking to get hitched. Things went downhill pretty quickly and there was a big ugly breakup. I met her at work, too, so we were still forced to see each other all the time and it was awful. It was one reason why I jumped at the job here."

"So was it just the girl, or are you one of those people who is violently opposed to marriage?"

"I wouldn't say *violently*…" Brendan shrugged. "Never thought much about it. Guess I figured it was something way in the future. Like way, way future."

Since it was all I thought about—not so much mine, but when it's surrounding you, it's impossible not to get a couple ideas—that seemed a bit crazy. But I supposed most guys didn't stay up late talking about fairy-tale weddings and finding the perfect dress. Or tux, as it were.

"Every relationship I've been in has felt suffocating," Brendan said. "Never-ending calls all day long to 'check in' or ask where I'm at and what I'm doing. Being told I never take anything seriously, and feelings hurt so damn easily that I start to feel like a jackass even when I was sure I wasn't being one. I feel exhausted just thinking about it."

"Yeah, relationships. *Pfft.* Who needs them? It's all just a big show with the couple looking happy from the outside in, anyway— hell, maybe they even believe it. But then they go home and spend their nights bickering about what to do or what to watch on TV. Even the littlest thing can turn into a battle." I wasn't exactly sure where that'd come from. I supposed I'd thought about it lately as I'd looked at couples, wondering if anyone was really happy. Grant and I had spent plenty of nights arguing over the remote, and there were a lot of things we didn't agree on, but I wouldn't have called us unhappy—I did suffer through a lot of documentaries, though, and he never watched what I wanted. And once in a while he'd zone out when I went over our schedules, but I knew he wasn't as crazy about his to-do list as I was, even though he asked me to keep his in order and then acted like I was inconveniencing him when I was inputting it for him. Maybe I'd been wrong all these years, and everyone who avoided serious commitments had it right. Life was certainly less complicated.

"If I had a drink, I'd raise a toast to no relationships," I said. "And I'm feeling rather anti-marriage as well."

"If I didn't know better, I'd think you'd had a drink." Brendan pulled into the parking lot of the shopping strip with the theater. "I wasn't saying…" He exhaled. "I'm not opposed to all relationships. But no matter how much I cared about a woman, I'd never let her force me into an engagement to make her happy. When I think about how hard relationships are, and the commitment it'd take to add the 'till death do us part' in the mix, I'll admit it makes me wanna run in the other direction. That doesn't mean I'm some player who's against being faithful to one woman, though. There are definitely nice parts of being in a relationship…"

The temperature in the car rose a couple degrees as his brown eyes bored into me, and my breath caught in my throat for reasons I couldn't explain, and honestly, didn't want to delve too far into.

"Now…" He patted my thigh. "Let's go watch zombies!"

"Well, one thing's for sure. Your commitment to blood and guts is certainly impressive."

He laughed and then got out of the truck. As we walked past the shops, I was pretty sure I heard my name called. When I glanced around, I spotted a girl waving at me. She was in the Adler/Friedman wedding. Angular cheekbones. "Hey, Angie."

"Hi," she said as she made her way over to me. "Guess what?" She thrust her hand in front of my face. "I'm engaged!"

"Congratulations!"

"I've been meaning to call you. I'm not sure how much I can afford, but I needed help finding caterers and a location, and I wasn't sure if that was something you'd do if I didn't have you there at the wedding?"

"Sure." I pulled a card out of my purse and handed it to her. "Give me a call and we can discuss pricing options and how involved you want me to be. I can just consult on setup if that's all that's needed."

"I've been reading your columns, too. I was so excited for you after your last one, then I read in the paper that you didn't get married. I'm so sorry."

The plastic smile I was starting to pull out in times like these automatically formed itself across my lips. I was also remembering why I didn't go out much. Between Grant and me, it sometimes felt like we knew the entire city. "It's fine. For the best, really."

"Well, it looks like you're doing all right to me." Angie's gaze moved to Brendan, then she flashed me a thumbs-up I was sure she thought was covert but was quite the opposite.

"Actually, Brendan's just a friend." I looped my arm through his, needing his support to continue the everything's-so-amazing ruse. "I've known him forever."

Brendan tugged on our intertwined arms, jostling me into him and making me stumble on my heels. "Feels like longer sometimes."

He shot me a goofy smile when I glanced up at his face, and I couldn't help giggling.

"An eternity, really."

"Like pre-birth."

At this point, the lines in Angie's forehead became more pronounced, so I decided it was time to bring the conversation back from the weird but funny path it had strayed down. "So congrats again on the engagement, and give me a call. It was really good bumping into you."

"Yeah, you, too," she said, though it sounded kind of like *I'm never calling you now, you weirdo.*

"You're great for business, you know that?" I said to Brendan once she was gone. We started toward the theater again, but a familiar figure caught my attention. I thought I must just be seeing things, but there, waiting to get into our favorite fancy Chinese restaurant, was Grant, and he wasn't alone. A beautiful blond woman stood across from him, and I could tell from her face she was smitten, though I couldn't see Grant's to try to gauge if the feelings were mutual.

My feet were still in motion, and my shoe slipped on something wet. I automatically clamped on to Brendan's arm to keep from falling and my ankle folded under me. I was pretty proud of myself for not landing on my butt, and would've continued the celebration of my awesomeness had I not tried to step down on the foot that'd been twisted and experienced shooting pain all the way from ankle to knee.

"You okay?" Brendan asked.

"Just go," I whispered, limping toward the corridor that would block me from being spotted by Grant at least. When we were safely out of sight, I wiggled my ankle around, grimacing when it caught again and again. Of all the stupid, embarrassing things. "I'm fine," I said at Brendan's raised eyebrows, but trying to put weight on it made me let loose a string of swear words. I crouched down, weight leaning on my left foot.

"Yeah, you're fine. Obviously." He squatted to examine my ankle, as if he'd be able to tell what was wrong by seeing it. I didn't need to see it to know it was at least sprained. He ran his fingers across where it had folded wrong, the ache inside at odds with the careful brush of his fingertips. "If you weren't wearing these crazy-tall heels…"

My mouth dropped and I patted my shoes. "There, there, he didn't mean it. It was whoever spilled the drink on the floor's fault. Not yours."

Brendan's mouth kicked up on one side. "I didn't realize you'd injured your head, too."

I smacked his arm. "Why do I bother hanging out with you again?"

"Because you don't have many other options."

"Oh, that's right."

"And then there's the fact that you've known me for an 'eternity.' Come on, let's get you home." Brendan grabbed my hand, glided me to standing, and had his arm around my waist in one smooth transition.

"Not home. We have a zombie movie to see."

"You can't walk."

I dared a glance toward the restaurant and could just see the back of Grant's head. Everything inside me, from my lungs to my stomach, felt heavy and wrong. Was he dating again? Had he given up on me? Did I want him to? So many confusing emotions swirled through me, but the one thing I knew for sure was there was no way I was limping back past him and the blonde. "Sure I can." Brendan hesitated, and I saw my opening. "At home I'd just be sitting anyway. Here I'll be sitting, but with a movie. And popcorn. Can't you smell it?" The buttery, salty scent filled the air. "By the time it's over, my ankle will totally be better. I'm sure of it."

Brendan glanced the way we came, then the few feet it'd take to get to the theater. "I'm carrying you inside, then."

"No way. I'll just take off my shoes." I eyed the floor, thinking of all the germs waiting to seep into my feet. Why hadn't I worn socks? I mean, the eighties were back, so while we were resurrecting ugly styles, I might as well rock the socks with heels, too.

Brendan turned his back to me. "Hop on."

My options were now a piggyback ride or being carried like a damsel in distress past my ex-fiancé and the woman he was possibly moving on with. Really, there wasn't any option. I jumped on Brendan's back. Of course I got the giggles, and they only got worse when everyone stared at us. "If we see anyone I know, I'll die twice."

"Just like a zombie," Brendan added. After we got the tickets—earning more strange looks—he ordered popcorn, soda, and an extra cup of ice. Somehow, we managed to get it all inside the theater.

He gently lowered me into a seat and took the one next to me. Then he pulled my foot onto his lap and rested the cup of ice on my swelling ankle. Brendan made a couple of jokes and comments about the previews, and the ickiness over the Grant incident faded into the background. After a few handfuls of popcorn and a long pull on my soda, life seemed pretty good, despite the throbbing in my ankle. I watched the lights flicker across Brendan's features. Who else would piggyback me through a theater and make sure I had ice for my ankle?

As the movie progressed, Brendan leaned over, the ice in place, his other hand hooked on my knee. He tapped his fingers, and every beat sent a zip of electricity up my leg.

Onscreen, zombies were biting people, the gory, thick sounds of beheading and guts splattering filling the air.

But all I could focus on was the contact. And how the guy I'd known forever was making me feel things I'd never felt before.

Chapter Fifteen

"Is there something you wanna tell me?" Grant asked as he stood across from my desk.

My brain was still trying to catch up to the way he'd barged unexpectedly into my office, and now he had his arms crossed like he was waiting for me to confess. And suddenly I felt like blurting out, *Okay, you caught me! I had thoughts about another man!*

Part of me believed I was moving on so well that I wouldn't want him anymore, but as I stared at him, old feelings rose to the surface. My heart tugged, and I probably would've stood and drifted closer to him out of habit if my ankle wasn't throbbing. I was rocking ballet flats today, and I'd argued with Brendan for a good ten minutes when he'd insisted I should wear my sneakers. He didn't seem to care that it was a fashion no-no.

"I thought you were still considering us," Grant said. "That's what you told me, and I've been sitting around, just waiting for when you were ready."

"I was. I am. I'm a little lost, honestly. What's going on?"

"The paper? Phoebe's column?"

My stomach dropped. I quickly turned to my computer, opened

up the *Beacon*'s website, and scanned down to the social column.

According to a source, our very own Dakota Halifax has already bounced back into the dating scene. Runaway grooms need not apply. Not sure if the man she was with last night was her one and only or the first of many, but looks like nothing can keep a good wedding planner down. Will she make another attempt down the aisle? And if so, how soon will it be?

So few words, yet they caused so, so much irritation. On the bright side, there was no mention of piggyback rides, and she did at least call me a good wedding planner. On the dark side, which I was pretty sure was where Phoebe's allegiance lay, it made it sound like I was about to embark on a dating spree. And that my only goal was another wedding.

"You believe this?" I gestured to the screen.

"Who is he?" The vein in Grant's forehead stood out. "Is this why you wanted space? To date?"

Knowing he was seconds from losing it, I worked to keep my voice calm instead of yelling back. "I was out last night. Went to the movies at our usual stomping grounds, actually." I waited to see if *he* wanted to confess, since he was so set on making me. He didn't say anything, so I went on with mine. "I was out with a friend. Not a date. Just two roommates who wanted to see a zombie flick."

"Roommates? I thought you were staying with Jillian?"

Shit. I meant to break my new living situation another way—I knew he'd hate it, and since it involved another guy, I also knew he'd overreact. "Look, this falls under my business, but like I said, I went to a movie with a friend, who happens to be male and is my new roommate. End of story."

His eyes narrowed. "So nothing's going on?"

Although my emotions were a bit confused around Brendan, we weren't even close to dating. "We're just friends."

"I don't like it."

"You don't have to. But while we're on the subject, what about you? Are you dating?"

The anger faded from his expression, replaced with something softer, and apprehension crawled across my skin. I wasn't sure I was ready to hear about the new woman in his life. "Funny enough, I was out last night, too. I met with Amy and Jaden—my son. You should see him, Dakota. He's smart and funny, and he's got my eyes and dark hair. I was nervous at first, but now that I've spent a little time with him… It's amazing. He's amazing."

I'd seen the woman, but I hadn't seen a little boy. I tried to remember the scene, but I'd been focused on her, on the way she looked at Grant. From the sounds of it, though, his focus had been on his son.

"I'm sure he's adorable," I said, and it was true. The glimpse I'd had of Amy last night, plus Grant's genes… Jealousy twisted my gut despite my best attempts to hold it back.

Grant rounded my desk and took my hand. "I want you to meet him. Next week I get him to myself. We're going to go to the park a few streets over. Can I come pick you up beforehand?"

Just when I thought my life was separating from his, he pulled me back in. He brushed his thumb across my knuckles and my skin warmed under his. Maybe I was just a hormonal mess, so deprived of a guy's touch that any would do.

I knew that wasn't true, though. Grant was familiar comfort, more than a year of shared togetherness, and getting through ups and downs. Brendan was new yet still familiar, a shared history and a sense of adventure that made me feel like a kid again. All it did was confuse everything again. "If you and I were actually going to work, wouldn't you have married me?"

"I couldn't go out and marry you without telling you about Amy and the possibility I was a dad—it wouldn't have been fair to you. But I'd waited too long. I've wished a hundred times I'd told you sooner. All I need is a little more time to get this part of my life figured out." His grip on my hand tightened. "Then I'll marry you. I will. In a big ceremony if that's what you want."

Longing wrapped itself around my heart. I could see me, Grant, and a little Grant look-alike sitting in his house. Running around in the backyard with Cupid. Secure. Stable. What I'd thought about several times in the months leading up to our wedding, even if the circumstances were slightly different than I'd originally imagined. It was still everything I'd wanted, offered up on a platter if I held out a little longer.

But would more time really make someone ready for marriage? I got waiting until you knew if you could stand the person for long stretches at a time, and dating to make sure you were compatible and that the chemistry didn't fizzle out after the lust phase—of course all of that was important. But Grant and I had already passed all those milestones and then some. What would make him decide he was suddenly ready and excited about it?

Then again, if he asked me to get married today, I couldn't say I was ready. Not after the past few weeks with Brendan and being unable to shake the lust phase feelings I got whenever he was around. I was starting to wonder if not getting married was a blessing in disguise. The kind of blessing that smothers you, then makes you feel grateful for air.

Like a Stockholm syndrome blessing. I laughed at my own joke, which was totally inappropriate right now. That was when I did my best laughing, really—I'd had to remove myself from a ceremony when the bride's grandmother started swearing in what I was sure she thought was under her breath. Of course thinking about that made me laugh more.

Grant's eyebrows scrunched together. "Dakota? Are you okay?"

I wasn't sure. But when I looked up into his eyes, I thought that a little more time might do us both good. "I'm willing to start talking again and see where it goes. I'm not sure meeting your son is a good idea, though. Seems like a big step."

"We'll keep it super casual. Just hanging out at the park, totally low-key, and I'll even introduce you as a friend—not that he'll pay much attention. He's two, so really his most pressing concern will be the slide and if I remembered the crackers and juice."

I rapped my fingernails on my desk, going back and forth.

"Honestly, I'm a little lost on the whole kid thing," he said. "Our few visits have gone well, but Amy's always been there. This is the first time I'll have him without her supervision, and I'm nervous I'll screw it up. You're good at this kind of thing, and I could use your help." He squeezed my hand. "No matter what happens between us, I hope I haven't lost you as a friend. That means you'll still be in my life, even if we can't work out our other problems."

When he put it that way, how could I refuse? "Okay. I'll go with you to the park, and at least help you with your first outing with him. After that…we can see how it goes."

Relief flooded Grant's features, and then he leaned down and kissed me. I meant to tell him to slow down, but instead, I closed my eyes and focused on how I really felt. Underneath the pleasant sensation of his lips on mine, did I get that tingly hope? Did he feel like the guy for me again?

I couldn't be sure, but hope was definitely not working its way through me.

When questioning your entire life, I don't advise walking into a community center that smells like moldy feet. Especially if you have to limp in there. Trust me, it only makes your life situation seem that much more dire. The fact that I was required to be here thanks to a glorified gossip communist who subsisted on carrot sticks and cocktails wasn't helping, either.

As I looked for room 105, irritation pulsed through my veins. You know how going to anger management class made me feel? It made me feel angry. Seemed counterintuitive to their goal, if you asked me.

As I stepped inside the room, I glanced around at all the mostly normal-looking people who were probably also here because of annoying coworkers. Whether you controlled your anger or not, some people needed smacked upside the head. I considered saying so, sure I'd get a few *Amens!* but the last thing I wanted to be known as was the anger management class troublemaker.

The tatted-up guy in the back with the goatee, scowl, and leather biker jacket looked like he might rip someone's head off if given the tiniest excuse, and I assumed he had a little more reason to be here than the rest of us. Hopefully they had happy pills on hand in case of an anger emergency.

I've just gotta get through this, and then I can move on with my life. I took a seat in the middle—not too brownnose-y, not rebel without a cause like Skull Crusher back there.

Another handful of people filtered in and then a small man with a comb-over and yellow pit stains under the arms of his white shirt stood at the front of the room. "Welcome. My name is Ron, and I'll be teaching you for the next two weeks. We all know what anger is, and we've all felt it…" He droned on and on about the heat, clenching your fists, your body tensing up, nearly losing your temper. But he was so monotone, it sounded pretty mild to me. I tried to pay attention, though admittedly I was rearranging floral displays for Valentina's wedding in my head.

Relaxing was the first anger-control strategy. Breathing, meditation, and the like. Here's the thing. I've been in yoga classes, with all the breathe in and out—hell, I even advise my brides to do it. But the only thing that ever helped calm me down was being in control. And not in a breathing in and out kind of way.

Great. I guess I do have some issues. Maybe I do belong here with Skull Crusher. I glanced back at him and he gave me a large grin, no malice but more a sense of solidarity. He rolled his eyes at Ron, and I decided Skull Crusher and I were going to be BFFs by the end of the course.

We were instructed to close our eyes and visualize a relaxing experience, also known as going to a happy place. I started to visualize a perfectly done wedding, only then it morphed into *my* wedding and sitting in my dress crying on the beach, that crippling sense of abandonment stealing my breath.

He doesn't want me. Talk about ruining happy place chi.

The intensity I'd felt that day was more than that moment, though. I wasn't sure why it ached so deeply, to the point that it was still there when I thought about it. It shattered my trust—the trust I'd fully put in Grant—that was for sure. But I shouldn't be feeling that. We'd made up. I'd agreed to meet his son.

I tried to picture us all together. Grant, me, and his son. But it felt like staring at one of the stock photos that comes in the frame when you buy it in the store. Pretty, but not yours. No memories attached.

Okay, anger management class is messing with my head. If sorrow put out anger, I was there. Anger-free and wanting to cry. *Damn emotions.*

"Great. I'm getting a really good vibe off this group," Ron said from the front, proof that his vibe-o-meter was missing a couple rainbows.

Changing the way we thought was next on the list of tips to ridding ourselves of anger.

"Silly humor"—Ron actually chuckled—"can help with rage in a number of ways. It helps you gain perspective. When you get angry and call someone a name or refer to them in some derogatory term, stop and picture what that word would literally look like. If you're at work and you think of a coworker as 'scum' or an 'unimaginative ape' for example, picture a piece of scum or an ape in place of your colleague, taking a call or typing on the computer."

Scum? Unimaginative ape? Talk about unimaginative. I can think of way better insults.

"You might even want to draw it," Ron continued. "It will help take the edge off of your wrath."

I pictured myself drawing Phoebe as a villain—a comic book type that had an accident with nuclear waste so that her face resembled a Picasso. I'll admit it actually was calming.

"One word of caution: don't give in to cruel, sarcastic humor," Ron said. "That's just another form of an unhealthy way to express your anger."

I wasn't sure if my deformed image would count as cruel, sarcastic humor. Probably. And just when I was borderline having fun, too.

We did another calming exercise involving counting, and during our short recess, I made friends with Skull Crusher—real name Wild Bill. Anyway, it was the name he gave me, although I doubted it was the one his mama used. He told me he'd give me a discount on a tattoo if I was interested, and I told him I'd refer my clients to him if any of them asked about ink. A lot got tattoos for each other pre-wedding. A romantic gesture, but something I'd probably advise against now. How awful would it be if Grant's name were somewhere on my person on top of having all the other fallout? Then again, if I had the tattoo, I'd probably feel more pressure to make it work now.

Either way, if my peeps wanted tattoos of any kind, I'd be referring them to Wild Bill, anger management co-conspirator. Although I'd probably leave off that last part.

Part two of the class covered changing your environment and habits. Getting rid of triggers, and recognizing when you were about to lose it.

Okay, so I totally didn't deserve to be in this course, but it got me thinking that maybe I could use a couple of the tips. I'd already changed my environment, but maybe I needed to avoid getting in the habit of thinking about Brendan in any way but as friends. And I'd think of Grant as a possibility. And I'd change my thinking about weddings, too.

First I imagined smashing a cake into a mess of icing and a cracked cake topper, ripping apart a bridal gown, and overturning decorated tables, centerpieces and flowers flying everywhere. Months of work destroyed in the most satisfying way. Then I mentally put it together again, a nice wedding puzzle that ended with picturesque perfection. It didn't make me super happy to think of my next event, but it did make me think it was bearable.

I was in control of my life. Phoebe could write about it all she liked, but I wouldn't let her change me. And I supposed I'd try extra hard not to punch her. Even make it a goal on my to-do list and everything.

After having Ron sign off on my slip, I bumped the knuckles Wild Bill held out to me, and told him I'd catch him next time.

Hope and tingly-happy feelings for weddings could wait. Right now, I was just grateful to be turning over a new leaf in my life. I crossed *Anger management class* off my to-do list, and moved down to the *Find a way to renew my hope in love* action item on the bottom. I figured it was time to change the color from Tangerine to Canary. Still elevated, but no longer high risk.

Yeah, I was all over this.

"How was Hulk class?" Brendan asked as I dropped my giant purse so I could give Cupid some attention.

I smooshed my doggy's face between my hands and told him what a good boy he was, then glanced up at Brendan. "It's anti-Hulk class, thank you very much. And it wasn't as bad as I expected. I even made some friends." I dug into my pocket and held up Wild

Bill's card as I moved closer to Brendan. "See. Good in a bar fight or if you're looking to sport some ink."

Brendan shot me a smile that I felt deep in my gut. "I'm so proud."

He's my friend. The friend glue that's holding my life together right now. I didn't know what I'd do if I didn't get to decompress around him—probably self-combust. Of course, decompressing wasn't easy once I started thinking about those undone buttons on his shirt and what would happen if a few more of them came loose.

I switched to the topic that'd help derail that line of thinking. "So, Grant came into my office today."

There was a slight tic in Brendan's jaw, so I decided to skip the part where Brendan and I were in the paper and Grant was upset about it, and focused on the part I could use help on—I'd call Jillian tomorrow, but I already knew she'd tell me Grant didn't deserve another shot, so I wanted another opinion. A less biased one. "He wants me to meet his son." I perched on the arm of the couch, happy to take my weight off my sore ankle. "I said I would, even though it kinda freaks me out, and I'm not really sure what I'm doing."

"Does that mean you're thinking of getting back together with him?"

"Honestly, I don't really know. He claims that's what he wants. For now I'm going to take it slow. See what happens."

For a moment it was dead silent. Apparently Brendan wasn't going to be giving me any advice, and now it seemed weird that I'd asked his opinion. Cupid was dancing around at my feet anyway, giving me sad eyes, so I walked into the kitchen and got him a treat. When I turned around, Brendan was right behind me.

"Meeting someone's kid isn't going slow, Deej. It's a serious step that implies you're planning on being in both of their lives."

"I worried about that at first, too, but it'll just be lunch at the park. Grant assured me it'd be casual, and he needs my help."

"Casual," Brendan muttered. "Sounds like he's manipulating you into meeting his son so he can use him to get you back."

"I heard that."

"Good." Brendan's eyes met mine. "You should be aware of what he's trying to do."

I sighed. "No matter how many times he says he still wants me, the only way for me to believe it is to see if I still fit into his life, kid and all. I'm trying to be careful, but it's not like there's a manual on how to act in this situation. If there was, I would've read it and had it highlighted and tabbed by now."

A little of the tension leaked out of the room as Brendan bit back a smile. "I have no doubt you would." He ran a hand through his hair and then glanced at me, his eyebrows drawing together as he noticed the way I was standing with all my weight on one side. "How's the ankle?"

I lifted it and rotated it one way and then the other. "I'm afraid you're going to have to piggyback me around for the foreseeable future," I joked, glad to be on to an easier topic.

"Fine by me. It'll be good exercise, packing you around." He brushed past me, opened the freezer, and peered inside.

"I'll try not to take that to mean I'm only good for weight training." I thought he'd turn and make another joke, but he was still digging around, his attention on the bags of frozen food. I leaned on the counter. "Actually, I'm surprised by how much better it feels. I should be back in my heels in no time."

Brendan glanced at me and then shook his head. He pulled out a bag of frozen peas, came over and put his arm around my waist, and then walked me back to the couch. I probably didn't need to lean on him as heavily as I did, but he was warm and solid, and wearing that amazing total-guy cologne he always did.

We set up on the couch, and when he placed the icy peas on my ankle, I flinched and sighed, the cool nice and uncomfortable at the same time. Which pretty much described how being around

Brendan always made me feel.

When I glanced up, I noticed a dark spot on his skin. "Is that a bruise on your chin?"

Brendan ran his fingers across his jaw, right where the hint of purple was. "Hmm. I didn't think it'd bruise. Guess I need some ice, too."

"Did someone hit you?"

"Barely glanced off me, really—not a big deal. Once in a while people take a swing, but they rarely land, and they only get one."

I blinked at him for a moment, thinking I shouldn't be turned on by the threat in his voice. "I'm now picturing you in the back room, going all *Sopranos*-style on a guy."

Brendan's expression didn't confirm or deny.

"Wait…so at your job, takedowns are encouraged, and at mine, just saying the word 'punch' lands me in an anger management course? Wanna trade?"

He cracked a smile. "No one wants me planning a wedding or writing an article about it. I'd end up saying red or pink instead of crimson or…"

"Watermelon? Dusty rose? Orchid? Salmon? I could go on all day."

"See. I totally fail at fifty shades of pink. And if it makes you feel any better, most days my job is more observing and keeping things in check than getting to take anyone down." He shifted the peas on my now-numb ankle, which was now looking rather pink itself. "You should come by sometime. Tell them you know me, and I'll give you the whole tour—the stuff no one else gets to see." His eyes lit up when he talked about his job. I could tell that he liked it and was good at it, and it gave me hope that he was here in town to stay.

"Hmm, a trip to the casino. Can I bring all my new anger management friends with me?" I asked, all false innocence.

"Uh, no." He leaned over me to grab the TV remote off the

coffee table, his firm chest pressing against my thigh, his face so close that I could see his pulse beating at his neck.

It'd be so easy to lean in and kiss his cheek, drag my lips across his skin. A swirl of desire went through me. Reminding myself that Brendan and I needed to remain only friends just got upgraded to Fuchsia.

Chapter Sixteen

The good thing about being crazy busy was I didn't have much time to think about my hot roommate or my also hot, maybe not-so-exed fiancé. The bad thing was, I kinda missed hanging out with my hot roommate. Not that I didn't miss my other guy. Not that they were my guys.

Okay, I think I fried my brain. Which means I need coffee to jump-start it.

I strode to the kitchen, risking heels for the first time in a week. As long as I was careful, I should be fine. I opened the coffee bag and inhaled, hoping it'd help me be awake enough to get it into liquid form.

Cool air came in from the open sliding door. Within an hour it'd be stifling again, which, don't get me wrong, I liked, but the hint of cool was nice. When I got to the window for a closer look at the morning light, I caught sight of a whole lot more than I bargained for. Brendan was shirtless, shorts hanging dangerously low on his hips, sweat glistening on his skin.

He must've just gotten back from his morning run. He tossed a tennis ball across the yard, the lean muscles in his back flexing under tan skin, and Cupid charged after it. I couldn't seem to tear my eyes away, and I was pretty sure I was drooling at least as much as, if not more than, my dog.

Apparently I needed to be busier. Good thing I had a wedding to put on.

As if he could sense me, Brendan glanced back at me and waved.

The jolt in my gut was more powerful than the caffeinated beverage I was waiting on could ever be. Words weren't forming, so I simply lifted my hand and smiled.

"Come on, Cupid," Brendan called. "I gotta get ready for work."

Cupid darted past me, the yellow ball in his mouth. Brendan was much slower, taking up the entire doorway before I realized that I should—duh—move out of the way so he could come inside.

I busied myself by grabbing a couple of mugs out of the cupboard. "Coffee?"

"Later." He poured himself a glass of water, and while logically I was sure he was just drinking it, it seemed like he was slow-motion drinking. "You've got a wedding today, right?"

Yes. The wedding. Good distraction. "Yeah, and the bride wants her cat to be the ring bearer, so I'm at Code Fuchsia already."

He leaned against the counter, crossing one ankle over the other, his chest still gloriously naked. In order to maintain cognitive thought, I focused on his face. But then I was noticing the stubble forming on his jaw, how the blond caught the light, and the tiny mole next to his nose. The dark brown eyes.

"Code Fuchsia?" he asked, and it took me a second to realize I'd brought it up, and that of course he didn't know what it meant.

"It s-started as a joke," I stuttered. "For bridal meltdowns. Like the terror code alert, but fancier colors. The brighter the color, the more dire the situation. It sorta seeped into my daily life, too. I even color code my to-do list. Keeps me on top of the high-action items."

He nodded like it wasn't an odd thing to do, but his twitching mouth said he was fighting the urge to mock me for it. "So what's under fuchsia?"

"The full code is actually Fanatic Fuchsia, Temperamental Tangerine, Wary Canary, Cautious Cobalt, down all the way to Low-Key Lime. Although sometimes Lime is just a level of shock that appears low-key but is masking Tangerine or even Fuchsia. "

"No purple?" Definitely mocking me now, a sexy smile curving his lips.

"Not on the code scale, but there's Purple Passion of course. So something I or my bride care a lot about, but there's not the meltdown factor involved. It's more like good job, there's some Purple Passion going on over there." I shook my head. "I can't believe I just told you all of that."

"I can't believe I've missed out on Purple Passion all my life." The mockery in his expression faded as he looked at me. His throat worked a swallow, his eyes darkened and—I could have sworn—dropped to my lips.

Oh holy crap. I gripped my mug like a lifeline, taking shallow breaths to calm my spiking heart rate. "So. Yeah. Code Fuchsia is happening today. I'm cursed with animals, and I don't trust a fluffy ring bearer."

Cupid barked, making me jump. Coffee sloshed over my cup, onto my hands. I hadn't even realized my dog had come back in the room. "Not you, Cupid. You're perfectly trustworthy."

He wagged his tail, apparently satisfied with my compliment. Brendan grabbed a paper towel and squatted down, dabbing at the coffee on the floor. He glanced at my feet, and I was acutely aware of my bare legs.

His eyebrows drew together—not the reaction I was hoping for. Not that I was hoping for one, but no girl wants her gams to be frowned at. "Heels?"

Oh. That. "Baby heels. My ankle's fine, I swear." I wiggled my foot to prove it. "I have spare ballet flats if I need them. You know me. Always prepared."

He straightened, so close now that I could feel the warmth radiating off him. He smelled like sunshine and dude, with a side of take-me-now.

Great, now I'm at Purple Passion. Nothing says ready to wed like a horny wedding planner. "I'd better get going," I said, embarrassed at how breathy my voice came out.

Brendan caught my hand as I started to turn. He gave it a quick squeeze. "Good luck with your fuchsia situation."

"I'll let you know how it goes. But with an animal curse on the line, my optimism is at Code White. Aka, nonexistent."

GET READY TO WED by Dakota Halifax
*Dogs, Horses, and Birds, Oh **My!***

Now, a quick word about involving animals in your wedding. Think of an infant, about a year old, running through your wedding, tugging on tablecloths and pulling off centerpieces. That's about the same thing as having animals present for your special day. Only their parents won't stop them. (Parents of small children, you really should stop them.) I'm just letting you know that when you invite animals in, you're also inviting chaos whether you mean to or not.

Horses kick, run, and try to eat the flowers; cats hiss, claw, and run through cakes—they also get tortured by those children whose parents aren't watching them—and dogs bark and feel the need to mark everything. Next thing you know, you've got pee at every table and surprises that need scooping up. Is that romance in the air? No, it's much smellier and totally unwelcome. Releasing doves at weddings, while romantic, also comes with a side of—well, you know. You've seen the nasty white globs on your windshield, so think twice about it. Those flamingos you think will add "flavor" to your big day? They don't always like humans in their space, and those beaks aren't just for decoration. They're really better left strutting around the wildlife habitat at the Flamingo where they have experts to take care of them in their own reserved space. Animals are an unpredictable variable that can cause the most planned to turn into the most hectic.

Is that Roscoe scratching at the door, begging to be let in? You better go get him. I know you're not listening anyway and you want him to be in your wedding. It's okay. You're the bride and you want what you want. I understand and I'll try to help you anyway. Just try to be as understanding when even I can't control what your hairy family member does on your special, now-more-hectic day.

Maybe I'd cursed myself. Maybe optimism would've prevented this. And maybe that tree branch would hold my weight.

Maybes were so much fun, no?

I'd abandoned my shoes, hiked up my skirt, and shinnied up the tree after the fluffy ring bearer who was hell-bent on making my job impossible. They say curiosity killed the cat. Right now, I was thinking she should be more scared of me. Why didn't I own a tranq gun? Why hadn't I thought of it before? Clearly an oversight on my part.

On top of that fun, Waverly, the bridezilla of all bridezillas, decided this morning that she should've gotten a white limo to drive away from the ceremony, and that no respectable wedding was without one. Had she expressed this desire before, I could've had one lined up. As it was, I'd managed to get a black limo scheduled, but it was going to cost twice as much, and the father of the bride decided I was trying to price gouge him.

Yes, all price-gouging wedding planners climb after Pookie when she darts up a tree. All part of the service that not enough money in the world would cover—especially if I exposed my underwear to everyone in the near vicinity. I told myself the same thing I did when Brendan was frowning at my heels as he cleaned up the spilled coffee this morning, close enough to be able to look up my skirt—at least I'd worn my sexy, ironically enough, purple underwear today. Although truth be told, I didn't want anyone to actually see it while I was in a tree.

Since I was starting to wish Pookie a horribly awful fate, I took a couple of deep breaths and pictured myself climbing down with the cat, both of us unharmed, and the perfect wedding that'd follow. Hey, I was nothing if not a fast learner, and I might as well put my anger management class tips to use.

"Dakota?"

Clinging on to a nearby branch, I searched the ground for Jillian.

"How's it going?" she asked, humor filling her words.

"Great. Just fancied a climb before the day's activities. Also, that white furball over there has the rings. Waverly got the creature when she was eleven, and while it's ancient in cat years and pretended it could hardly walk, it suddenly decided to shoot up the tree when the florist arrived."

"Ah, the curse. What a bitch." I wasn't sure if she meant the curse or the cat, but both seemed especially bitch-like right now. Jillian glanced from me to the cat, probably calculating the distance between us. "Fire department?"

"I was hoping to avoid it, but I'm afraid Pookie and I are at a stalemate." Honestly, she was ahead, what with her ability to balance on a tiny branch and claws for support, but I had too much pride to admit that. "Come on you little piece of—"

"Is she okay?" Theresa, the mother of the bride, peeked up through the branches. Her hair was in curlers and she was wearing a long silk robe.

"She's great." *Until I get my hands on her.* "Did you bring the food?"

The woman held up a can and the fishy scent was strong enough I was sure the cat could smell it. Its ears twitched and then she mewed and turned away.

"I was afraid of that. She just ate. And once she settles into a place, even Waverly can't coax her out." Theresa clutched her robe closed with one hand. "If Waverly hears she got out of the house, even after she specifically told me to watch her—and that she's up the tree… Well, you know how high-strung she is. She's been freaking out about everything this morning."

"I'm totally on it," I said, careful to not remark on her high-strung statement either way—I'd learned that could come back to bite you if you weren't careful. "Just go make sure everything's on track with her, and I'll have the cat down in no time."

Theresa went back inside and I eyed the cat. She was only a couple feet out of reach, curled at the base of a skinny branch. If I could just… I clamped on to the branch above and inched forward, but froze when I heard a crack. No dice. I looked down at Jillian.

"On it," she said.

"Ask for Larry Donovan, and tell him Dakota Halifax needs him." His son had been one of my dad's players several years ago, and he'd become a family friend, which rarely happens when it comes to a kid and their coach dynamic. But he and Dad had risen above all that, and he'd helped me out before. Speedy and nice were his specialty. Plus he'd have gloves, whereas I did not, and I preferred my skin without the claw marks I was sure to get if I actually got a hold of the cat. At this point, I was hoping the rings around her ribboned neck would simply fall off, so worst-case scenario we could go on with the ceremony.

But this was the animal curse we were talking about, so I wasn't going to hold my breath. I managed to get out of the tree semi-gracefully. My almost healed ankle throbbed, so there went that. And hey, if it turned purple, at least I'd match the lilac and mint wedding colors.

Twenty minutes till start, the chairs in the reception hall were filled, and the cat was still up the damn tree. After I'd climbed down, it'd gone a few feet higher and caught the silver ribbon around its neck on a sawed-off branch. Not enough to get it to come loose— apparently Teresa had tied it tight so the rings wouldn't come off. So now there was the fear the kitty would cause itself harm, and while I wasn't exactly fond of the cat, I didn't want that either.

But all of this was on the DL, qualified as Things the Bride Doesn't Need to Know Right Now.

Waverly glanced away from her reflection as I entered the room. "Can you believe I'm finally getting married? I've waited for this day for so long!"

It was one of the weddings where I was counting down with the bride, mostly because I needed it to be over. The last month with all of my extra drama had made it even more difficult than it should've been. Some clients were impossible to make happy, and Waverly was one of them.

"You look amazing," I assured her, pinning up the train of the dress so it wouldn't drag and catch before she made it to the aisle. I almost asked her if she needed anything else, but for once in my life I bit off the question. I was tapped at what I could handle, and if those firemen didn't show up soon...

I caught a flash of red out the window. Speak of the yellow-coated heroes. My phone vibrated with a text from Jillian, telling me the firemen had arrived. And that one of them was "all kinds of sexy."

Which worked out, because I was so relieved, I wanted to kiss them. "I'll be back in a few to make last-minute checks and then we'll be good to go." I pulled the curtains that overlooked the front yard with the tree, shot a meaningful glance at Theresa so she'd know to continue keeping Waverly happy and distracted, and then left them in the room, closing the door behind me.

There was no time to fake nonchalance, so I sprinted down the stairs and out the front door. "Hey, Halifax," Larry said, slapping me on the back, the way he always greeted me. Apparently daughter of a coach meant treated like a sports player.

I explained the cat sitch and the time crunch. "Bonus points if we get him down within the next ten minutes and the wedding can start on time."

"Antonio will go up."

Antonio flashed me a smile—dark hair, bronze skin, and a strong dimpled chin. Even stronger physique. There was general attraction, of course, but not anything that had me tempted to flirt with the guy. In fact, my mind went to Brendan this morning, shirtless and playing with my dog.

Heat pooled low in my stomach. I thought of him in my kitchen, teasing me about my color codes. I bit my lip, allowing myself a moment to indulge in a scenario where I'd run my hands across his skin and he'd pull me to him and kiss me, long and deep, before wishing me good luck with the wedding.

Wedding.

I straightened my shirt because in my imagination, that kiss would've definitely rumpled it. "You guys got this?"

Antonio was already heading up the ladder; Larry nodded at me. "We'll have 'er down in five."

Five minutes. I knew I didn't have much time, yet I found myself pulling out my phone. I wasn't sure what I was going to say, just that I wanted to hear his voice.

"You're never going to guess what happened," I said when

Brendan picked up. By the time I'd relayed the cat story, with him laughing the entire time, the culprit was down, nice and subdued in the fireman's arms. "Okay, I gotta go."

"See you tonight," Brendan said, and I couldn't help replaying that imaginary kiss one more time.

I hung out in the kitchen area, helping Jillian, since she'd helped me earlier. "Speaking of the only animal that didn't cause me problems at the wedding, what was in the chicken? It was amazing."

"A new cream and white wine sauce I'm trying."

"I'm now recommending it to all my wedding parties, just so I get to eat it."

"One of the groomsmen asked me out," Jillian said.

"Which one?"

Her eyes were glued to the pot in her hand, scrubbing extra hard though it was already shiny silver. "The best man."

I wrinkled my nose. "The one who made that awful toast?"

Jillian rolled her eyes. "I knew you were going to bring that up. So he's not the best at wedding toasts."

"He actually said, 'I hope you guys are happy and stuff. I'm sure it's going to last longer than his last wedding.'"

Jillian winced and then put her eye-blindingly shiny pot into one of the rubber supply bins she'd brought with her. "But you saw how cute he is, right? I think he was just nervous. And it's been a while since I was on a date. I usually just say no to groomsmen, but he didn't ask for tonight. He asked me out for the weekend."

"That does show promise, and he is cute. Have fun and stuff on the date." I shot her an extra wide grin. "I'm sure it'll last longer than your last one."

Jillian smacked me with a towel, but she was laughing.

I stacked a few of the clean dishes and put them in her other bin. "It's not like I can really talk about who to date or not, anyway.

I'm considering a guy who didn't show up to our own wedding because he claims he still loves me, while having conflicting feelings about my super-hot roommate, who I happened to see shirtless this morning, and all I can really say about it is *damn*."

"Two guys to choose from? If that's your Poor Me speech, it needs serious work."

"I'll add a few sob stories later. Or maybe I'll just wait and see what Phoebe says about me in the paper." I hefted the bin so I could take it to her van. We loaded the last of the supplies with the help of her staff, and then said our good-byes.

I'd just gotten in my car when my dad called. We exchanged pleasantries, and when he asked if I'd found a new apartment yet, a subject that I'd accidentally on purpose avoided—easy enough since I hadn't talked to him since I'd moved—I decided it was time to come clean.

"I'm, uh, kinda sorta living with Brendan West now."

The silence on the other side was deafening.

And just when I thought he might never speak again, he asked, "You go from one guy who can't complete the play to what? A backup boyfriend? Just sitting on the bench waiting for a shot?"

"It's not some random guy, Dad. It's Brendan. He had an extra room for rent, and we're friends. Have been for a long time, remember?"

"Mm-hmm. Don't get me wrong, I like the kid, but I don't see why you've got to live in the same house. If you need money—"

"I don't need money."

"You've got a perfectly nice bedroom at home. And with how often I'm gone, it'd be like having your own place most of the time. You could help me scout some teams in your spare time. Or if you're set on soccer, I bet I could get the school to consider you for an assistant coaching spot."

"What about the fact that you're allergic to Cupid and my room looks like a football locker?"

"It's got a few things. I could move them."

I noticed he didn't offer up a solution about my dog, so after a beat I said, "I'm good where I am, Dad. It's nice to not live alone, but to have my own space, and it's also nice to be so close to work and for my dog to have a yard to play in. And just to be clear, I don't want to coach soccer or any other sport. Running my own business takes up all my time."

Sometimes it felt like neither of my parents got me—they certainly didn't understand the wedding planner gig. But I'd always had a soft spot for Dad. Probably because he'd stepped it up when my mom left us, doing the best he could. "I appreciate the offer, I do. But like I said, I'm good, okay?"

He grumbled a bit, then said, "Okay. But you've gotta at least come to our opening game next weekend."

For the first weekend since I got back from my honeym—er, cruise—I didn't have a wedding going on. "Can I bring Brendan?"

"Sure."

"And will you be nice?" I asked, and he paused long enough for me to know he had to think about it. "Dad!"

"I will, I will. It's just, I finally got used to the idea of you getting married, and then…"

"And then I didn't. I know. I was there. Grant was not." I opened my mouth to explain why exactly, and that things between him and me were still complicated, but decided there were some things a dad didn't need to know. If it became absolutely necessary, I'd fill him in later.

"I wanna make sure you're okay, kid. It's my job, you know."

My heart swelled. It was impossible to be mad at him for looking out for me, I supposed.

"Next weekend, then," he said. "Bring Brendan, and I'll set you guys up with a nice seat."

I wasn't even sure if Brendan could go, or if I should've dragged him into it in the first place, but I knew that I'd rather go with him than anyone else.

Part Three

WARY CANARY - ELEVATED

(SIGNIFICANT RISK OF ELEVATED BLOOD PRESSURE, QUICKENED HEART RATE, POSSIBILITY OF TEARS, AND BEING IN NEED OF TISSUES)

"Between men and women there is no friendship possible. There is passion, enmity, worship, love, but no friendship."

—OSCAR WILDE

Chapter Seventeen

After my Sunday spent kicked back with Brendan and Cupid, I felt ready to take on Monday, despite its well-deserved bad rap. What I didn't expect, though, was Grant's mother waiting outside my office door.

"Evelyn. Hi."

The woman threw her arms around me. I was surprised by the overwhelming surge of affection tumbling through my body. I hadn't realized I'd missed her until she was here, and now I didn't want to let go.

She pulled back and gave me a sad smile. "You look so lovely."

"Thanks. You too."

"Oh, you're too nice." She pressed her lips together. "It broke my heart that you didn't come back from that cruise as my daughter. That I didn't get to help throw that reception. Which, by the way…" The blue checkbook she dug out of her purse was slightly crumpled. "How much do we owe you for that? I'm sure there were deposits you never got back. I meant to call and offer before now, but I wasn't sure how to approach the subject."

"Oh, it's—"

"Please, Dakota." She turned her blue eyes—eyes so similar to Grant's—up to me, and I couldn't deny the desperation in them.

"Why don't you come inside my office and I'll make coffee." Yes, I was going to need even more coffee than I'd originally planned to deal with today.

After we each had a drink in front of us, I told her that Grant and I had already taken care of the costs. Actually, I'd taken care of most of them, but I figured I was the one who'd wanted the fancy centerpieces and the china I figured I'd use forever but now never wanted to see. The boxes were shoved in the back of my office, and I thought someday when this was all a distant memory, I'd see if another bride wanted to use them. All those extras were why my bank account looked so ragged, but at least Grant had taken care of the cost of the cruise.

We made small talk for a few minutes, but even after the conversation died down, Evelyn remained in her seat, a strange look on her face.

"Did you…need something else?" I asked.

"Settling the cost of the reception wasn't the only reason I came to your office today." Evelyn scooted to the edge of her seat. "Grant told me he's tried talking to you, but he's not sure you'll ever give him another chance. So I don't care that this conversation might be uncomfortable. I'll do whatever it takes to convince you that my son—along with the rest of us—still wants you in our family."

Oh jeez. What was I supposed to say to the woman who was looking at me like all her and her son's hopes and dreams rested on me? Talk about pressure. "Did he ask you to talk to me?"

"No!" Her eyes went so wide it might be comical in a different situation. "Right now he's trying to focus on his son, although he keeps talking about you and saying how much better things would be if he had your help—he always says, 'Dakota would know exactly what to do in this situation.' He knows he made a mistake.

I just want him to be happy again."

I didn't know what to say. I wanted to point out that he'd been the one not to show up, and his life was different now. With her staring at me, I felt the weight of his well-being, though, and I didn't want to hurt him. "I want him to be happy, too."

She continued to stare as if that wasn't good enough, and maybe it wasn't.

"We agreed to take it slow. I needed space after everything that had happened, but we already arranged to get together this week."

"Oh, thank goodness." Evelyn took my hand in both of hers, and I couldn't help thinking of how quickly she'd accepted me, always saying positive things about the parts of me my mother always picked at. "Maybe we can go to lunch sometime, too? I miss having you around."

She smiled and my heart squeezed. For a moment, I was the little girl who just wanted a mom who cared. "I miss you too, Evelyn."

Over the past few weeks I'd started thinking things had turned out the way they did for a reason, and I just needed to figure out what that reason was. As I looked into Evelyn's face and the hope filling it, and thought of her words about Grant and the ones he'd said to me over the past month, I thought that maybe he and I had needed a trial to make our love and family stronger, so our marriage could withstand that much more. Stronger in the places we were broken and all that.

Without my hope in love, though, I wasn't sure I believed that. Wasn't sure I could ever fully trust Grant again, despite what he or his mom said. But Evelyn had reminded me of everything I'd almost had, and I wasn't sure I was ready to totally give up on it, either.

On a lot of ways, the Aces Resort and Casino was like every other casino I'd been in. The place was newer, everything shiny and bright, and the air was filtered better than the older places where a heavy cloud of smoke constantly hung in the air. But there were still no clocks on the walls, and the layout was meant to keep people inside the maze of flashing machines and tables with good-looking dealers. In true Vegas fashion, there were also several cocktail waitresses in little skirts walking the floor.

The one difference, though—the only difference I cared about—was that it was where Brendan worked.

"You finally came," he said, meeting me by the service desk.

"You did promise me the behind-the-scenes tour. I just wanted to be able to rock five-inch heels like all the other girls here before it happened." I lifted my foot to show off my glittery and spike-toed shoes.

"Hot," he said and my stomach got that fresh-from-the-roller-coaster sensation. "But if you fall on your butt or twist your ankle again, you know I'll never let you live it down." He put his arm around my shoulders, and I couldn't help noticing it was a friendly type gesture. Which felt a bit like the universe reminding me what he was to me. There was a closeness with him I didn't feel with anyone else—besides Jillian, of course, but it was still different. But kissing him would be a mistake. He'd helped me survive a few of the roughest times of my life, back when I was younger and again after my failed wedding. I needed him as a friend to lean on. The person who could make me laugh, even as he was mocking me.

If all that failed to keep me on the safe side of the line, there was the memory of him going off about relationships and how he hated how much work they were.

"Don't you worry about me, B.S. I've got this. And in case you didn't notice, these heels could double as weapons, so you should be extra nice to me. I didn't put on my leaves-nothing-to-the-imagination dress, though, so I don't pretend I'll be able to keep up with the rest of the women here."

Almost on cue, a group teetered by on heels, wearing low-cut dresses that displayed lots of cleavage and enough of their legs I was sure I was about to see if they'd remembered underwear.

"You've got a dress like that?" Brendan asked.

I raised an eyebrow. "What do you think?"

His face was so carefully neutral, I couldn't read him. He never mentioned other girls to me—except for that tiniest bit of info I'd dragged out of him about his ex and her ultimatum about marriage. I wondered if it was only a matter of time before he got a girlfriend, but I also couldn't help but wonder if maybe—just maybe—he got a little flustered around me, the way I did when he was shirtless in the kitchen, or sitting close on the couch or—

The temperature rose despite the arctic air that blasted through all casinos, and I reminded myself those were the type of thoughts I was supposed to be avoiding.

Brendan put his hand on my back and led me toward a corridor without further comment on the tiny dress discussion.

Maybe it weirds him out to think of me in something sexy. It weirded me out when I first thought about him being sexy as opposed to my childhood friend. My gut dropped. *Or maybe he's not even semi-attracted. I'd rather it be weird than gross to him.*

"What I'm about to show you is highly classified, and could get you killed in some circles." He flashed me a smile, his expression open again. Then he stopped in front of a door marked STAFF ONLY and swiped his badge.

Admittedly, when it opened, a mix of excitement and anticipation, along with a tinge of pride and attraction for the guy giving me staff-only access, tumbled through me. Whenever we encountered another person, they'd nod at Brendan in a way that made me think he was an even bigger deal here than I'd already thought.

"There are a lot of places I can't take you, of course, but the surveillance room is a trip. Wait till you see it." He scanned his pass, typed in a code, and opened a door. Screens lined one side of the wall, and a couple of guys were stationed in front of them.

Brendan introduced me around, then talked about different cameras, the kinds of security, and showed how they kept track of it all. Not enough that I could, like, pull off an *Ocean's Eleven,* but by the end, I knew better how casinos worked, and how foolish people were to think they could get away with cheating or stealing.

When we stepped into the hallway, he double-checked the door had locked behind us, then put his hand on my back, guiding me the way we'd come.

I smiled at him. "You know, I thought there'd be more super-dark Ray-Bans and a fancy earpiece you constantly gave instructions into."

His hand moved a few inches lower on my back and heat spread outward from his touch. "Sorry to disappoint."

"'Disappoint' would be the last word I'd use. That room was really cool. Thanks for the backstage pass."

He pulled me to a stop and then turned to show off a tiny earpiece. He pushed a button and asked for an update on the pit.

He nodded at whatever he'd heard. "Keep a close eye on them for me," he said, and then turned his attention back to me. "It's more Bond-like if people can't spot the earpiece right away. As for the dark glasses, they'd look cool on me I'm sure, but they'd also make it harder to see."

Oh my, I was about to melt into a puddle in the hallway.

Right before we reached the exit that'd take us to the casino floor, Brendan paused at an office door. He knocked, and a deep voice beckoned him to come on in. "Hey, Mr. Maddox. I just wanted to introduce you to someone. This is Dakota Halifax."

I had a split second to process the name before the guy glanced up. Massive was an understatement. His muscles were visible underneath his white shirt, his neck strained against his collar, and his hands were more paws than hands. His forehead creased, his expression so serious I was sure Brendan and I were about to get into trouble, the way we used to in elementary school.

Then he snapped his fingers and pointed at me, and my mouth went completely dry. "You're the wedding planner," he said. "I knew I'd heard the name before."

Brendan glanced at me. "Wow. You really are well-known."

Enough that the local paper reported on my social life, but not enough to have any real clout. But I was pretty sure that wasn't why William Maddox knew my name. "It's nice to meet you," I said, trying not to let the fact that the guy totally intimidated me show. "I'm currently planning your daughter's wedding. I didn't realize you ran this place, too."

Mr. Maddox stood to shake my hand. He wasn't quite as tall as Brendan, but he was twice as wide. "My daughter and wife just go on and on about how wonderful you are. They've even insisted on reading me a few of your columns."

"Sorry about that," I joked.

He laughed—always nice when my jokes landed, because they didn't about as much as they did. "You should've seen their faces when I suggested they could have the wedding at one of my casinos."

"Well, we're going to pull off a beautiful ceremony, don't you worry."

"Try to keep them at least close to budget."

I flashed him the assuring smile people tended to like when talking money. "Don't worry. I know where to find all the good deals."

"I was about to head out for the day," Brendan said when Mr. Maddox glanced at him. "Unless you need me to take care of anything else."

"No, go. You two have fun." Mr. Maddox winked, and I got the feeling he had the wrong idea about Brendan and me. I was about to tell him that we'd known each other forever, but decided it wasn't important. With how many people assumed we were a couple, though, I was starting to think maybe they were on to something. Or maybe that was because seeing Brendan at his job had tripled his hotness factor, and he'd been no slouch in that area before. "It was nice to finally meet you, Miss Halifax. Be good to our boy. We want him to stick around for a long time."

"I'll do my best." What was I supposed to do? Say no to a guy who could break me in half? Plus, I wanted Brendan sticking around for a long time, too.

We reentered the casino, and Brendan double-checked the door locked behind us, the same way he'd done with the control room.

"That dude's ginormous," I said now that I was sure I wouldn't be overheard. "They should just put a giant picture of him on the wall, with a notice that says 'This guy will come after you if you steal, so don't.'"

"Then we could call it North Korea instead of Aces."

I grinned at Brendan. "You're *so* funny."

"That's what I keep trying to tell you. It's about time you listened."

"Brandon?" A leggy, raven-haired girl approached. She put her hand on *Brendan*'s arm and the muscles in my shoulders tightened. "You're not on tonight?"

"Just finished my shift."

She glanced at me, and when she turned back to Brendan, her lips stuck out in a pout. "I was hoping you could come chat with me when the bar's slow."

Considering I suddenly wanted to rip her arm off, it was probably time for another anger management class. *Deep breath. In and out. He's not mine.*

"Maybe another time." Brendan gave her a polite smile and then turned to me. "Ready?"

What was up with his all-business work face? It made it impossible to tell if he was interested in the waitress. Did he usually hang out for her shift? I sure as hell didn't like the sound of "another time."

"Who the hell's Brandon?" I couldn't help asking as we walked away.

"She called me Braden the other day."

"Wow, she must like you an awful lot, then."

Brendan stopped and narrowed his eyes at two girls next to the blackjack table. They weren't playing but watching. He glanced around and then raised a finger, catching the attention of one of the guys on the floor in a dark sports jacket. He tipped his head toward the girls, and the guy headed over to them. The girls shook their heads and sighed, and then they stormed off toward the hotel area.

"I knew they weren't twenty-one," Brendan said as he gave the nod toward the guy who'd asked for their IDs.

If we didn't get out of this casino where he was totally rocking the Bond vibe, I was going to be throwing myself at him like that cocktail waitress wanted to.

He cupped my elbow, and butterflies swarmed my tummy. "So now that you've seen the place, you ready to get out of here and have some real fun?"

Oh, I could think of a lot of ways to answer that question, and most of them were contrary to my goal to keep Brendan's and my relationship firmly on the friends side of the line.

I lined up my club with the golf ball, my heels sinking into the ground. "You picked this sport on purpose, didn't you? You knew it was your only shot at beating me."

"Less talking, more swinging," Brendan so helpfully said. Apparently his family had been friends with the owner of the course back in the day, so the guy let Brendan play, even when they were closed. With the sun all but gone, there was a 90 percent chance we'd lose every ball we hit. Especially mine—I always hit off to the right.

I swung, following through like Dad had taught me. I lost sight of the ball over the trees, but it was, of course, off to the far right.

Brendan stepped up next to me and propped his golf ball on a tee. He'd lost the coat and tie in the truck, and the top buttons were undone by the time we arrived at the first hole. By the second, he'd lost the cuff links and rolled up his sleeves. Not that I was paying super-close attention to every spare inch of visible skin or anything.

He lined up, readjusted his grip on the golf club, and then swung, the movement swift and fluid, as if his body already knew exactly what to do. I watched as his ball soared up the middle of the fairway, bouncing in the green grass not far from the hole.

Yeah, I was definitely losing this game, and it'd barely started. "How about a late-night soccer game instead?"

"Your shoes are better suited for golf," Brendan said, giving the studded heels a pointed look.

"Hey, no one told me we were going to be playing sports, or I would've brought other shoes to slip into."

"I thought you were always prepared. Is this like a *Code Tangerine* situation?"

At his mocking grin, I gave him a quick shove and hurried into the driver's side of the cart before he could. My golf game might suck, but I could drive a golf cart like no one's business. For a while we played, hitting the balls we could find, and managing to even put a few in the holes. By the time we were on the eighth green, though, it was pitch black and I couldn't find my ball.

I sat down just short of the hole and lay back in the grass. "I give up."

Brendan plopped onto the ground next to me. "Probably for

the best. I was afraid you were going to bean me in the head with that last ball. Then *you'd* have to piggyback *me* to the cart."

"I'd drag you by a leg, so don't get any ideas."

He laughed and lay down, so close his arm was resting against mine. Part of me wanted to roll over to look at him, and the other, more scared part remained staring at the stars overhead. As a general rule, I wasn't much for surprises. Probably since the ones I got were like guess what, the flowers aren't here yet. Or *surprise!* That one iffy uncle is drunk and making passes at the bridesmaids.

But the kind of spontaneous freedom of playing night golf with Brendan was a good surprise. In fact, every time we hung out, everything was so natural that plans seemed unnecessary. I knew we'd end up having fun, no matter what we did. "I'm glad you came back here, and that you looked me up."

"Me too," Brendan said, his fingers brushing my forearm. "Part of me thought it was silly to track you down in hopes we'd still connect like we did all those years ago. But I had to know how you turned out."

I finally twisted my face toward his, the blades of grass tickling my cheek. The moonlight lit up his profile, yet softened his features, reminding me of the boy he used to be. "I thought about you a lot over the years," I said. "I sometimes wished we would've kept in better touch, but I was sure you'd probably forgotten all about me."

"You don't forget the first girl who punches you."

I laughed. "Never gonna live that one down, am I?"

"Afraid not."

I stared into his dark brown eyes, the corners crinkled in amusement, and gratitude and happiness warmed my chest. "Seriously, Brendan, I can't thank you enough for everything you've done the past month. I needed a distraction from my life and a place to live, and I don't know how I would've managed without your help."

"Happy to help. Though I'm sure you would've thought of something."

"Probably. But it wouldn't have been near as fun."

Most of the time I was so focused on my bubble of weddings and events that I forgot to take the time to slow down and appreciate something as simple as the feel of grass on my skin and a star-filled sky overhead. The heat from the day was soaked into the ground still, and the damp earth scent filled the air.

Instead of getting antsy about everything I needed to do over the next few days, I simply closed my eyes and relaxed, enjoying that for a moment at least, life was perfect.

The next thing I knew, someone was gently nudging me. "D.J.?" Brendan's hand moved to my cheek, and I realized my other one was resting on his shoulder. And that my leg was curled over one of his.

When had I fallen asleep? And even more important, when had I moved *onto* him? I quickly shot up, my cheeks burning. "Sorry. Guess I was more tired than I thought."

Brendan hopped to his feet and extended a hand to me. "Home?"

I liked the sound of that. "Home."

Chapter Eighteen

GET READY TO WED by Dakota Halifax
Orange as a Wedding Color

Have you ever looked at your pale reflection in the mirror and decided that you'd look better with an orange face and streams of orangey-brown streaks down your arms and chest? I didn't think so. Yet I've seen it happen with bride after bride. You try on your wedding dress, think you're not as tan as you want to be, and decide to get some last-minute color. And more often than not, it goes horribly wrong.

So what do you do when your skin suddenly matches the neon orange of the infamous sign welcoming people to "Fabulous Las Vegas, Nevada"? Exfoliate. Try a sugar body scrub on a washcloth. After bathing, rub baking soda in circular motions onto your damp skin. Once you've dried off, put lemon juice on a cotton ball and go to town. This might take a couple bottles of lemon juice and a bag of cotton balls. Lemon juice is also drying, so be sure to apply some lotion afterward. Dry, flaky skin or orangey color? You decide.

Now if you're set on getting a tan, here are some tips for preventing the color that nature never intended: Exfoliate *before* you apply self-tanner. The mist or foam application works best. Take several weeks to build up your tan, a light layer at a time. The instant you see spots, take a break. Count on your honest friends—you know the ones who claim to be brutally honest so they can be mean without apologizing? Yeah, them. They'll tell you if you're getting too tan or weird-colored. If you go the spray booth method, make sure to rub for your life the instant the spray stops. No amount of dancing around inside the booth seems to prevent streaks. I've seen rivers of dark colors on legs and arms from this method, not to mention the disastrous effect it has on your face. You don't want anyone wondering if you're dirty or if that's supposed to be tan. I'd even go so far as to suggest not tanning the face at all. A light bronzer will give you that same glow without the more permanent, sometimes scary, side effects.

A lot of tears had been shed in the Ready to Wed office since I'd opened. Brides, mothers of the brides, grandmothers, friends. Even the occasional tear from me at seeing a beautiful love story unfold—not going to go into the ones I shed my first day back after my wedding didn't happen, because that was depressing and beside the point—and then there were the brides. Yes, I know I mentioned them first, but they got two mentions because they did the majority of the crying. Take a typical situation and the emotions involved, mix in a wedding, and the emotions and drama tripled at the least. I wasn't sure the exact science behind it, just that it was, without a doubt, true.

Add every little thing that could and would inevitably go wrong, like hair, dress, whitening teeth, and the godforsaken self-tanner, and it was amazing any bride was ever not crying.

There was no doubt Helen was upset, the telltale sobs reaching me before her features came into focus. The instant she stepped up to my desk, though, the reason behind the tears was obvious. She was orange, and some parts of her were more orange than others. Over the years, I'd gotten good at masking my reactions. Nothing made things worse than a gasp with a muttered expletive. It was a good way to take a Code Tangerine—literally in this instance—to Code Super Fuchsia, with no chance of Canary or Low-Key Lime for the rest of the day.

Helen was about to get married for the second time. The first had been a shotgun one that ended three years later. Between the emotional toll of the divorce and being a single mom, it had taken her a few years to get back into the dating scene, and even longer to find the right guy. She kept telling me that this time she wanted to do it right. Apparently not right enough to pay attention to my packet that included self-tanner woes.

Don't any of my brides actually read the packet or my column? That was neither here nor there, though, so I said what I always said. "Don't worry, we'll fix it." I led her to the bathroom and pulled the kit I kept for this very reason out of the drawer.

Noticing the puddle on the floor, I squatted down. I opened the cabinet and was greeted with more water, the wood on the bottom of the vanity nice and soggy. "Shit."

"Does that mean you can't fix it?" Helen shrieked.

Double shit. "Of course we can fix it. My sink's got a leak, that's all." Honestly, it'd probably be a quicker fix than her skin. A tightening here or there, once I found out where the pipes were loose. Helen would need to be scrubbing her skin like mad for two days to make her face streak-free for her wedding.

After applying baking soda and lemon juice to a washcloth, I showed her how to make circular motions to start taking off the color. "The good news is, it's also a great acne fighter, so your skin should be crystal clear on your big day."

Once she saw the color coming off on the washrag, her mood mellowed, somewhere between Canary and Cobalt. I gave her instructions to continue with the treatment, wrote down a list of good foundations and bronzers to help counteract any leftover color, and finalized a few last items for her wedding. Multitasking at its finest.

As soon as she left, I cleaned up my to-do list, got out my toolbox, and went to fix my leak. Living in an old house meant everything needed fixing at one time or another, and Dad had taught me basic home repairs, insisting it was important to learn to be self-sufficient. But as soon as I got under the sink, water seeping into my shirt in the ickiest way, I realized my problem was bigger than I'd originally thought. The water was coming from a cracked hose, so not something I could simply tighten.

I turned off the water and attempted to get the hose off. The problem was the pipe was where I needed to be, and from this angle, my arms weren't quite long enough to get the strength to really turn it. I tried to prop binders under me to make it work, but they only made the angle worse. I tried swearing and beating the spot where the hose was screwed in with the wrench, but it was sadly ineffective as well.

My bank account was still looking sad enough that I hated to call a plumber, and more than that, it was a problem I really should be able to fix myself.

I heard Brendan's voice in my head. *It's okay to have help now and then, you know.* Then I remembered that he was off work today.

But I don't want him to have to spend his day off fixing my sink.
I thought about the other night at the golf course, and how

much I was starting to crave being around him. Living together, you'd think I'd be getting sick of him or need space, but the opposite was true.

I whacked at the stubborn bolt one more time, then gave up and called Brendan.

"*I*t's rusted on," Brendan said. The faux marble sink obscured his top half, and his jean-clad legs stuck out of the vanity. I'd never thought legs could be so sexy, but there was definitely something sexy about his. The way his thighs filled out the denim, how the material was perfectly distressed in all the right places. "Every time I turn the nut, the bolt turns, too."

Was it wrong that his words sounded dirty in the best possible way?

Get a hold of yourself, Dakota. He's fixing your sink, and you're looking at him like some kind of sex object.

My cheeks heated, and I cleared my throat, telling myself to be a professional. "Should I just call a plumber then? It's not a big deal if you can't fix it."

"Hell no! I've got this."

"Now who's refusing to ask for help?"

He scooted out, ducking his head to keep from hitting it. "You actually called me with a problem, which I know is big for you, and I'll be damned if I don't fix it."

"So I have to ask for help, but you don't?"

"Exactly." He flashed me a crooked smile. "Actually, I'm gonna ask you for help—see, not a hypocrite. I need you to hold the bolt in place while I twist the nut."

I should've known that handyman Brendan would be even hotter than usual Brendan. He hadn't shaved today either, so the stubble was back, and I wanted to run my fingers across it, even though I knew that was pushing the friends boundary on multiple levels.

I knelt down. "Okay, tell me what to do and I'll do it."

He stared at me for a beat, long enough my pulse quickened. "Uh, I'm gonna lie back, and then you lean over me."

Now how was I supposed to not be thinking dirty things? It was like the universe was setting me up. Brendan handed me the pliers, his fingers curling over mine for a moment, and a thrill shot through my stomach. This was getting out of control. Gripping the wrench, he maneuvered himself under the sink again.

I leaned over him, trying to keep my body hovering above his, but there was no room for that. Finally, I just gave in and dropped on top of him, our bodies pressed together in a way that was sure to give away how fast my heart was now hammering.

Brendan shifted and his hips bumped against mine. My breasts were pressed against his firm chest, and every shift sent an addictive shiver of electricity through me. Heat built between us—or maybe it was just me. But I was *definitely* feeling the heat. Judging from the slight twitch of his eyebrows and the shallow exhale he let out, he wasn't totally unaffected.

His gaze slowly lifted as he raised the wrench and secured it on the nut. Forcing my focus on to the bolt, I gripped it with the pliers. Brendan's muscles flexed under me as he twisted the wrench, and I bit my lip, working to tamp down the swirl of desire twisting through my core.

The nut finally broke free, sending a shower of rust down on us. I ducked my head to keep from getting it in my eyes. I heard the wrench hit the bottom of the cabinet as Brendan dropped it.

When I lifted my head off Brendan's chest, my eyes met his. He stared right back at me, his brown eyes darker than usual, and I swore it was more than the lack of light. His hand moved to my back, his fingers spreading there and pressing me closer.

And that's when I felt the thing. Not *the* thing. But the spark of hope in my heart. What I used to feel during weddings and when

I used to look at Grant and think about being with him forever. What I hadn't felt since Jamaica. What I was starting to think I'd never feel again.

The longer I stared at Brendan, looking at me like he liked what he saw and would do anything for me, the more tingles erupted, zipping across my skin in hot pulses that made it hard to fully catch my breath. Or care that I couldn't.

Brendan lifted the hand not pressing into my back, cupped my cheek, and whispered, "D.J.?"

My hand slid up his chest to his jaw. I indulged in what I'd wanted to do all day—for weeks, really—brushing my fingers over his whiskers and settling them on his lips.

Brendan made a low noise in the back of his throat, and I was definitely feeling all the things now.

"Dakota? Are you here?"

I jerked up at the sound of Grant's voice, banging my head on the top of the cabinet. Rubbing the spot I hit, I slithered out of my precarious position. Of course that meant basically running myself down the entire length of Brendan's body, and all my nerve endings were still firing at full speed. My face was too hot—bright red for sure—and my shirt had come up, exposing my stomach. I quickly tugged everything into place as I stood.

"There you are," Grant said, appearing in the doorway of my office bathroom. His gaze moved to Brendan, who was pushing himself out from under the sink. I didn't dare take too long of a look at him, because I wasn't sure if what had just happened was an in-the-moment-type thing for him, or if he'd been experiencing attraction from the beginning, too.

"H-hey, Grant. This is Brendan. He was helping me fix my sink. Brendan, Grant."

"Her fiancé," Grant added with a cross of his arms.

"Ex-fiancé," I said, then felt a stab of guilt when he shot me a look, even though it was true. He couldn't go around calling himself my fiancé still. I'd agreed to talking and attempting to spend some time together, but I wasn't even calling him my boyfriend yet.

"I was her *first* fiancé," Brendan said with a smirk, adding a whole new layer of awkward to the conversation.

An angry muscle flecked at Grant's jaw, and I searched for a subject change to try to diffuse the situation. Words weren't coming, but I did notice the time on the clock over his head—I couldn't believe it'd gotten so late. "That's right. We're taking your son to the park today."

"You forgot?" His tone was both incredulous and accusatory. I supposed the incredulousness was deserved at least—I never forgot appointments thanks to my color codes and alerts, and usually I didn't even need them. My cell sat on my desk, out of hearing distance of the alerts I'd no doubt missed.

I ran a hand through my hair. "Not forgot. The sink was just an unexpected problem, and I lost track of the time."

Brendan put his hand on my back, something he'd done dozens of times, but now it was stirring up memories of when it had been there moments ago, pressing me closer. "I'll take care of the sink and lock up, so don't worry about a thing. See you at home."

He tipped his head at Grant, polite but not exactly warm, but somehow not rude or challenging, either. Grant's hands slowly curled into fists, and I hoped he didn't lose his temper and try to challenge Brendan—even though I'd never call Grant weak, I had no doubt he'd find himself on the ground so fast he wouldn't know what hit him.

I positioned myself between the two of them, grabbed my phone and purse, and turned to Grant. "Shall we go, then?"

"What did he mean, your first fiancé?" Grant asked as soon as Jaden was preoccupied on the slide/jungle-gym area. "You never told me you were engaged before."

I'd wondered when that was going to come up. When we'd picked up Jaden, Grant had introduced me as his friend. From the way the kid's mom looked at me like I was Suspect Number One, I gathered he hadn't told her I'd be going on the outing. Finally, after a round of twenty questions, she'd handed over the kid, who was adorable and so clearly Grant's I couldn't believe he'd ever questioned it. Then we'd walked to the nearby park, Jaden practically sprinting the entire way.

"Brendan asked me to marry him when I was nine," I said.

The crease in Grant's forehead softened. Clearly he was relieved, but he probably wouldn't be if he knew I hadn't stopped thinking about that moment with Brendan under the sink since it happened. My roommate was becoming more than the boy who'd proposed with a Life Saver. Right now he was crossing over to an amazing maybe that I was tempted to try.

But here I was with the guy who I'd once promised to marry, and after our initial strained interactions post-failed-nuptials, this one felt more like the us that used to be. Still needed some work, but the comfort that he knew me and I knew him was there.

Grant took my hand in his, the way he'd done hundreds of times before. "Thanks for coming with me today. It means a lot." He beamed at Jaden as he came down the short slide, pride glowing in his eyes. "I was so scared about being a dad, but I didn't realize how awesome it'd be."

Jaden ran over, a giant grin on his face. As he excitedly told his dad something about the slide in his little kid talk, I could see that glimpse of the family I'd always wanted with Grant. Unlike when Grant sent me the pictures of his son that felt like someone else's generic family in a frame, this one was an image I could reach out and touch—especially with Grant's warm hand still wrapped around mine.

The memory of Brendan telling me Grant was trying to manipulate me popped into my head. Admittedly, seeing him with his son did soften me toward him. But after watching their interaction, I didn't think he'd use his son to win me over. Sway, maybe. More than anything, I think I was just the person he'd gotten used to coming to for help problem solving, because he knew I'd find a way, despite the cost to myself.

Jaden took off again, and Grant waved at him, then he tightened his grip on my hand. "Like I was saying, I didn't realize all the fun that'd come along with the responsibility, but something's missing." He brought my hand up and kissed the back of it. "You're good with him. I really think we could make this work."

The imprint of loving him was still written on my heart, but I wasn't sure I was in love with him still. It felt like I was standing on a ledge. Step one way and slide back in love with Grant. Become a part of his family, with a mother-in-law who treated me like a daughter and a son I'd eventually call my own, too. It wasn't the way I'd expected it, but I had to admit it had its allure. The security I'd always wanted. And it'd be so, so easy.

On the other side of the ledge was the unknown. Risky, yes, with no promises or guarantees, but totally mine. There was a possibility of Brendan in the mix, but even without it, I wanted to know that I was worth keeping around for more than my problem-solving skills. I wanted to know I could be strong alone if I had to, even if it wasn't the most fun path, and even if it was the harder one.

Being alone was better than being with the wrong person, and in this moment, I wasn't 100 percent sure Grant was the right one.

The real question, though, was could I live always wondering what if?

Brendan was on the couch when I got home, remote in one hand, his other resting on Cupid's head.

My boys, I thought with a smile. The day with Grant still had my gut tied in knots, and a heavy side of guilt that I couldn't give him the definite answer he'd wanted was rolling around in there, too. Add the confusion, and I was like an emotion collage, all pasted pieces in a mess that made it hard to see anything clearly.

But at least being here made all the clashing noise in my brain move to the background.

"You have a good time?" Brendan asked, turning down the volume of the TV.

I shrugged. "It was good to see him, nice to meet his son, and he said all the right things. But the more I'm around him, the more confused I feel."

"I don't see why. Seems pretty clear to me."

"Then explain it to me, because I could use some clarity."

The muscles along his jaw tightened. "He's an ass. End of story."

"You don't know him," I said, irritation rising up and dissolving my momentary contentment. "He's a nice guy, actually, and he's been going through something huge."

Brendan was off the couch and in front of me with a couple long strides. "Nice? He left you on that shore alone, D.J. If he cared about you at all, he'd know you have abandonment issues. He would've known that there was no worse way to hurt you."

A hole opened over my heart, raw and aching. "I don't have abandonment issues."

He placed his hands on my shoulders, his eyes softening. "You don't have to pretend with me. You don't have to be tough. Your mom sucks for leaving you the way she did. And your dad was a good guy, but he was gone a lot, too. If your *fiancé* knew you like I do, he would've grown a pair of balls and told you about his pre-wedding jitters instead of leaving you waiting there for an hour. If you want him, that's your choice. But don't expect me to not hold that against him."

A lump formed in my throat and suddenly I was blinking back

tears. Grant didn't know that about me, but part of it was my fault. I'd never told him that I still had internal scars from my mom, because I didn't want him to see my weakness. I'd been trying so hard to be *his* support system, the girl who made everything okay and was on top of her life.

Brendan ran his hands down my arms, the sensation of his skin on mine calming the storm inside. "I guess that makes me a hypocrite, though, because I left you, too. I told my parents I didn't want to move, but there was only so much I could do, and that killed me."

"You didn't abandon me."

He let out a long exhale that seemed to carry the weight of the world. "I did. And I can't help thinking if I would've been around— if I would've moved back here sooner—I could've prevented the whole Grant thing from happening in the first place."

I was going to tell him that was silly, but the fierce determination in his eyes and the set of his jaw told me he was dead serious.

"But it's not about me," he said. "It's about you. What do you want?"

"It's not that simple," I replied. "Grant regrets what he did, and he's trying so hard to make it up to me. Everyone makes mistakes—I can't punish him forever for it."

"That's not what I asked." Brendan's hands moved to mine, and he stepped closer. "What do *you* want?"

I was about to tell him that I didn't know—that was the problem. But as his fingers curled over mine and the tingly love hope I'd felt earlier came back, zipping underneath my skin, I knew that wasn't true. At least in this moment, I knew what I wanted. "To finish what we started under the sink." I squeezed his hands. "Only I'm afraid that I'll feel guilty about it, or that it'll mess things up between us, and I just got you back, and my life is still pretty messy and—"

"All I've been thinking about for the past few hours is finishing what we started. Actually, I've been thinking about kissing you for weeks." He leaned in until his warmth and cologne invaded all my senses, and his voice dropped even lower than usual. "Will it make you feel less guilty if I initiate the kissing?"

I swallowed, finding it more difficult than usual.

Brendan pulled me flush against him and my breath lodged in my throat. My heart thudded against his as he lowered his lips and brushed them over mine. "You just stand there. I'll do all the work." I felt him smile, and then he pressed his mouth firmly against mine. Using his grip on my hands, he pulled my arms over his shoulders, then his fingers ran down my back, settling on my hips. He parted my lips with his, and after that, I couldn't stay still anymore.

I curled my fingers into his hair as I opened my mouth, inviting him to deepen the kiss. His whiskers brushed my skin in the most delicious way, and I gently sucked his lower lip. His tongue moved to meet mine, a gentle sweep that made me burn from head to toe, and my body melted into his.

"I…" Thoughts were fuzzy, but I knew if I didn't say something, I might let him carry me into his bedroom, and that'd be way too fast. I sucked in a deep breath, working on catching my breath. "Like I said, I'm still a bit broken, and I think it's a bad idea to just dive into another relationship."

"Okay," he said, brushing my hair off my face and resting his hand on my neck. "But I don't think I can sit back while you continue to date Grant. I'll still be your friend if that's what you choose to do, but I need to know, one way or the other. I can go slow, but I can't be second string. I'm not built that way."

For the first time today, things were crystal clear. I was going to have to fully break things off with Grant, no halfway, dragging out the pain anymore. Not just because Brendan didn't want to be a standby, which I understood, but because I still felt the thorn of his rejection in my heart. I'd pretended I could get over it, but I couldn't. I wasn't even sure I could ever let someone else in fully because of it.

As I focused on Brendan again, all I knew for sure was that I couldn't go back. "I want you. Just you."

A slow smile curved his lips, and then he gave me a gentle kiss. "With how often you kept telling everyone we were just friends, I was worried this was totally one-sided on my part."

"Definitely not one-sided." I moved my hand directly over his heart, smiling when it was beating as fast as mine. "I was serious about going slow, though. Kissing, dating—that's all fine. But the rest…" I glanced toward our *separate* bedrooms.

"Slow. Got it. I won't make a move in that direction"—Brendan tilted his head toward the hall—"until you tell me you're ready. Deal?"

I nodded. "Deal." Then worry seeped in, because my brain hated me. "What if we don't work out? I mean, we're freaking living together, and this could ruin a friendship that started when we were seven."

Panic wrapped its tentacles around my chest, trying to choke out the happiness I'd experienced moments ago.

Brendan lowered his forehead to mine. "I've loved you one way or another since the first day we met, Dakota Jane Halifax, and I'll keep on doing it, no matter what happens. Even if we find out we're better as friends."

I tipped onto my toes and kissed him again, because I wanted to, and because I could, and because most of all, I believed him.

Chapter Nineteen

 tied the seafoam-colored ribbon around the bouquet of pink and white peonies on my desk and held the knot in place with one hand as I glanced at my ringing cell phone. When I saw it was Tess, I picked up, sure she was checking in on the course she'd required I take. "I'm all over the anger management thing, I swear. I've got my second session in a few hours." I tucked the phone between my ear and shoulder and looped the ribbon into a bow. "Unless I can just skip it? I'm good now, really. Got it all figured out."

"That's actually not why I was calling, though I think completing the entire course will be good for you."

"I plan on passing with flying colors." I resisted adding *So Phoebe can suck it*, since it might undermine the statement in Tess's eyes.

"That's what I like to hear. Now, I wanted to talk to you about your next column."

"I'm still brainstorming a few ideas and should have a better idea on what topic I'm going with by the end of the day." It wasn't due yet, and she didn't usually call to check in, but I wanted to assure her I wasn't slacking. I'd actually started one titled "How

not to look like a desperate hussy while catching the bouquet."
Funny, but possibly too mean, and too short—how many ways
could I really say "please don't give the other females competing
black eyes for a superstition that started back in medieval times"?

Of course, then I could go into how people used to think it was
lucky to get a piece of the bride's gown and that led to the bouquet
toss, which was supposed to avoid ripping dresses, not encourage
you to rip someone else's off.

"Well, that's what I wanted to talk to you about," Tess said. "I
usually give you free rein to write whatever, but…"

I flinched at that "but," worried it held all kinds of things I
wasn't ready for.

"People want to know about you. How you're doing after not
getting married. Your dating life. How you feel."

"How I feel?" Ugh, it was even worse than I'd imagined. "Why
would people care?"

"You've made a name for yourself, and with you planning the
wedding between Valentina and Marcus, the buzz is only getting
bigger. Our readers like your advice, and the way you put it in your
cute, witty way."

*Cute? People think my columns are cute? Here I thought I was
more "edgy."*

"But seeing you struggle with love has hit a nerve," Tess
continued. "I can't tell you how many emails we've gotten about it.
They want to know more."

My fingers went to the silky petals of one of the peonies, rubbing and rubbing until a few of the petals were balled between my
fingers. "I, uh, don't know about putting my personal life out there.
I regret doing it in the first place."

"I hear you, and I'm not going to force you to do it. But this is
what people are asking for. Either they hear it from you, or Phoebe
keeps trying to get the scoop on your life. Which would you rather
see in the paper? Her version or yours?"

"Hey, Wild Bill," I said as I settled into the seat next to the guy I'd first thought of as Skull Crusher. Honestly, I was a little tempted to ask if he'd care if I called him that. But I supposed it was a bit contrary to the calm mood Ron was so diligent in trying to cultivate.

The lights were dimmed—well, maybe that was just bad lighting and not Ron—and he'd put on instrumental music. Harp was heavily featured, with a little flute mixed in. I swore it made my heart rate hitch instead of calm.

Wild Bill held out his fist, and I knocked mine into his.

Then Ron cleared his throat and held up his hands, announcing it was time to get started. As his monotone voice filled the air, I sat back in my chair. My mind was still spinning over what Tess had asked me to do, and those words: *Which would you rather see in the paper? Her version or yours?*

Good thing I was all versed in controlling my irritation now, because I'd wanted to ask why the option wasn't not being in the paper *at all.* But I'd held it in.

"…bottled-up emotions are also dangerous," Ron said, and I swore he was looking right at me, too.

I'm working on it, sheesh!

He kept on glancing my way as he talked about how harmful that method could be, leading to hypertension, high blood pressure, or depression. It was like a problems buffet where you got way more on your plate than you wanted and felt ill afterward—why I avoided the buffets on the Strip, by the way. "All you can eat" sounds like a good idea until you eat your body weight in shrimp and the mere smell makes you want to vomit.

"Now, that doesn't mean you express all your feelings, either," Ron continued. "The 'let it all hang out' way of dealing with emotions is a dangerous myth. People use it to make it okay to yell at others. And is that okay?"

I wanted to play devil's advocate and say it depends on what that person did. But I kept my mouth shut—just like my emotions. Fingers crossed, high blood pressure was all I got from it. Ron waited till he'd gotten the required head shaking and murmured nos before moving on.

"Angry people can be cynical. Almost paranoid. They can believe that others do things on purpose to annoy or frustrate them."

I had printed proof that Phoebe Pratt went out of her way to frustrate me, so I didn't like the implication that I was paranoid.

"We all need to work on building trust," Ron said. "Time for an exercise."

"If we're doing trust falls, I get Wild Bill," I said, smiling at the grizzled guy beside me.

Wild Bill winked at me. "I'd catch you."

At the front, Ron crossed his arms. "This is a group activity. We'll all be sharing something. Miss Halifax, since you're so eager to volunteer, how about we start with you?"

All eyes turned to me.

What was it with everyone wanting me to open up today?

"How about you start with why you're here?" Ron asked, his eyebrows jumping up in a hopeful way that made me despise him a little.

"My boss made me come."

"Because…?" Ron arched his eyebrows even higher.

I held up a finger—not the one I really wanted to, but one to ask for a moment. Was I really going to confess? In front of all these people I barely knew? Tess wanted me to tell the entire city, so I supposed a handful of people who understood feeling out of control of your life at times was as good a place to start as any. "Well, it all started when I got stood up at the altar."

Wild Bill leaned across his desk. "You point me in the right direction, and we'll take care of that guy good." Yes, he was threatening my ex, but anger wasn't the right word for the way he did it. More like solidarity, and I'd be lying if I said I didn't appreciate it.

Ron shook his head and sighed. "Healthy ways, Bill. Violence isn't the answer, remember?" He cast me a glance that made it clear he blamed me for the outburst. And he wondered why I didn't open up more. "Go on."

"Anyway, this awful woman at my work—"

"Healthy words."

Seriously, dude, I'm trying not to be angry here, and you keep prodding me. I took a deep breath, hoping it was the cleansing kind people talked about. "She wrote in the *Las Vegas Beacon* about how I got stood up, and then she questioned how I could plan others' weddings when mine fell through."

Gina, the woman on my left, gasped. *See. She gets it. Of course, she did Carrie Underwood her cheating ex's truck, baseball bat to his pretty little ride and all.* Truth be told, I was kind of jealous. I bet it was fun to get all that rage out in physical form, an object to destroy instead of only feeling destroyed inside.

I flashed her a thanks-for-understanding smile.

"And then?" Ron asked.

"Then I ended up here. You fill in the blanks."

Our instructor pursed his lips. Light bounced off his shiny bald head as he tipped his chin down and looked at me over his large glasses. Seemed like an odd choice to put such an annoying guy in front of people who were in trouble for acting aggressively. I'd appreciated the tips I'd learned, but homeboy needed to back off.

Or maybe that was my bottled emotions talking—Ron had said that could cause a person to take out his or her anger on someone else, lashing out at people who didn't deserve it. "I wasn't *actually* going to punch her in the face. Whatever happened to jokes?"

"Jokes about bodily harm aren't funny," Ron said.

Wild Bill shot me a sidelong glance, as if he didn't necessarily agree but didn't want a lecture.

I let out a bit of the anger churning inside me, just a tiny leak as I tried to explain my side of the story. "I never asked for her to cover my *personal* life in her *public* column."

Ron took a few steps closer, a hint of actual sympathy on his features. Finally he got it. That I was justified. "Can we control other people and what they say?"

Control. That was what it came down to, right? Well, I liked to have it. I liked to give orders and organize my weddings. I knew the answer was no, but what I really wanted to know was why not? Things would be better.

On the other hand, the lack of control when I was with Brendan, how he surprised me—how my emotions ran out of me unbidden—were all things I liked about him. He made losing control fun.

Gina nudged me with her elbow and shook her head, mouthing "no" as if she really thought I was stumped on the answer.

I recited what we'd learned last class. "We can't control the unpredictable actions of others. Only the way the events affect us."

My words were meant to get Ron to back off, but I'll be damned if it didn't help cool the heat winding through my body. It was like my brain needed to hear that I couldn't control everything. Didn't mean I didn't want to, or that I'd be happy about what Phoebe said from here on out. Or even that I'd never be tempted to say things about wanting to punch her. But surely that was still progress, right?

I looked my anger management instructor in the eye and said, "Thanks, Ron. You just made me realize something."

He blinked at me a couple of times, a goofy smile curved his lips, and then he moved on. I was still thinking about my column, though. The only thing I could control about the *Las Vegas Beacon* was what *I* wrote in *my* column. I was going to give the people what they apparently wanted and write Tess her article, and I'd make it more popular than Phoebe's gossip section if it was the last thing I did.

The thought of letting out all the feelings I'd been holding at bay made my stomach clench. What if I couldn't get the floodgates to stop once I started?

Worse, what if I didn't like who I was once it was all out there?

Either way, it was time to reclaim control of my life and finally put my failed nuptials behind me. And I knew just where I had to start.

The hopeful lilt of Grant's voice when I'd asked him to meet me for a late dinner had done a number on my resolve. I kept telling myself that he left me, so I shouldn't feel bad about what I needed to do. I'd even called Jillian, filled her in on Brendan and my make-out session, and had her amp me up for the conversation I needed to have with Grant. But it didn't stop the churning in my gut.

Good thing I'm trained to break bad news in a way that makes it seem okay.

Grant strode into the restaurant, an ear-to-ear grin on his face.

You're killing me, Smalls. Of course a quote from *The Sandlot*—a movie I'd watched with Brendan a dozen times growing up—popped into my head. But it helped me be strong. To remember why I needed to do this—this was for my future wellness, and so I could give my relationship with Brendan a real shot.

Meeting at my place would've been weird considering I lived there with Brendan, and Grant's place would've been difficult, but I was also rethinking the out-in-public option I'd chosen. Too late now to do anything about it.

"I'm so happy you called," Grant said as he settled across from me.

I repeat. Killing *me.* "Grant, you know I care about you, and always will…"

His smile faded. I should've prepared something more original than the classic breakup starter-kit speech, but there was no reason to dance around the point any more. I sucked in a deep breath and focused on everything I needed to say, hoping it wouldn't get all twisted up on my tongue before I could get it out. "These past few days I realized something I didn't see before. I loved you, so I guess I didn't want to see it. But we don't want the same things."

The more I'd thought about our relationship, the more I realized it'd been off-balance. I was the fixer. I'd held back talking about my problems or the stress in my life to take care of his. "I tried so hard to be the perfect girlfriend and then fiancée, and at the time it seemed nice because I was helping and doing what I did best. But I got lost along the way—I'm not blaming you for that. It was who I thought I needed to be."

"I'm not asking you to be perfect."

"I know. But Grant, what would you even do if I had a breakdown and started crying?"

"But you never cry."

From his perspective I could understand his confusion, since I'd never let him see me cry, not really. It wasn't until Brendan showed me what it was like to feel whole even when broken that I realized it was okay to not just have flaws, but to allow people to see them. If I couldn't let go with Grant, how could I possibly expect us to work? "When it comes down to it, our connection doesn't run as deep as it needs to for it to hold up a marriage."

Then there was the fact that I'd always remember how he left me standing alone on the shores of Jamaica, and it'd come up in every fight. Every time we went through a rough patch. I could forgive, but I couldn't forget, and that meant we'd always have trust issues. Maybe that made me a bad person, but if that were the case, at least I was an honest bad person. Since I didn't think rubbing salt in a wound was the way to go, I held back—healthy words and all. "I admire you for stepping up when you found out about your son. I know the transition was a bit rocky, but you're going to be a great dad—you don't need me for that. And someday you'll find another girl who you won't hesitate to marry."

Grant's eyes narrowed. "It's that other guy, isn't it?"

Something inside of me snapped. I'd tried to keep this civil, but I could feel angry heat traveling through me. He'd always had a tendency to blame things on everyone else, and I used to rub his back and tell him I understood. That so-and-so from his office was hard to work with. A hundred other excuses I'd provided trying to be supportive. See? Fixer. But that wasn't my role anymore.

"Do we really need to replay how you were the one who stood me up at the altar? Who ran away instead of talking to me? That's on you. Take some responsibility and live with your decisions."

Grant stared, mouth slightly agape, as if he didn't recognize me.

I rose from my seat, pride welling in my chest. It was time I take responsibility, too. I'd let him in again, lied to myself, and allowed his mother to influence me. Regaining control of my life had taken me longer than I'd thought it would, but I'd keep getting back up and trying, day after day, until I got it right.

The last part of my course today, right before Ron signed off on the form saying I'd completed it, had been on being assertive, but not attacking. I'd told Grant how I felt without swearing or yelling, and it was nice to get it out there.

"Good-bye, Grant," I said. "Best of luck with the rest of your life." I walked out of the restaurant and inhaled the fresh air. I had upcoming weddings to finish preparing. And for the first time in a long time, I was actually excited about it.

Part Four

CAUTIOUS COBALT - GUARDED

(GENERAL RISK OF ODD BEHAVIOR, FAMILY PRESSURE, STRESS, AND COLD FEET. TEARS HELD AT BAY, BUT CAN QUICKLY TURN EITHER WAY)

"The course of true love never did run smooth."

—WILLIAM SHAKESPEARE

Chapter Twenty

Living with a hot guy who was willing to drag me into the bedroom whenever I was ready, but not taking advantage of it, was like walking by a table of beautiful slices of wedding cake and not taking a bite. Not even a little swipe of the finger to taste the icing.

In other words, so hard that I thought I must be mental for even attempting it.

I was starting to think that he was purposely parading around half naked, too, knowing he was slowly driving me crazy. A lazy grin spread across his face as he looked across the kitchen at me. His faded blue jeans hung low on his hips, his hair was still wet from his shower, and he hadn't shaved today. "Hey."

My heart took off on a high-speed chase, practically leaving the rest of me behind. I bit my lip as I took in his toned chest and the sexy vee of his obliques. I put down the peanut M&M's I'd been snacking on, closed the distance between us, and wrapped my arms around his waist. The dampness from his skin soaked into mine. He slid his hand into my hair and lowered his mouth until our lips finally met. As we kissed, I ran my nails up his firm back muscles, smiling when he groaned. If he was going to drive me crazy with desire, I might as well not be the only one.

If we were in a normal relationship, I'd need several dates to see if we were compatible, and if he was more or less attractive the more time we spent together, before deciding if I was ready to add sex to the mix. Brendan and my compatibility was off the charts— we liked the same food, movies, sports. He was much messier than I was, but his attractive factor was growing exponentially by the day, so it negated the points I usually would've taken off a guy's overall stick-aroundability score.

But jumping in too fast made it feel like a rebound relationship, and I didn't want Brendan to be just a rebound. And while I knew we were way past that, I also didn't want to move too quickly.

Every day, every kiss, was chipping away at my resistance, though. Making it harder to remember why I'd decided to go slow.

Brendan gripped my waist, lifted me onto the counter, and wedged himself between my legs. My breaths came faster and faster, and then he moved his lips to my neck, sending goose bumps across my skin. I hooked my feet behind him, unable to stop a moan from escaping and filling the crackling air between us.

The bowl of fruit on the counter got tipped over in the process, but as his mouth came over mine again, I hardly noticed the apples and oranges rolling across the counter and floor. Fire burned through me, hotter and wilder with every stroke of his tongue. I traced his muscles with my fingertips, going lower and lower, until they were brushing the top of his pants.

It sometimes felt like we were playing the dirtiest game of chicken ever. Testing the boundaries, seeing how far we could push it. Who'd crack first. If only frustration wasn't the end result, it'd be the most fun game ever, too.

"Living together is a bad idea right now," I said on a breath.

"Nuh-uh," Brendan so articulately disagreed, his hands sliding up my thighs. If I'd been wearing my usual skirt outfit, I would've been a goner—I practically was anyway. His touch burned through my denim and left me wishing for a skirt.

"You know we need to leave in, like, five minutes."

"Five minutes is all I need," he said. I smacked his shoulder and he laughed. "I was kidding." His gaze ran over me, burning everywhere it touched. "I'm gonna need *much* longer."

My heart beat even faster, somewhere around hummingbird speed now. "You're evil, you know that?" His whiskers tickled my fingertips as I brushed them across his jaw and over the indention in his chin. "You knew we needed to leave, and you had to stand all half naked and wet in the kitchen."

Mischief danced in his eyes. "I never said I was a good boy." He kissed me hard on the mouth, then turned and strode to the fridge, the muscles in his back and shoulders tight. He opened the door and stood there for a moment, taking deep breaths. I fanned myself with my hand, trying to get control of my hormones as well. Here we were about to go hang out with my dad, and my head was nowhere near where it needed to be.

Brendan grabbed two bottles of water. He took a generous swig of one, and then offered me the other—we'd been going through a lot more water lately. "Need help with the apples and oranges?" he asked.

"No, go finish getting dressed so we'll be on time. I might just leave them till later, anyway."

One corner of his mouth twisted up, the skepticism in his expression clear. "Mm-hmm."

After downing half my water bottle in one gulp, I turned my attention to the fruit scattered across the floor. Part of me wanted to leave them to prove I could. The other part of me was screaming louder, though. I mean, who leaves food on the floor like that?

I gathered the apples and oranges and stacked them neatly in the bowl, thinking of how he used to just leave them on the counter. They probably wouldn't have scattered everywhere with his old method, but the bowl looked nicer, and I liked that we did the kind of kissing that knocked things over.

Picking up my purse, I wandered into the living room and glanced at the time again. I was about to call for Brendan when he came out of his room. Along with his jeans, he was now wearing a baseball tee and his faded black Niners cap. *He's just as irresistible clothed, too.* Fortunate and unfortunate all at the same time. He raised his eyebrows in a way that said he'd caught me ogling him, and I gave him my most innocent smile with plenty of batting my eyes.

I'd never felt so...silly in love. I'd gotten butterflies, and there'd been desire and attraction, sure. But when I was with Brendan, I sorta felt like Cupid—bouncing around, jumping whenever he came into the room, and a whole lot of panting.

It was a total how-did-this-amazing-thing-happen-to-me feeling. But I didn't quite trust it, either. My relationship with Grant was more serious, but I'd loved him with everything in me, and I wasn't sure I could do that again, which also seemed unfair to Brendan.

Although he'd made it clear he wasn't big on long-term commitments, and at the time I'd been experiencing enough angst over relationships to stupidly agree, not realizing it might come back to bite me.

"Don't worry." Using his thumb, Brendan smoothed the spot between my eyebrows and then cupped my cheek. "We got this."

I wasn't sure if he meant hanging out with my dad, or more— like all the things I worried about. But then he kissed me again, and it didn't really seem to matter.

"This is a trip," Brendan said as he pulled up to my dad's tan ranch-style house. The yard was rocky, with a few stumpy, short palm trees, and the red door with the fancy window Mom had insisted on stood out in the game of "which one of these things was not quite like the others."

"Not much has changed." I climbed out of the truck and waited for Brendan to round the hood. Besides the door, the tiny two-bedroom home hadn't been updated since it was built in the seventies. It seemed like the entire neighborhood had upgraded, but not Dad. He was of the if-it's-not-broke-don't-fix-it mind-set. Apparently "in need of serious update" was not "broke."

I reached over the chain-link fence and opened the gate. When Dad answered the door, it took him all of two seconds to give a pointed look to Brendan's hand on my waist.

"Hi, Dad." I stepped forward to hug him and whispered, "Remember to be nice."

Dad made a *phfft* noise that didn't give me a whole lot of confidence. But he pulled out a smile when he turned to Brendan and shook his hand. "Brendan. Been a long time."

"Yes, sir."

"You still play ball?"

"Just a pickup game here and there whenever I can."

Dad nodded, assessing him the way he did his players, as if he could tell everything about him with a good once-over. "You had a good arm. I remember that."

"So did D.J.," Brendan said.

Dad patted me on the shoulder. "That she did."

"I came by it naturally," I added, thinking I might as well keep the happy mood going.

We headed inside, and Dad jerked a thumb at the cardboard boxes on the coffee table. "I got pizza. Hope that's okay."

"Pizza sounds great." I sat on the couch next to Brendan and grabbed a slice of pepperoni, and Dad set up in his trusty recliner with all the fancy compartments that hid remotes and held his drinks. It was a lot like Brendan's couch, actually.

Dad eyed us again, and I fought the urge to scoot away from

Brendan—I was a grown-up in a relationship I was excited about; no reason to hide it. I even smiled to show everything was A-okay.

The lines in Dad's forehead deepened as the corners of his mouth pulled down. "When Dakota mentioned bringing you, I didn't realize she was already dating someone new."

I wiped my mouth with a napkin. "When I mentioned it, Brendan and I weren't dating."

"Just living together," Dad said as his eyebrows shot up—they were starting to turn gray and a bit out of control, giving the motion more emphasis.

"But we're not even—" I cut myself off. So not going there. "We're dating. Taking it slow. I just got out of a serious relationship and—"

"You almost got married. First you decide to go get hitched on some distant shore, where I can't even give you away. Then that dinklewad doesn't bother to show up. Don't you think you should take some time before you get another boyfriend? You were always like that, in love one minute, out the next. I could hardly keep up."

An ache rose, the same one I used to get when he asked how I could let my feelings get hurt so easily, or when he told me to just suck it up and get out there again. Always the coach, emotions were something to shove away. A weakness.

Was it any wonder I constantly held them in, and would nearly kill myself instead of asking for help?

Brendan put his hand on my knee. "D.J. and I are taking things a step at a time. I know she's worried about moving too fast, and that dinklewad, as you so accurately put it, hurt her. I care a lot about your daughter. I always have. I'll take care of her, I swear."

Dad pressed his lips together. Tension hung in the air as he deliberated his decision about Brendan's statement, mouth moving one way then the other. I held my breath, feeling like a little girl again, waiting for my daddy to tell Brendan sleepovers weren't allowed anymore.

Dad leaned back in his chair and sighed. "Suppose it's none of my business. I'm just her father. She keeps insisting she can make her own decisions."

"And I can, though I appreciate the concern," I said.

The rest of the meal went slightly better—I mean, when you start at Awkwardsville, there's not a whole lot of places to go but up. We kept to safe topics, talk of NFL and who we thought had good potential for the Super Bowl. (Always the Niners, of course.)

After we'd eaten, I left Brendan on the couch and followed Dad into the kitchen. I cornered him as he pulled a soda out of the fridge. Unlike him, I was better at filtering emotions through what was or wasn't said now. "I didn't realize you were upset about not being able to walk me down the aisle. You said you didn't care, but I should've known that you'd want to."

He shrugged and popped the top of his orange Crush. "I don't care. I was just making a point. You were going to get married, and you were happy, so I was happy for you. He seemed like a nice guy there till the end."

"I just don't think we were quite right for each other. Maybe he did me a favor. But it still hurt me pretty badly."

Dad reached into the fridge and handed me an orange soda, as if it was all that was needed to fix everything. When I was a little kid it seemed to. Scraped knees? Homework neither one of us could figure out? Have an orange Crush. I probably drank a six-pack the few days after Brendan moved—every time I'd teared up, Dad had just passed me another one.

I popped open the top and took a swig, enjoying the familiar fizz of the bubbles in my throat—with my coffee addiction demanding my attention all the time, I forgot how satisfying an orange soda could be. "I didn't expect to start dating again so soon. But he makes me happy, Dad, and I didn't even think that was possible a month ago."

Dad scuffed the faded linoleum with his shoe, and I could tell he was having a hard time figuring out how to say what he wanted to. "I know I wasn't any good with the mushy stuff. You probably could've used a female around. But I don't want you hurt, kid. Like I said, you always jump in so fast. One minute you love a guy, the next the fire department's coming to undo the damage of your séance."

I rolled my eyes. "It wasn't a séance. Just a...cleansing. And that was a long time ago."

"Then there was the guy after that, and the one in college, and that gambling addi—"

"I get your point, Dad. No need to rehash the dating hall of shame."

"Go slow. Think things through."

"I'm trying." *But sometimes love doesn't make logical sense.* I knew that better than anyone. I'd seen mismatched couples that somehow worked and heard love stories that went against everything you'd normally call romantic. But I kept that in, because he'd call it nonsense. And despite what he said, I could tell his not being at my wedding, even though it didn't happen, *had* bothered him. He was too stubborn to say it, of course. A trait I'd probably gotten from him, though in his eyes I was a soft girlie girl.

After growing older, I understood better why he and Mom couldn't make it work. Yes, she'd left for her career, but she needed understanding, and Dad didn't do that, just like she didn't take the time to see that he had feelings if you looked hard enough.

"You'll always be my little girl," Dad said.

"And you'll always be my old man."

Dad chuckled at that, then glanced into the other room at Brendan, who was still on the couch, giving us space. "He was always a good kid. And I appreciate what he said about taking care of you." Dad cracked his knuckles, as if even that admission needed a total guy gesture to bring it back to an acceptable level of manliness. "Gotta get my gear together, then we can go to the field. Unless you changed your mind about the game?"

"Wouldn't miss it for the world." I lifted my can and he clinked his against mine. Then he headed to the garage for his pregame get-ready ritual that took seven point five minutes.

I wandered back into the living room and Brendan stood. "Everything good now?" he asked, even though he sounded like he already knew the answer.

I tilted my head. "Are you telepathic?"

"Little bit," he said with a sly smile. "I could tell you were talking, and from the smile on his face, I'd guess it went well. Plus, my tea leaves said as much this morning."

"That's more clairvoyance, I think. Or maybe divination."

He shrugged one shoulder. "I do a little of this, a little of that."

I put my hands on the sides of his waist. "So what else did your tea leaves tell you, then?"

"That you were dying to drag me to your bedroom." He nipped at my bottom lip, making my pulse skid underneath my skin in hot bursts. "I have so many memories of sitting on your bed. I wanna see how much it's changed over the years."

I glanced toward the garage, then took his hand and pulled him down the hall—might as well make some of his predictions come true. I pushed open the door to my old bedroom. There was a lot more football gear than used to be in there, discarded helmets and shoulder pads, along with an old-school TV/VCR combo so Dad could watch tape. He'd finally gone digital last year, though it took a lot of swearing and threatening to throw his iPad. But some of those tapes were of classic NFL games, including Super Bowl highlights, so there was no way he'd give up the VCR completely.

I shook my head at the mess that a part of me itched to organize. "And he wonders why I didn't want to move back in. There's not even a spot for me anymore."

"You still have all the soccer posters," Brendan said. There was one of David Beckham for the obvious reasons, and one of Mia Hamm, the athlete I used to want to be. The high school team pictures hadn't been there when Brendan was last here. While I loved playing, I also learned that I didn't want to play on a professional level. I had too many other interests, and after four years of playing in high school, I was burned out with the training.

"Here's the hint of girliness creeping in," Brendan said, pointing at the pictures of my girlfriends and me in our prom dresses. "No dates?"

"I tore the pictures with them down when the guy I went with broke up with me. My friends and I burned them in a Cleanse Yourself of Your Jerk Ex ceremony, actually. Cathartic, really, until one of the shrubs in the backyard caught on fire and we had to call my dad's friend Larry, who's a firefighter."

Brendan flopped on the bed, pulling me next to him. "Man, this brings back memories." He reached back and opened the window, then stuck his finger in the small slit in the screen. "It's still there."

"Yep, so next time you need to sneak in, let me know and I'll unlock the window."

"I was so scared your dad was going to find me, kill me, and bury me in the backyard. I kept thinking it wasn't worth it, but then I'd come in here and we'd kick back and talk and laugh for hours, so I'd go ahead and sneak in again the next time."

I ran my fingers across the line of his forearm. "I looked forward to those nights. But I was also terrified my dad would catch you. And then kill us both." I closed my eyes and thought of the two of us back then, so young and innocent, lying on my bed talking about sports, joking around, and coming up with new strategies for our next game of Fugitive. "I was so crushed when you left." I opened my eyes and glanced at him. "I wanted to be the tough girl who didn't cry, but I did. For weeks. Once you were gone, the dynamic with the other guys fell apart and I was a loner for a couple years."

"It kills me to admit this, but I *might've* shed a couple tears myself." His cheeks colored and he ran his palms down his jeans. He shook his head. "Can't believe I just told you that."

I bumped my shoulder into his. "It's okay. I won't tell anyone."

He took my hand, threading our fingers together. "There at the end, a few months before I left, I started thinking about kissing you."

My throat went dry. "Oh yeah?"

"I kept chickening out. Thinking it'd be weird. Then after I left, I wished I had."

"And now…?"

He leaned in, our breath mixing together for a moment before he pressed a kiss to my lips. "Now I'm just glad I finally did."

"Me too."

I heard my dad's heavy footsteps in the living room, meaning the car was ready to go. Over the years I'd spent countless weekends on the sidelines. Once I got to be the same age as the players, I was a "distraction," so I'd had to move to the bleachers. That was when I'd stopped going to away games, too. Luckily I had my friends from the soccer team by then, and I spent a lot of nights at teammates' houses, learning about makeup and bras and gossiping about boys.

I kissed Brendan one more time—just a quick peck—and then we headed into the living room.

Dad looked up from the clipboard in his hand. "What are we waiting for?" He pulled on his green and orange hat. "We've got a game to go win."

We. That was why, even though he sometimes yelled to get his point across and brought up the point I fell in love too quickly—a fact I was painfully aware of, especially when I looked at Brendan and realized how attached I already was—I'd forever be a daddy's girl. He was there when I needed him most, and even when life got hard, *we*'d taken it on together.

And if I ever did attempt another walk down the aisle—a big freaking *if* that made my blood pressure rise just thinking about it—he'd sure as hell be the one giving me away.

Chapter Twenty-One

Brendan sent me a text that there'd been an incident at the casino so he was pulling a double shift and wouldn't be home till tomorrow night. If you asked me, "incident" was a funny word to use to describe anything that caused that kind of reaction, but for all I knew it was a simple card counting violation.

In a way, it was good. When Brendan was around, it was hard for me to concentrate, and I needed to start my column. The blank screen and I had a standoff, that stupid cursor blinking over and over. And over. But I'd made a goal to let the city of Las Vegas into my life on my terms, and I was nothing if not goal-oriented. Even though I thought I'd come to terms with it—and I had—laying it all out made it feel like someone had reached into my chest and gripped my heart, squeezing tighter with each line I wrote. I didn't like feeling vulnerable, and I liked the thought of anyone actually reading it even less.

It took five drafts to put the spin on it that I wanted, and it was way longer than anything else I'd ever written, but it was time to turn my poor-jilted-bride image around. Preferably before Phoebe made me sound like some kind of pathetic serial dater who couldn't wait to land another man. The fact that I hadn't really waited very long was beside the point. But I didn't want to make it sound like I didn't care about what had happened either, all *Cheerio, mates! Being stood up's the best, you should totes try it.*

Not sure why that side of me was British, but anyway...

As soon as I'd gone through it again to check for typos and see how it read in one fell swoop, I sat back and sipped my second glass of wine—maybe that was why I felt better about what I'd managed to write.

Part of me thought I should sleep on it, but if I waited, I might chicken out. So I wrote up the email to Tess, attached the file, and moved the cursor over the send button.

In one quick motion, I pressed it. The second it left, a thrill battled the wave of nausea in my stomach. Not a combination I'd recommend, but it was done.

Now I got to hope it wasn't a giant mistake.

The rest of the week passed by in a blur of too-short tablecloths, a massive search for fabric in the perfect shade of blue, and a meeting with Valentina and her mom to finalize food and flowers where Mr. Maddox actually made an appearance. Brendan was working a lot, and I was going nonstop to fix all the tragedies that'd sprung up—it'd been that kind of week. But tonight we had plans, and I was counting on that excitement to get me through the day.

Only then I noticed the *Beacon* in my stack of mail. Even though I knew what the article would say, I had to open it up and see it in black and white.

GET READY TO WED by Dakota Halifax
When I Dos Turn to I Don'ts

Did you ever want something so badly that you'd do almost anything to make it happen? Have you ever felt like you lost sight of what was important? Wondered how you became the person you are now? Well, a couple of months ago, I wrote a column about how happy I was to be getting married. In case any of you haven't read about it already, my wedding never happened. Was it from lack of planning? No. It was well planned, I assure you. That was the one thing I got right.

While I was raised by a wonderful dad who means the world to me, and who did a fantastic job, I dreamed of a life with two people who loved each other under one roof, raising a family together. The so-called normal families all my friends had—or seemed to have, anyway. I'm a determined person, and once I set my sights on that dream, I worked to figure out how to get it. I was so close, that dream inches from my grasp. And it wasn't just about reaching my goal; I was in love. Alas, it didn't end up the way I'd hoped it would.

Did it hurt to wait for a groom who never showed? I can't even describe how much that tore me apart inside. I've had my fair share of heartbreaks, but this was deeper, like my life was crumbling around me, and I couldn't do anything but cry. Yes, I cried. I hate crying, by the way. Not a fan. *At all.*

I found out a few things by getting stood up at the altar, though. I'd lost myself a little in the whirlwind of wedding details and the fact that I was about to achieve my dream. Love didn't fit in the neat, tiny box I'd placed it in. So I'm rediscovering who I am. Figuring out how to stand on my own again. Thinking about love in a new light. And you know what? So far I've learned that I'm stronger than I thought I was. Also, who says what's a normal family and how you need to get there? There's no deadline. No race. No perfect checklist that'll give it to you—if there was, I swear I'd have found it. I love me some checklists.

No matter how well planned out your life is, though, it's got ups and downs. The unexpected happens. Sometimes it seems like there's a good reason, and sometimes it seems like the universe is having a good laugh at your expense. I'm glad for these unplanned adventures—some more than others. Am I happy that people know me as a wedding planner whose wedding didn't go according to plan? Not exactly. Am I happy that I didn't get married? Well, I've had a while to think about this, and even after the pain and the heartache, yes, I am.

Wanting something, no matter how badly, doesn't always mean it's right for us. You've got to learn when to hold. When to fold. So my advice to everyone—and especially to the brides out there—is to make sure you take time to figure out what you really want. Don't settle (unless it's a budget issue, in which case I'm an expert at figuring out cheaper ways to achieve the same effect). I've rediscovered the girl I used to be. I've been blessed with good friends who've helped me through this last unexpected adventure. I would have never gotten through this without them.

So if you've been hurt before, then know you're not alone. I've been there. I'm still there some days. But it gets better. And I'm excited to see what happens after better.

"I think I'm going to puke," I said to my empty office. People were actually going to *read* that. What had I been thinking? It was like those dreams where you were running around naked, yelling at yourself to *put on some clothes already!* Only there was no putting on clothes. It was out there. And now people were going to know that I cried. That I was human.

"I think I preferred robot mode."

My office phone rang, and I answered it on autopilot.

"The DJ just pulled out of the wedding," a hysterical female shrieked at Code Fuchsia level. I shuffled through my brides, trying to put the voice with a face. "We've had him booked for months because he's one of the only DJs who even had Hindi wedding songs, and now he bails on us? What am I going to do?"

Padma. Of course. My mental state was obviously in a bad place if I'd failed to recognize her voice the second I heard it. "Don't worry," I said in my soothing, let's-take-things-down-a-few-color-levels voice. "I'll have you a new DJ, with the music you want, by the end of the day."

When I got home, Brendan and Cupid were playing fetch in the house. They both froze in place as I stepped inside. Then Cupid brought me his slobbery squeaky ball, which I guess was his way of saying he still chose me when it came down to it. Despite the drool, I appreciated it. I took the ball from his mouth and tossed it down the hall. He bounded after it, tongue hanging out, nails clicking against the floor.

Brendan took one look at me and opened his arms wide. "Bring it in."

With a sigh, I closed the distance between us and let him envelop me in a hug. "Do you have any idea how hard it is to find a good DJ who plays Hindi music?"

"Can't say that I do. But I have a feeling the sad face is about more than trying to find a DJ."

Was it really that obvious? Guess that was what happened when you let everyone see inside your life—actually, I knew it was more about Brendan being able to read me so easily, which was comforting, but not enough for me to suddenly be okay with everything. "I feel so vulnerable and naked. I don't like it."

Brendan dragged his nose down my cheek. "Naked sounds nice."

"I'm not the good kind of naked right now." I shook my head and closed my eyes, sinking further into his embrace.

Cupid came over, dancing around with his ball in his mouth, but when neither of us moved for it, he gave up and headed into the kitchen.

"I read it," Brendan said. "It was good."

I winced. "I don't know. I thought I'd be happy to have my version out there. But right now I feel like hiding from the world and never going out again." Nothing in the column was a news flash for Brendan—after all, he'd seen the pain firsthand. Knowing he'd read every word was both nice because he was being supportive and nerve-racking because I'd reminded him of that broken side of me, something I was still working to be okay with. "I thought I'd gotten over it—and I have for the most part—but putting it out there and knowing people are reading it has brought back all those icky emotions."

"Give yourself a break. It'd be strange if you felt nothing." He ran his fingertips down my arm. "It was obvious you put your heart and soul into that column. It was brave and hopeful, and people will relate to that."

I tipped up my head and peered into the dark brown depths of his eyes. "Thanks, but I still don't like it. It was supposed to be empowering and I just feel like a mess. At least I'm not crying all the time, the way I was in my office that first day you came to see me." I shook my head. "I can't believe you didn't run—you probably should've. It's not too late, although with our living situation, it's gonna be trickier, so that's your bad." The joke didn't come out quite as light as I'd been going for.

Brendan gently cupped my chin. "Do you really not get it? That first day I walked into your office, I knew I was a goner. I thought it'd be fun to see you again, but when you lifted your beautiful face, black smudged across your cheek, I forgot my own name. As we were talking, I told myself to calm down—that you were D.J., my childhood friend. But from that moment on, I couldn't get you out of my head."

The anxiety squeezing my chest eased, a happy flutter taking its place. "You made a pretty big impression, too. I kept telling myself to stop thinking about how hot you were. And then you were so easy to talk to, and having our friendship back made all the crappy stuff not so crappy anymore…" I leaned into him again, taking a moment to soak in his familiar cologne and his warm skin next to mine. "Without you, I don't know how I would've made it through these past few months." I twisted my head and placed my lips against his cheek. "You know I'm a little bit crazy about you, right?"

The skin around his eyes crinkled as he smiled. "Just a little bit?"

He was obviously joking, but a sharp jab of apprehension shot through me. I thought about how Dad had pointed out my tendency to fall in love so quickly. It was true. I wanted to be tough, and I played it cool, but inside I was always crushed when a guy didn't call later, or when a relationship ended.

Brendan was not only the guy I was falling hard for; he'd also become my best friend all over again. This was a different kind of falling. It was jumping out of an airplane without checking to see if I'd gotten a parachute, and if it didn't open, I'd be splat on the ground, no chance of recovery.

"So did that help?" Brendan asked, pulling back to look at me.

"Are you out of Code Pink now?"

"Code Fuchsia," I automatically corrected, but I was thinking that I was in Code Fuchsia trouble with him.

Brendan pulled me toward the couch. "Maybe we can get it to Purple Passion…" He sat and tugged me down so I was straddling him. His hands slid up my thighs, and my worries, as well as every other thought in my head, went hazy. He drew me closer, until nothing but our quickened breaths separated our lips, not an inch of space between our bodies.

He dipped his head and ran his lips across my collarbone, sending the room spinning. I arched back, rocking my hips at the same time, eliciting a groan from him. The next thing I knew I was on my back on the couch, his body pinning me with his delicious weight. Then his tongue and limbs tangled with mine, a blur of kisses and fingertips grazing skin. I tugged his shirt up and let my fingers drift over the taut muscles of his abdomen. I pulled my legs up on either side of him, my skirt inching high enough to expose most of my legs, which Brendan took advantage of, his hands skimming my thighs.

This was it. Maybe I was falling, and it was a little scary and a little fast, but I couldn't wait anymore. Figuring out everything else could wait.

Brendan's phone rang, vibrating against my hip bone, and he swore under his breath. He lifted himself onto his hands, his arms locked, and took a few heaving breaths as the phone continued to ring.

"It's the ringtone I have for Mr. Maddox. I'm so sorry, but I need to get it." As he reached for his phone, I was pretty sure he muttered, "Looks like I'll be dealing with the color blue tonight."

I covered my mouth to hide a smile, because it wasn't really funny. I was all hot and bothered, too, the imprint of his hands on me a torturous and pleasant memory, all at the same time.

"They're back?" Brendan asked, running a hand through his

hair. "No, I understand. I'll be there as soon as I can." He hung up and let out a sharp exhale. "We've got these clients who need extra security, and they've taken a liking to me. Which is good, only they want to have access 24-7. They're going to be here all week." His eyes met mine, and a flush of heat traveled across my skin. "I had plans to take you out tonight."

I hooked my finger through one of his belt loops. "I had a feeling we were on our way to staying in."

Brendan groaned. "You're so not helping." He dragged his thumb across my bottom lip. "I'd say you should come stay at the hotel with me, but you're too distracting, and I might kill someone if they interrupted us. Can't you be a little less sexy?"

I wrinkled my nose and stuck out my tongue, giving him my best total-weirdo look that'd surely send even sex addicts running for the hills.

"Nice try, but it's still far too cute." He leaned in, his lips close to my ear. "Later, you and I are going to finish what we started." The combination of his words and his breath against my neck sent a pleasant chill down my spine. He kissed the sensitive spot under my ear and straightened. "And stop worrying about your column, okay? It was a good one."

Warmth filled my chest, different from the heat still pumping through my veins. One more kiss and Brendan headed to his room. He came out a few minutes later in a black button-down and a shiny black tie, looking every bit the security guy those very important people wanted. If it meant getting him full time, I'd be tempted to hire him as my personal security guard, too. I probably couldn't pay what they did, though.

Not with money anyway.

Okay, dirty thoughts are not making this better. Brendan paused at the door and I blew him a kiss. Yep, I was a goner. As soon as the door was closed, Cupid came wandering back into the room.

I reached over and petted my trusty companion. "I think I'm

in trouble, Cupid. Did you shoot me with your arrows?"

Cupid gave me an appropriately confused look, considering I was talking to a dog about arrows. "I think I'm already in love with him," I said, though there wasn't really any thinking involved.

The problem was, Brendan always made this face whenever the words "marriage" or "wedding" were mentioned. Which was kind of often, considering my job. I couldn't help flashing back to the conversation about his girlfriend who'd been obsessed with it, and how he'd made it clear he wasn't really into the idea. It wasn't like I was ready for anything like that—it terrified me now, actually. I just wasn't sure if it was a good idea to be falling so hard for someone who wasn't interested in it at all.

Chapter Twenty-Two

$\mathcal{A}$t the end of anger management, right before Ron signed off on the course, he'd challenged us to try to befriend someone who'd wronged us. He warned us it wouldn't be easy, and if we felt violent urges, we'd need to remove ourselves from the situation. Apparently if I got to know Phoebe, I'd be less likely to attribute malicious intent or my problems to her.

Color me doubtful, but I'd made an action item on my to-do list to attempt a decent conversation, and on my way to talk to Tess, I figured I might as well start the process. So when I neared her desk, I propped up the corners of my mouth in a smile and said, "Hi, Phoebe."

Her eyes widened as she spun her chair around. She scrambled for her phone and held it up like a weapon. "What do you want?"

When she'd acted like she was scared of me all those weeks ago, I'd thought she was putting on a show, but she did appear to be frightened by me now. I couldn't help get a pinch of satisfaction over that, although it wasn't exactly helpful on the befriending front. "I was simply saying hi. How're the Vegas social circles? Spy any cool people lately?"

She lowered her phone a fraction of an inch. "You'll have to read my column to see."

"Can't wait."

She eyed me like she didn't trust the niceness, and I forced my lips to lift even further. There'd be no hair braiding, but there wouldn't be any hair pulling, either—not that I did the catfight thing. I'd spent far too many years hanging out with boys. But Phoebe looked like a hair puller. I figured maybe even this goodwill attempt would keep my name out of her column.

A couple waves and nods to the rest of the people working away at their desks, and then I continued to Tess's office. I knocked on her open door to announce myself. "Ready for our meeting?"

"Yes, yes. Close the door and have a seat." Tess held up a large manila envelope, so full the sides were bulging. "Do you know what this is?"

"No idea."

"It's letters to the editor."

"People still write letters?"

"Some do. I get a lot of emails, too. But these"—she tossed the envelope across the desk—"are responses from your column. I printed out the emails and put them in there, too. I thought you should see what people are saying."

I pinched the corner and lifted it like it might bite me. "I'm not sure I wanna know."

"Trust me, you do. There were only a couple of mean ones, and I didn't include them," Tess said.

How reassuring.

Tess picked up a pen and tapped it against her desk. "You struck a nerve. People relate to breakups, to hurting. To trying to pick themselves back up. I knew it'd be popular, but even I underestimated the response—we got hits from all over the country."

All over the country? Whoa.

Come to think of it, things had been busier at the Ready to Wed office lately, with lots of referrals calling in. "Thanks for pushing me to do it." I still wasn't 100 percent sure I'd enjoyed opening up, but it had been cathartic, even with the "feeling naked and exposed" freak-out. Plus, it was helping me open up with Brendan. Thanks to the VIP clients he'd been doing security for all week, phone conversations and the one dinner we'd snuck in at Terra, the restaurant in Aces, were our only interactions. The clients were set to go home on Saturday, though. I just had to get through the Jones/Taylor wedding and then Brendan and I would both have our entire Sunday free to spend together. I was pretty sure I knew how we were going to spend it, too, and I was counting down the hours.

I hugged the envelope to my chest, thinking I'd read all the letters tonight, Cupid by my side, a cheesy romance movie on in the background. It was scheduled in and everything. Originally I thought I'd cry and feel sorry for myself through romance movies from here on out, but now that my faith in love was restored, I was ready to watch fictional people fall in love. As long as the *M* word wasn't involved, because I was spending way too much time stressing over it, regardless of telling myself to knock it off.

"I look forward to your next column," Tess said. "You can keep it fun and light most of the time, but remember the impact of a well-placed one that goes a little deeper. You're practically famous around these parts, after all."

I laughed at that, but thanked her anyway.

I was steps away from the bright afternoon sunshine when Phoebe cut me off. "I hear you're dating one of the security personnel from the new Aces Casino now. Apparently he's Mr. Maddox's right-hand man, too?"

My gaze homed in on her iPhone, held at the ready, no doubt recording this. I'd tried to be nice, and now she was taking advantage of that so she could get dirt for her column. Dang Ron and his challenge.

"I decline to comment on my personal life, Phoebe."

"Guess I'll just have to dig the old-fashioned way, then. Wonder what I'll find? What people will say about you two?"

No one knew much about our relationship. I supposed Jillian, my dad, and the people Brendan worked with were the most informed, but they wouldn't talk about it. Then again, I didn't exactly want Phoebe tailing us in some pathetic attempt to get a scoop that wasn't there.

"You know what's really unfair?" Phoebe asked, and I raised my eyebrows, too scared to ask what, but not wanting to break up the nice-fest if it was actually happening. "I thought you'd finally be taken down a notch."

Guess I don't need to break out the nice-fest balloons after all.

Phoebe shook her head. "But you just move on like nothing happened. Find another guy like *that*." She snapped her fingers. I wanted to tell her it involved being nice to people, but then actual tears filled her eyes. "You think I like covering everyone else's relationships? That I don't want one of my own? Do you know how hard it is?"

Well, this conversation skipped all the other colors and went right to WTF Fuchsia. Usually people ramped up to it. I'd never seen a flip quite like this before, but if there was anything I was equipped to deal with, it was a breakdown over love.

This would be the point I hugged my brides, but I thought Phoebe might slap a sexual harassment lawsuit on me or something if I attempted it, so I lightly patted her shoulder. "I know tons of guys who'd love to go out with you." If she attended any wedding, pretty much anywhere, groomsmen would be on her like white on the rice tossed at the departing couple. "You go to the hottest clubs in the city. Everyone knows who you are. You're successful."

"Not as successful as you," she shot back, then punctuated it with a sniff and chin quiver.

Really? Not just an ounce of niceness while I'm trying to console you?

"Which is probably why Grant chose you," she added.

Now the conversation was seriously giving me whiplash. "Grant? What does this have to do with him?"

"He and I dated. I thought things were going well, and then he just stopped returning my calls. Next thing I know, he's with you. When I confronted him in person, he told me that it hadn't even been an official relationship, and I needed to move on. He even offered to set me up on a pity date, like I couldn't get my own. So yeah, you win. At work and at love. Congratulations."

For a moment I could only stare. I didn't want to think about Phoebe and Grant, or the fact that he'd clearly kept that from me on purpose, but at least she'd made it pretty clear it'd been before he and I got together. Whenever I used to talk about her, I thought he'd just flinched because he knew I was going to go on a rant. I briefly wondered if it would've been easier to dump him right away if I'd known, but then I thought it was better that pettiness or who he'd dated in the past weren't responsible for our parting. It was about knowing he wasn't right for me, and the fact that he hadn't been completely honest with me about more than just finding out he might have a son proved it.

Next order of business: figure out what to say to the now-crying Phoebe. Apparently she wasn't made of stone. "Look, love's not a competition. Even at work, it's not like you and I are opponents. There's no reason to compete with me—you can have it."

"I don't want to just have it. I want to *win* it." She narrowed her eyes and I saw a flash of her usual self. She looked away for a few seconds and when she turned back, her sad, woe-is-me look was back. It didn't seem false, but more like she didn't know how to wield it. "You know how well liked I am? My ride didn't even show to pick me up like she promised. My car's in the shop, and not only is she thirty minutes late, she won't even answer my calls."

Phoebe stared for several seconds out the glass door I was dying to walk through, then looked at me. My muscles automatically tensed, bracing for her next comment. "I know I don't deserve it, but I would appreciate it if you could give me a ride home."

The urge to tell her I'd rather pay for her cab fare than take her myself was strong, but I took one of those deep, cleansing breaths that were all the rage, telling myself this was progress. "Of course."

She'd actually been almost decent to me, but it was her statement "I want to win it" that scared me. It felt like more of a challenge. Bitchy Phoebe I could deal with—even control my temper around, thanks in part to anger management classes. But vulnerable Phoebe freaked me the hell out.

As we headed to my car, I said, "I didn't just find another guy, you know. Like I said in my column, I was hurt when Grant stood me up at the altar. I was planning on waiting to date, but when a good guy comes into your life, you thank your lucky stars, not tell him he has to wait. And we've been friends for a long time, too, so it's not like he's just some guy I barely met."

"So is it serious, then? Is he the one?"

Alarms screeched in my head. Regardless of her fragile state, I had to be careful. While just the thought of Brendan was enough to cause ecstatic happiness to tumble through me, I didn't want him reading that I was talking about us like we were super serious and having him feel the need to run in the other direction. If only I hadn't agreed so enthusiastically with his stance against relationships that night at the theater, I wouldn't be so afraid for him to find out how hard I was already falling for him.

Me and my big mouth.

We got into my car, and Phoebe turned to me, clearly expecting a response. "He's the one for right now," I slowly answered, measuring every word.

The ride passed in silence, only the music from the radio filling the air. When we got to her house, Phoebe started out of the car, and then abruptly turned around. "Thank you, Dakota." She gave me an almost-smile and then closed the door.

I stared after her as she climbed the stairs to her condo, feeling a bit like I'd just made a deal with the devil, and wondering if I'd accidentally signed away something I wanted to keep.

Chapter Twenty-Three

GET READY TO WED by Dakota Halifax
Playing With Fire

Candles seem to be all the rage these days. And why not? Candles have been linked with romance for centuries. You know what's the opposite of romantic, though? Seeing your wedding go up in flames. If you choose this route (the candles, not the up-in-flames part), keep a close watch and have plenty of water and fire extinguishers. Also, think about things like curling irons left on, irons you used on your dress or tux, and any other item that might start a potential fire. For fireworks, which are also a big hit at weddings, you'll need to look into the legality of lighting them off. Sometimes it's a no-go, and sometimes a send-off with sparklers is a nice, low-key, and low-cost option.

Fires are dangerous, and I'd like you to remember that there are other options, such as battery-operated candles and white lights. No matter what you decide, though, you still need to be prepared. Wedding rule number one—I know, I make every rule number one, but who can keep track of all of them and, honestly, whatever's going wrong in the moment feels like number one. So, ahem, *Rule Number One*: if it can go wrong, it probably will, so being prepared will make the entire day run smoothly. I'd like to give a shout-out to our local firefighters, who've saved me several times with their quick responses.

As for a different kind of playing with fire, I'd like to give a not-so-honorable mention to being stupid at bachelor and bachelorette parties. Do you really think a room full of semi-wasted people can keep a secret? *Really?* Well, spoiler alert, they can't. That whole "what happens here, stays here" motto has made some of us a bit overly confident in our indiscretions. So I'm here to break the devastating news that it's a Vegas urban legend, and what happens at those parties can—and often does—follow you around like the Ghost of Strip Clubs Past.

Don't do anything you wouldn't want your significant other to see, hear about, or do. It's been the demise of several cute and loving couples, and it could happen to you. It must not have been meant to be, you might argue, but if you ask me, it's just playing with fire. You don't send a drug addict to pick up your prescriptions, so don't put yourself in a situation you can't handle, especially while inebriated. A fleeting moment of debauchery while your friends egg you on isn't worth ruining your future with someone who loves you. So be smart or you might just end up burned.

"It's fitting that she wants three hundred and sixteen candles," Jillian said, "because her bridesmaids' dresses look very *Sixteen Candles.*" She lifted the frothy pink ruffled dress that I'd draped over a bench. It'd taken some extra fabric, innovation, and a lot of swearing from a tailor and me, but hopefully the dress would fit the now-pregnant bridesmaid. Why she'd waited three days before the ceremony to see if it still fit—only to discover it didn't zip up all the way anymore—I had no idea. Apparently it was all part of trying to keep the first part of her pregnancy secret, although she'd spilled the beans to her friends a few weeks ago.

"*Sixteen Candles* was Kara's inspiration, actually," I said. "We even duplicated a floral headpiece from the movie for her flower girl."

Since Jillian was all set on the catering end, I'd roped her into helping me place candles around the front of the chapel. It should've been done yesterday, but the monogramed candles got held up in Saint George, Utah. All three hundred and sixteen of them, one for each day Kara and Jack were together before he popped the question. So I'd left at six in the morning, driven to Saint George, and buzzed back here. All kinds of fun, let me tell you. This wedding was hell-bent on falling apart, just like I was hell-bent on not letting it.

All I've got to do is make it to tonight. Brendan was supposed to be done basically babysitting his VIP clients tonight, and I couldn't wait to curl up on the couch with him. Or, if either of us had the energy, maybe do something that required less clothing and more cardio.

I pictured us cuddling, how we'd exchange details about our days and listen if either one of us needed to vent. There'd be a few jokes in the mix, then his eyes would darken and he'd flash me the seductive smile I couldn't resist. My pulse skittered as I thought of undoing the buttons he hadn't gotten to yet, and the way his hands would grip my thighs and pull me closer, and an intoxicating mix of desire and affection flooded my veins.

The crunch of tires on gravel pulled me out of the pleasant scene going on in my head. Doors slammed, and then words carried in on the wind, snippets here and there about getting ready and asking if anyone knew where Elise was. Elise was the pregnant bridesmaid, so I made a mental note to find her if they hadn't in the next few minutes.

Kara came into the chapel, blond hair in rollers, wearing yoga pants and a tank top with the word BRIDE across the chest in rhinestones. She scanned the candles that'd besieged the floor. "You got them! Oh, thank you so much!" The exuberant hug she attacked me with caused me to stumble and knock over a few of the candles near my feet. "I always wanted candles. It's just like I pictured when I was a little girl!"

A moment ago, I'd been inwardly grumbling about impossible demands, three hours' worth of driving, and an exact number of candles. But with Kara hugging me, the wonder in her voice, I got that tingly fairy-godmother-granting-wishes sensation. My hope had been slowly working its way back to fighting shape, but I worried I'd never get that excitement for another one of my brides. I was glad it'd shown up for Kara. She'd loved *Sixteen Candles* as a little girl, and she said that Jack was the type of guy she never thought she'd get. He adored her, in addition to being quite wealthy, and said she could have whatever wedding she wanted. She'd chosen low-key in a chapel, her biggest demand candles. And when her bridesmaid had announced she was expecting at Kara's bridal shower, something I'd seen brides fly off the handle for, Kara had cried tears of joy for her friend.

She pulled back, her eyes glistening. "Can you believe I'm getting married today? For a while there, it seemed like it'd never actually get here."

"I'm so happy for you," I said, genuinely meaning it. The rest of her family and bridesmaids came into the chapel, all except the mother-to-be.

"Still no Elise?" Kara asked her maid of honor, who shook her head.

I put my hand on her shoulder. "I'll try to get a hold of her. You go start getting ready."

"Okay. Apparently she spent most of the morning puking—morning sickness. Said she thought it'd be gone by the time we got here. Last I heard she was going to be about ten minutes late, but she's not answering her phone." Thanks to the dress debacle, I had all of her numbers, not to mention her address if it came down to it.

Raquel came in, her boxes of hair supplies in hand. I waved at her. "You guys are all set up for hair in the back room. I'll get the 411 on Elise and let you know what's going on. Don't worry." I gave Kara a reassuring squeeze, along with a smile to match. "Everything's going to be perfect."

One hour later, I wasn't so sure it was going to be perfect. Every time a guest came into the chapel, a gust of wind would extinguish several candles. I'd already singed the hair on my arms, along with the hem of my skirt, while reaching and stepping over the sea of lit wicks. It was why I'd suggested battery-powered over open flame, but I could tell from the crestfallen look on Kara's face that she'd wanted the real thing. So I tiptoed through the burning maze once more, lit the smoking candles again, and hoped no more guests would arrive.

Then there was the fact that Elise was three shades of green and hadn't stopped puking since she'd arrived. The dress fit though, so...yay?

Jillian had made up ginger tea and Elise was sipping it, hands wrapped around the cup like it was her lifeline. I figured a church was a good place to pray for it all to go off without a hitch. Or you know, without anyone getting puked on.

The mother of the bride strode up to me, her features tight, and a knot formed in my gut. It was an expression that said something's gone horribly wrong—the grim look on her face said runaway bride, but Kara wasn't the type, so that couldn't be it.

"Do you smell smoke? I think I smell smoke."

After lighting all the candles, I felt like I'd never *not* smell smoke, but now that she mentioned it, it did seem to be stronger. I glanced across the sea of candles but didn't see any telltale swirls.

"I think it's coming from the hallway where the groomsmen got ready," Dianne said, putting her hand on my arm as she glanced in that direction.

The groomsmen were outside—I'd okayed them to get fresh air but not to go far, because I'm bossy like that at weddings. Instead of asking more questions, I scooped up an extinguisher and rushed toward the west wing.

When I got to the door of the guys' makeshift dressing room, smoke was barreling out from under the door in forbidding dark plumes. I lightly tapped my fingers on the doorknob to test it— scalding hot. I wanted to charge in and use the extinguisher, but I knew a hot doorknob could mean backdrafts and who knew what else. Enough that I knew better, that was for sure.

"Call 911," I said to Dianne, who'd followed me. "Tell them to send the fire trucks."

"Cigarette fire," Larry told me when he, Antonio, and the other two firemen came out of the chapel. "Lots of smoke, not much flame."

"Thank goodness," I said. Then I glanced at the wedding guests, all dressed up and waiting on the lawn as the sun dipped low in the sky, making the clouds purple and pink with a few orange stripes of sunlight still trying to fight through the impending dark. The bride was around back so that the groom wouldn't see her, although they'd been on the phone most of the time, checking in on each other. I'd already been a fan of Jack, but he won me over even more when he'd reassured Kara that no matter what, they'd find a way to get married because he couldn't wait to call her his wife.

The last thing I wanted to do was disappoint him or Kara. "How's the smoke in the chapel?"

"Not bad. It's safe if you want to continue with the wedding."

"I'll double-check, but I think it'll be a go."

Larry slapped me on the back, teammate style as usual. "You know, the boys down at the station are starting to make bets on when you'll need us next."

Stellar. Just add "fire hazard" to my public profile. "Well then, how about you save me the trouble of having to call again and just stick around, because my bride wants three hundred and sixteen lit candles, and she's getting them. I could use a little standby assurance besides my extinguishers, though."

His gray mustache twitched in a way I was pretty sure meant he was smiling underneath it. "Anything for you."

"Thanks, Larry. And tell the rest of the boys I appreciate them, too. You all are gonna get wedding cake at the station. Like, till you're sick of it."

I confirmed with Kara that she wanted the show to go on, and when she said she did, I ran around the hazy part of the chapel throwing open the windows. I even found a fan to help blow the smoke out of the window in the room where the fire had been. Within thirty minutes, everyone was reseated, the candles were relit—thanks to extra help from Larry and Antonio—and the "Wedding March" was filling the air.

I quickly fluffed out the train of Kara's dress so it'd be fully displayed as she walked down the aisle, but not so full it'd catch any candles, then left her to her father.

The muscles in my neck ached, the pain radiating down to my shoulder blades, and my feet were sore from all the extra running around in heels. Giving myself a quick shake to keep myself going, I squeezed into the narrow gap between the wall and the seats so I could head up front and keep an eye on everything.

Even under the veil, I could see Kara's brilliant smile as she came down the aisle. If it'd been most any other bride, she'd be flustered or possibly even blaming me. Instead, she wore the dreamlike expression of someone who was more concerned with the love she had for her groom than anything else in the world.

My hope bank filled up just a little higher, and I found myself wrapping my fingers around my phone, wanting to call Brendan and tell him how much he meant to me. Only I worried that was the wedding buzz in the air talking and that I needed to press on the brakes before I scared him.

I've gotta go slower this time. I considered the plans I'd had earlier tonight, and thought maybe I should slow those down, too.

No, I definitely was ready for that next step. Right? *Crap, now I'm messing myself up again, making problems that aren't there.*

I shook my head. *Just focus on the love, focus on the love.* Jack and Kara faced each other in front of the preacher, both wide-eyed and wearing grins like they couldn't believe their luck. I was so wrapped up in it, I almost missed it—one of the candles was shooting its flame several inches higher than the rest. It licked at the ribbon on Elise's bouquet, taking a taste and looking like it wanted more. I waved, trying to get her attention—on the bright side, her skin was back to her normal color and she didn't look like she was going to hurl—but she was focused on Kara and Jack as well, unmoved by my subtle gesture.

Can this wedding please just give me a break already? There was no way to completely hide myself, but I figured being seen was better than having a second fire. People might start to talk about hellfire and the union being unsanctioned or something, and that was *not* happening on my watch.

I sneaked behind Elise and nudged up the arms holding

the bouquet, whispering, "Hold it higher. It's hitting one of the candles."

Her eyes widened and then she nodded, holding it even higher than needed.

The vows ended, the bride and groom kissed, and I did an internal happy dance celebrating the lack of fire hoses for the ceremony. But then the flower girl kicked over a candle on her way down the aisle. One of the groomsmen stepped forward with a canister in hand, extinguished it with a burst, and the entire place cheered.

On his way past me, he held up a hand for a high five, and I smacked it. Then I nodded at Larry and Antonio to let them know we were clear on this end. Once all the guests were out of the chapel, my local friendly firefighters helped me make sure the candles were all out.

"Till next time," Larry said.

I gave the candles one last glance. "Kinda hoping there won't be one."

"Like I said, till next time." Larry gave me another hard slap on the back and then I hauled butt over to the reception hall to make sure everything there was going off as planned, and with any luck, fire free.

As I walked around Kara and Jack's reception, I couldn't help wondering if I was playing with fire jumping into a relationship so quickly after the demise of my last, and if I was going to get burned. It was like seeing Jack and Kara gave me enough of my love hope back to start worrying that when it came down to it, Brendan's goals in life weren't the same as mine.

Way, way in the future—that's what he'd said about even the *possibility* of marriage. Did that mean someday he'd suddenly want it? Grant told me the reason he hadn't shown up was because he wasn't ready, and he *hadn't* been against it from the start. I didn't need a promise of forever right now, but I didn't want to be the only one in the relationship thinking about a future together.

As much as I was trying to completely forgive my ex, I hated that he'd shaken my faith in my judgment and my trust in other people. It was bad enough to have my faith in love ripped away. Why'd he have to take more?

I stopped, trying to change my line of thought. It wasn't fair to take my issues out on Brendan, but it didn't mean I shouldn't be careful. Where was the careful line, though, and how did *fun for now* fit into it?

There I go, jumping in too fast again, the way I always do. More than anything, I wanted to be able to say it didn't matter if we ever defined our relationship, but the control freak in me liked things defined.

On the other hand, I didn't want him to think I was pressuring him like his last girlfriend did.

As if he sensed I was thinking about him, my phone buzzed with a text from Brendan, telling me he was officially off duty and asking me what I was up to.

Me: Taking care of this reception at the Grove. I'll probably be here fairly late.

I felt like I should add something to the text about how much I'd missed him and couldn't wait to see him, but too many thoughts were buzzing through my head now, and I worried it'd sound desperate. I obviously didn't know how to have a relationship anymore. There was too much pressure. Too many ways it could crash and burn and leave me crushed and scarred.

Crap, I'm gonna mess it up.

Me: Don't feel like you need to wait up.

There. I'd left it up to him. Maybe a cowardly move, but at least it wasn't desperate. Eventually, though, I needed to know if he and I were on the same page, and that meant finding a way to broach the topic. I couldn't set myself up for another heart-shattering ending. I was working on becoming stronger, but break something enough times and eventually the pieces would no longer fit together.

I slipped my phone into my bra and circled the reception hall again. After the problem-ridden ceremony, I almost didn't trust how flawlessly the reception was going, even though I had planned it to be that way.

I headed over to the food tables, where Jillian was starting to clear the main course away. Only a few minutes until cake time, which was always magical—cute bride and groom interaction followed by a sugar high. Talk about win-win. "How's everything on your end?" I asked Jillian.

"Running smoothly. I was a little worried about the new guy, but he's good." Jillian pointed her meat fork at a young waiter running food back and forth.

"He looks sixteen."

"Eighteen. Cute, though."

"Slow down, cradle robber," I teased. "By the way, how are things with the best man who needed toasting lessons? Tim, wasn't it?"

"Already over. Fun while it lasted, though. But speaking of hot men…" Jillian leaned in. "I talked to Antonio again, and he asked for my number."

"Score. Actually, that was my plan all along. Set the church on fire so you could get a date with a hot fireman. Hope I'm not going to hell for it."

"I'll let you know if it was worth it later," Jillian said with a laugh. I left her with the food and went to check on the wedding party one more time.

The cake came and went, there was dancing, and then everyone blew bubbles as the newlyweds headed to their car and drove off.

I stared at the Just Married written in the middle of the white shoe-polish heart and got a swimmy, twitterpated feeling about their new union. Maybe I still had other doubts about my life, but at least my career was finally back on track. As long as Phoebe didn't write another column implying I didn't know how to follow through on things, it should remain that way.

"D.J.?"

I turned, thinking I must've imagined the familiar voice. But there was no one else who called me D.J, and no one else's voice caused my heart to leap in my chest like that. My earlier doubts melted as I took Brendan in, from his suit to his slightly messy hair that looked like he'd raked his fingers through it several times, to his perfect lips lifting in a slow smile.

"I came to see if I could help you out with anything." He held up a coffee cup. "And I brought you a hazelnut macchiato, just in case you needed an extra boost."

A lightness filled my head as I wrapped my arms around his waist. "My knight in shining Armani."

Brendan glanced down and tugged on the bottom of his suit jacket. "I don't even know who this is, but I'm sure it's not Armani."

I grinned and took the cup from him. "Well, nothing else rolls off the tongue the same."

As I took my first sip of the heavenly brew, Brendan slid his hands behind my back and linked them, bringing my body against his. "Man, I missed you."

My heart expanded. He missed me, too. "Right back at you."

"I love my job most days, but that…" He sighed, adding to his adorably crumpled vibe. "I guess when you drop three and a half million in a week, though, you get what you want."

I almost choked on my drink. "Seriously? They lost that much?"

Brendan nodded. "The wife's crazy about the slots, and the husband likes poker and blackjack."

"You could've gone home. Rested up."

"I couldn't wait any longer to see you." Brendan brushed his lips across mine and then gave me a gentle kiss. Every glance, every gesture, his touch, all made me more of a believer in us. "Plus, I thought if I came and helped out, I could get you home even sooner." The half-growling way he said it sent desire winding through my core.

All my questions from before suddenly seemed silly and inconsequential. And to think I was jumping in too fast was silly. The guy in front of me knew me better than most anyone in the whole world—he knew how I loved my coffee, about my neat-freak tendencies, odd bridal terror-alert color scale, that I held back my emotions, and all the other little things that made up the real me.

I wanted to believe that I wouldn't get hurt again, but I knew there were no guarantees. Holding back in a relationship was dooming it to fail, though. Sometimes you had to simply dive in without knowing the endgame. And I wasn't just saying that because my self-control was hanging on by a thread and I didn't know how much longer I could wait to get him home and rip off his clothes.

I figured pulling out my phone to add a to-do list item might ruin the mood, so I mentally added *Stop being scared of a real relationship with Brendan and just let it happen* to the top of it. I set my coffee cup on a nearby table and tugged on the lapels of his jacket, pulling him down so I could reach his mouth with mine. Closing my eyes, I focused on the sensation of our bodies pressed together and bit lightly at his bottom lip.

He made a low noise in the back of his throat and splayed his hand on my back, eradicating the minuscule space between us. I slid my hands inside his jacket, feeling the strong muscles underneath his shirt and mentally calculating how long it'd be before we could get home and get rid of the layer between us. A distant part of me remembered that there were people around and I should at least use a little discretion. But the close part of me was enjoying having our bodies so entwined I didn't know where he ended and I began. My breaths were his, our rapid heartbeats merged into one high-speed rhythm.

Then someone cleared her throat.

"Sorry to interrupt this get-a-room moment," Jillian said. "But apparently the pregnant bridesmaid is puking again." She held out her hand to Brendan. "Jillian, by the way. You must be the famous Brendan."

At this point, I wasn't sure why taking care of Elise was my job—the wedding and reception were all but over, the planning and execution done. But I supposed the staff would need to be notified, and the poor pregnant lady would probably need some help. I'd learned earlier today that her husband was a sympathy puker, too, and the last thing I needed was more people losing their dinner.

I knew this reception was too good to be true. I sighed. "Duty calls. Puking's sorta the trump card."

"I'll keep that in mind," Brendan said with a smile, then leaned in and kissed my cheek. "While you take care of that, I'll just have Jillian here show me what I can help with."

Jillian got a canary-eating grin and an alarm sounded through my head. She'd probably interrogate him as soon as I left them alone—possibly even threaten him while waving a knife around. I didn't want her to scare him off now that I'd finally decided to stop putting our relationship under so much pressure. We didn't need similar goals or to be defined right now. We needed light, fun, and the opposite of our past relationships.

I wanted to pull Jillian aside and ask her to take it easy on him, but then I saw Elise lean over and heave into the bushes strung with twinkling lights, her husband beside her looking like he might go next, and I had no choice but to leave my two best friends behind and hope for the best all around.

Chapter Twenty-Four

There's nothing quite like seeing your mother waiting on your doorstep when you think you're about to have sex with your boyfriend for the first time. Total ice bucket of water over the head.

For a moment all I could do was blink, thinking—more like hoping—I was seeing things. "Mom?"

She stood up and hugged me. "Hey, hon. I was starting to worry I got the wrong address."

I wanted to ask what she was doing here, but I knew she'd be offended, and it's not like we saw each other very frequently.

"I sensed you needed me," she said.

As usual, her mom senses were *way* off. "If you would've called, I'd have told you that I'm fine."

"Yes, but you'd say that either way. Besides, you didn't call me back when I tried to get a hold of you earlier this week."

Because I'd been up to my eyeballs with wedding problems and hadn't had the energy to deal with anything else. And while we'd come a long way in our relationship, I didn't think we were quite at the drop-by-unannounced level.

Brendan drove his truck up the driveway, the headlights blinding me for a moment before disappearing inside the garage. I heard his truck door close and then he walked over, the lack of light making it hard for me to make out his features until he was right next to us. Mom had met him a few times in passing, although I doubted she'd recognize him now. If she'd gotten my address from Dad—she certainly hadn't gotten from me—he'd probably told her I was living with him. Possibly that we were dating, but they rarely said much when they did speak, so maybe not.

"Brendan, you remember my mom?"

His shoulders tensed slightly. "Yeah. Cheryl, right?"

Mom extended her hand and shook his. Then we all stood in the doorway for an awkward beat.

"So…" I glanced at her car at the curb. "Where's Frank?"

"Oh, he was busy with something or other. Like I said, I just sensed you needed me, so I got in my car and drove. I was thinking we could go shopping tomorrow. It's so rare I get a girls' day, and Frank simply abhors shopping."

Something about the way she said his name made me wonder if her impromptu visit was more for her than me. No doubt she was getting antsy again, feeling trapped by being settled in one place. Classic Mom. She'd left every good man she'd had, all in the pursuit of a magical *grass is greener on the other side* option, whether it be the next job, the next town, the next guy.

And now she'd chosen my life as a distraction from hers.

"I hope it's okay if I stay with you. Just for a couple of days." Mom draped her arm over my shoulders. "I missed my girl."

Brendan glanced from her to me, and his eyebrows rose in a silent question. Telepathy would come in really handy right now. I shrugged, and Brendan looked back at Mom. "Of course. Can I get your bag?"

"Oh, aren't you a gentleman!" Mom hooked her arm through Brendan's, her mouth moving a mile a minute as she led him to her car. He got her suitcase, walked her inside, and set her up in the spare bedroom.

When she ducked into the bathroom, I turned to Brendan. "I'm so sorry. I didn't know she was coming."

"Do you want her here?" he whispered.

"'Want' is a strong word." I ran a hand through my hair. "I have a feeling she's having trouble with her job or with Frank. That's when she tends to visit, and I don't know how to say no. She's my mom, and I don't get to see her very often."

"I understand. I can't help feeling protective of you, though." Brendan grabbed my hand and kissed the top of it, holding it next to his lips as he spoke. "I know your mom's hurt you before, and I don't want her to do it again."

"It's okay. I'm all grown up now. And she's…well, still her, but I think she does the best she knows how." I'd wasted plenty of time as a kid wondering how she could have left me, and like a lot of kids, couldn't help thinking I'd done something wrong. Now that I was older, I knew it was her issues that had made her leave, not mine. Still, part of me worried that one day I'd find out I was also a sucky mother. But even if I struggled, I'd never leave my kid, no matter what. I'd figure it out.

"Well, I'm still going to run defense, just to make sure."

My mom came out of the bathroom and I could feel my muscles tense, preparing for whatever she'd say next. Brendan pulled me close and shot me a glance that said he had my back. What other guy would try to protect me from my mom?

She looked from me to Brendan and a crease formed between her eyebrows. "Oh. Your father didn't tell me you two were dating. But that makes sense. Dakota never could go long without a boyfriend."

I flinched, but Brendan took my hand, lacing his fingers through mine.

"Anyway, I came here to gamble as well as see my little girl, but I'm rusty." She reached into her purse and withdrew a deck of playing cards that was still sealed in plastic. "Who's up for a game of Texas Hold'em?"

I filled up Cupid's food bowl and patted his head. "What do you think, buddy? Our new home's working out pretty nicely, isn't it?"

He turned and licked my hand, and then went back to his food. I covered a yawn and eyed the coffeemaker, hoping that'd speed it up. Mom had kept Brendan and me up until two thirty in the morning, "prepping" for hitting the casinos. After the hectic week we'd both had, we were dragging and hardly good company, but she'd insisted we keep going, finding excuse after excuse to drag it out a little longer. One more round. Could Brendan explain craps to her? Somewhere in there she'd also asked Brendan to tell her how she could get the inside track and take it to the house, swearing she wouldn't use it at the casino he worked at. He'd taken it all in stride and, with a polite smile, told her she'd just have to play the odds.

Odds. Also known as the reason I wasn't a good gambler. I liked knowing the outcome, not hoping for it, and Lady Luck always seemed to give me more of a passive-aggressive smirk than smile down on me.

"Morning!" Mom's greeting was cheery and high-pitched.

Exhibit A of my bad luck, ladies and gentlemen. Guilt pinched my gut for even mentally referring to her as bad luck. Seriously, though, her timing last night couldn't have been worse. Now I had to deal with being frustrated and on guard.

I reached for the coffeepot. The drops sizzled when they hit the now-empty warming plate. As a goodwill gesture I filled Mom a cup, too. The hazelnut creamer clouded the dark liquid as I poured it in, and I could hardly wait for the cup to hit my lips.

Mom tossed a copy of the *Las Vegas Beacon* on the counter next to me. "You're in here."

I slid one of the mugs over to her. "Yes, I write the Ready to Wed column. I've told you that before."

"That's why I picked up the paper to check it out. But I don't mean your column. I mean this." She stabbed a finger at the middle of the page, and I saw the heading to Phoebe's social column. Right there at the top was my name. My stomach bottomed out when I saw the name next to it.

Dakota Halifax is currently dating Brendan West, one of the security personnel at the brand-new Aces Resort and Casino. While she and her current beau started out as friends, she assured me they've moved past that. But she also said that "he's the one for right now," and sounded pretty hesitant about even that. Guess we'll have to see who she steps out with next, because this reporter is pretty sure her rebound is about to be bounced.

"Does Brendan know?" Mom asked, leaning back and craning her neck toward the hallway. Brendan hadn't come out of his room yet, and I hoped he wouldn't choose now to do so. "I could sense something was up between you, but I had no idea that—"

"It's not true." I doubted Brendan would ever read that section in the paper, but since this apparently was going to become a thing, I should probably let him know we'd occasionally be featured in the social column. "Damn Phoebe! I should've known better than to say one word to her. I should've made her walk home."

Anger started pumping through me, and I didn't want to use the tricks I'd learned in anger management classes to tamp it down. I wanted to let it wash over me and burn strong. Doing what Ron had asked me to had only gotten my relationship publicly smeared.

"Well, if you were feeling too much pressure living with him already, it'd be totally understandable," Mom said. "It's not a bad thing to need space."

"I care about Brendan, and I like living with him. I don't want him to read this and think I'm a heartbeat from running." I took the paper and jammed it into the bottom of my workbag, so he wouldn't see it on the counter, Phoebe's awful words about him faceup. As soon as I got a chance to talk to him alone, where my mom wouldn't be able to add her ever-so-helpful comments, I'd explain. Guess having that talk about our relationship and how we were going to define it was no longer optional.

Mom tipped back her coffee and then set the mug in the sink. "Come on. Let's get out of here, go shopping, and forget about everything else for a while. It'll do you some good."

I was pretty sure she meant it'd do *her* some good, but the walls did suddenly seem to be closing in. "Later, Cupid," I said, running my hand over his head and then scooping up my purse. As I followed Mom outside, I thought maybe a couple of new outfits would make me feel better. It was probably a healthier alternative than driving over to Phoebe's place.

Because if I saw her right now, I'd be doing way more than threatening.

*M*om and I were three shops and several bags into our excursion when she heaved a sigh. "I don't know if Frank and I are going to work out."

I replaced the silky top I was looking at on the rack and turned to her. "I thought you were happy about setting up roots. That you were ready to slow down."

"Well, I thought so, too. But here's the truth, Dakota. You and I, we're not the settling-down type, no matter how hard we try to be."

My shoulders tensed, the way they often did around her, and I got a hollowness in the pit of my stomach. "No offense, Mom, but speak for yourself. Maybe *you* aren't the settling down type, but I am. It's all I've ever wanted."

"It's what you *think* you want. But you didn't get married, did you?"

The last few months of progress unraveled at her words, all

that healing undone in one sentence. Yes, I'd moved past being left, but the fact that my own mom didn't even acknowledge how much that hurt me stung. "I wanted to get married. Grant didn't."

"On some level, though, you were probably sabotaging it. It's why it all fell apart there at the end."

My temper was rising and I clenched my jaw, trying to keep it in check. "He found out he had a child. Trust me, I had no part of that process."

"Okay, but didn't you say you're glad you didn't end up getting married? I do read your column, you know."

The raw edges of the pain she'd caused me over the years smoothed out a bit, because at least she made an effort to read my column, but why'd she have to use it against me? I blew out my breath, afraid we were about to talk in circles. "Yes, because it wasn't right. And it led me to Brendan, who I think I have a real shot with."

"I always think I can make it work with each guy, too. I move from one to the next, just like you. In and out of love from one day to the other. It's what we're good at. The sticking, not so much."

"I can stick. I've been in Vegas for most of my life."

"Yes, and I worry that because of that, you don't even know who you really are—you even said so in your column. You wrote that you'd lost part of yourself. I remember, because I thought, that's exactly how I felt right before I got divorced. I was a mom and a wife, but everything that was me was gone."

The edges of pain re-sharpened, digging in again. I hadn't been enough, and neither had Dad. Dad and I had made her feel lost. I got that, I supposed, but it still hurt.

"I don't mean that I didn't enjoy some days. You know I love you." Mom moved closer and reached out her hand like she was going to put it on my shoulder. Then she hesitated as if she wasn't sure she should touch me—I wasn't sure either. "What I'm trying to say—not very well, I'll admit—is that I don't want you to feel like a failure if it doesn't work out with Brendan. Or if you find you want something else in a few months, or even discover that you need to be alone from time to time."

She let her hand drop on my shoulder, her eyes locked on to mine, and I got the feeling she wanted me to tell her that she could walk away, too. If she was going to, fine. But I wasn't going to tell her that it was okay. Or maybe this was her way of telling me why she walked away when I was younger, as if she couldn't help herself. Well, it wasn't okay, and if she wanted reassurance, she'd have to go somewhere else.

I turned and grabbed the first three shirts I saw, not even bothering to check the sizes, and headed into the dressing room. I did need some alone time—from her. The logical side of my brain said that she had no idea what she was talking about. She didn't even know me—not really. But there was a sliver of doubt digging its way in, making me wonder if I'd unknowingly sabotaged Grant's and my relationship before he'd stood me up. If I was currently ruining my relationship with Brendan without knowing it.

One place, one person, and kids, eventually, had always been my goal. Was it because I wanted it, or was it so I could prove I wasn't my mother? This weekend was supposed to be spent getting closer to Brendan, and instead I was spending it with the one person who could mess me up and make me question everything.

On cue, my mother said, "Dakota? How about after this we hit the casinos? We can grab food somewhere along the way, and I want to try out some of those famous Vegas cocktails, too."

"Yeah, fine," I called, mostly because fighting her was always a losing battle, and I didn't have the energy.

The pink fabric of the shirt I pulled on snagged on my bra before finally smoothing down. I turned and stared at my reflection, asking it what I really wanted. Hoping it'd tell me that I wasn't broken. That I could get over the trust issues Grant left me with and that I was, in fact, the sticking type.

Chapter Twenty-Five

When I awoke the next morning, it took me a moment to realize I was in Brendan's bed. Brendan was next to me, his face peaceful in sleep. My lungs suddenly weighed a hundred pounds, and when I tried to swallow, it felt like I'd drunk a bucket of sand. An angry rhythm was pounding at my temples, but I tried to push past it and piece together last night.

Blips slowly came back to me. Shopping with Mom, her dropping the bomb that we're just no good at sticking. Asking me if I even knew who I was. Being dragged to several casinos as she went from slots to blackjack to Texas Hold'em, and ended at craps. I'd played a couple of games here and there, got up seventy bucks only to lose thirty of it. That was when I'd walked away. But Mom dropped a grand along the way. Even weirder, she seemed happy about it.

There'd been drinking, too, quite a bit of it. The most powerful Long Island iced teas I'd ever had, and for some reason I kept ordering them—that's right, I was freaking out that I was like my mom, which had been heightened by all the men she'd flirted with. But there'd been laughing and dancing, too, and the fact that

I'd had fun with her had only worried me more. Made me think maybe she was right.

Which made me order more drinks. Damn Vegas! I thought after all these years I was immune to her charms.

Okay, so I'd take a little of the responsibility—forgetting about everything for a while had definitely been nice.

My stomach rolled when I remembered a guy pulling me close on the dance floor.

Then I got the image of pushing him away and telling him I had a boyfriend—phew.

There was a faint memory of climbing into the back of a taxi, but I couldn't remember the rest. Namely, how I was in bed with Brendan West. Here I was in the place I'd desperately wanted to be, and I didn't remember how I got there. Or how far things had gone—I wanted to remember our first time, and worrying I might've missed it left me cold inside.

Apprehension churning through me, I slowly peeked under the covers. And breathed a sigh of relief. *I'm wearing the same clothes I was in last night.* They smelled smoky, too. Ugh.

Brendan stirred and lifted his half-hooded eyes to me. "Hey. How's the party animal this morning?"

I pressed my fingertips to my throbbing temples, wishing they'd stop. "Fuzzy. And confused. How did I get in here? Did you have to carry me? Because that'd be so embarrassing."

"No, you walked right in." Brendan covered a yawn with his hand. "Told me that you were going to make my wildest dreams come true, and then you stumbled over here, kissed me...and passed out on top of me."

I groaned and pulled the blankets over my head. "Even more embarrassing. Great."

Brendan laughed and tugged down the blanket. "It wasn't so bad, really. You say funny things in your sleep." I shook my head, and he drew me to him. His hair was mussed, his torso bare. I rested my head on his chest. His skin was warm and his heart beat out a steady rhythm under my ear.

I sat up, immediately regretting it when a sharp pain shot across my head. "What about my mom? Did she make it back okay?"

"She's fine. I checked in on her after you crashed. You guys must've had quite the time last night."

"It was...interesting, anyway. One minute I was in a dressing room, mad at her and wishing she'd never come. But then we hit Caesar's Palace, and she's got this frantic energy that's hard not to catch. And then there was the drinking... I'm pretty sure she's leaving Frank and that's why she showed up here. I thought she might actually settle down this time, but..." I couldn't help remembering how she told me we weren't the sticking kind. "I guess it's just not her thing."

Was it mine? I didn't believe that I *couldn't* stick—I could do anything if I put my mind to it. I'd dated plenty of guys who were wrong for me, but I'd also dated guys who were genuinely good people who simply didn't work out, no "sabotage" on either side. But what if my goal to get married and have a family was a silly notion I held on to because I didn't know how to give up?

Brendan would probably just be relieved if I said I didn't want those things.

Brendan cupped my cheek. "D.J.?"

"I'm fine," I said, flashing him the best smile I could manage. "Pretty hungover, and sorry last night was a bit of a mess, but fine. I think I'll go take a couple Tylenol and see if my mom needs some, too."

He caught my arm as I moved to get out of the bed. "I need to talk to you about some things, D.J."

His foreboding tone turned my insides to stone and the drumming in my head increased. "Let me take some pills, grab a quick shower, and get some coffee first? My headache's screaming too loud for me to really process anything."

He dropped my arm and nodded. The grim set of his mouth made my blood pressure spike, and worst-case scenarios were already filling my head, but thanks to the hangover, they were too jumbled to really catch one and hold on to it. As soon as I could properly function, I was going to have to stop being such a chicken. Just lay out my fears and ask what he wanted, so I could see if we were even close to being on the same page—hopefully a little clarity would help me figure out what the hell page I was on.

Ugh, I'm seriously never drinking again. Dealing with problems while impaired left the margin of error far too large for my liking.

By the time I got out of the shower, Mom was already awake, and she'd made coffee—I almost forgave her for everything right there. But as the caffeine jolted my system awake, I knew we needed to have a real conversation, too.

"Mom, what's going on with you and Frank?"

"You know what we should do?" Mom dug out her phone and showed me a picture of a little cottage in San Diego with a beach view that was for rent. "We could live there. Get a break from everything for a while. Life could be just like it was last night, you and me hanging out and having fun. Wouldn't that be nice?"

Apparently Mom now viewed me as a partying buddy, and I wasn't quite sure how to break it that we weren't. Yes, it had been more fun than I could've imagined, but it wasn't really me or who I wanted to be. "I have a life here. Friends. A boyfriend. A job. And you've got your place with Frank, right? Aren't you guys almost done remodeling?"

Mom lowered her phone and sighed. "I don't think it's going to work with Frank. He's a dear man, and I've enjoyed the time we spent together, but I need a new adventure."

At least she'd finally admitted what had brought her here. Only it didn't make me feel any better. "Life doesn't always have to be an adventure. Sometimes you need to deal with boring or tough times. You can't just run when it gets hard." Okay, I was being a bit of a hypocrite, considering I'd been holding back with Brendan, but I was more bobbing and weaving than running, and I was going to stop.

"I'm not running," Mom huffed. "Like I said, you and me, we're just not the settling-down type."

"No, *you're* not that type. I'm the type of girl who got abandoned by her mom when she could've used her." I was surprised I'd put it out there, but relief filled me that I didn't have to bite it back anymore. Shopping, a dinner here and there, getting drunk together, and dancing all night—it didn't fix the past.

Mom paled. "So that's what this is all about. I've apologized. I can't change the past."

"You say that you're sorry you weren't made to be a mother, but that's not the same as apologizing for not being there. So maybe you run from your responsibilities, but I've got obligations here, and I follow through."

"I admire you for that, too. I just hope you don't wake up one day and feel like you've wasted your life." Mom set down her coffee cup and smoothed a hand down her hair. "I think it's time for me to go."

Wasted her life. Was that what she thought of the time she was actually in mine? "At least tell Frank that you're leaving him. He deserves that. Not just waking up one day and finding you gone, the way I had to." Pain stabbed at my heart. I hadn't meant for the conversation to go this way, all the old wounds reopening. I'd wanted to talk to her about Frank, and ask her if she'd be okay. Have a real, honest conversation. But suddenly I found myself angry all over again. That she'd left. That I'd had to hold in how much it hurt for so long. Bottling up my emotions had made me bitter, and the truth was, they'd needed to come out for years.

Maybe what I needed to do to be someone who could have a stable future was to face the past and let it go.

Mom headed out of the kitchen.

"I hope you find what you're looking for someday," I said to her back.

Mom hesitated and turned. "You, too, Dakota. You, too."

Tears were forming, and I was about to go find Brendan when my phone rang.

"I take it you saw the paper," Jillian said, not bothering with a greeting.

I sniffed, trying to cover the fact that I was so close to crying. "I saw. I'm pissed, but I suppose it could've been worse."

"Wow. Maybe that anger management course did change you. I certainly wouldn't be so calm if my ex wrote a letter to the editor and my boyfriend was in the social column for canoodling another woman."

The second Jillian opened the door, she held out her iPad, the *Las Vegas Beacon* already pulled up for me, not bothering with small talk or telling me to be cool. One way to forget about a fight with your mom is to immediately have a disconcerting information bomb dropped on you.

Actually, it was all sucky, and I wasn't sure I could deal with any of it, but I knew I couldn't be at home where Mom was most likely packing and walking out of my life—maybe forever—and Brendan was… Well, who knew anymore.

My hands shook as I skimmed down to the social column. The first few paragraphs were about which celebrities were seen at which nightclubs and with whom, but then I saw Brendan's name and my lungs stopped taking in air.

Brendan West was seen last night at the Aces Casino. Considering he works there, that wouldn't usually be news, but he wasn't sitting in Terra with Dakota Halifax this time. No, the canoodling was happening between him and a dark-haired beauty I'm told also works at the casino. And according to a source, Dakota was seen out last night as well, at Pure, dancing and drinking and looking very much single. Not sure who did the bouncing, but it looks like they're both already moving on. So, gentlemen, if you were looking for a chance with our recently jilted wedding planner, good luck. I hear she's rediscovering herself.

My legs buckled, and I flopped onto the couch that used to double as my bed. As if the information wasn't bad enough, the snark there at the end was like pouring lemon juice on the wound from the knife Phoebe'd jabbed into my back.

Not to mention I was feeling more lost than discovered today.

"There might be a good explanation," Jillian said. "I mean, if she made up the stuff about you at Pure, then—"

"I was there. How the hell does Phoebe find out everything so fast?"

Jillian's eyes widened, the question in them clear.

"My mom showed up two nights ago, and she and I…we went out. Gambling led to drinking and drinking led to dancing. But I wasn't out as a single girl, and I certainly didn't think Brendan was either. Single guy—you know what I mean."

Jillian wound one of her dark curls around her finger. "Well, I saw the way he looked at you the other night, and you've known him for years, so…maybe it was just like your outing. Completely innocent."

Since she was a skeptic about love, that was probably her best pep talk. The doubtful voice in my head said despite knowing him for several years, I hadn't been around him for a lot of them. But then I thought back to him bringing me coffee, how I'd decided he knew me better than anyone, and the way he was so protective when my mom had shown up.

What had he said this morning, though? *I need to talk to you about some things, D.J.* Ominous to say the least. Was this what he was going to say? That he'd developed feelings for someone at work? That he wanted to date other people? Rip out my heart?

"I don't…know. I want to say of course not, but…" A lump rose in my throat. I never would've guessed Grant would stand me up, either, and I'd dated him for a lot longer. There were so many things I'd been proven wrong on lately, I just didn't have much faith in my judgment anymore.

"Maybe I shouldn't have told you," Jillian said. "But when I saw it… I'm supposed to be the one who reads this stuff and lets you know what's important, and try to keep you from the bad. But this… Well, I can't just sit back and ignore it if he's cheating on you."

Tears burned my eyes and I squeezed Jillian's hand. "I'd rather be here with you than have to read this on my own." I blinked to clear the tears and let out a long exhale. Time to see what my ex had said in this letter to the editor.

LETTER TO THE EDITOR:

When I don'ts turn to I dos

Did you ever want something so badly that you'd write a letter to the editor? Realized that you wanted something the instant you let it go? My name's Grant Douglas, and if you wonder why it sounds familiar, I've been mentioned in Dakota Halifax's Ready to Wed column a few times recently. I was her groom-to-be.

Dakota was right. Our wedding was well planned—she did it all, and I'm sorry to admit that I didn't help or support her like I should've through any of it. I'd thought a cruise wedding would be the easy way. That it'd take away the pressure I was starting to feel about getting married, and help her to not stress over the planning. I loved her, and I wanted to make her happy. I wrote off all my fears as cold feet that a lot of people get before their wedding.

Then, along with panicking that our wedding date was approaching so quickly, an ex-girlfriend showed up and announced I was the father of her son. I didn't handle it very well. The pressure I'd already been feeling had worn me down, and I lost myself as well. I wish I'd have been stronger, and that I would've talked things through with my fiancée. I hate that I hurt Dakota. That I made her cry. As she pointed out, the unexpected happens. I think we both lost sight of who we were and what we wanted. Like her, I've been working on finding myself these past few months, so I'm writing this letter to take responsibility for my actions.

I screwed up. It's something I'll always have to live with. But I'm enjoying my new life, where I'm the father of an amazing son and I'm slowly learning how to own up to my mistakes and become a better person. I hope that this letter will at least make up for some of the pain I put the people I love through. I'm sorry, Dakota, especially to you. Maybe now I can move on, too.

Grant Douglas

Las Vegas, Nevada

"Holy shit," I said, shaking my head and blinking back a new wave of tears. "I so didn't expect that. Especially after I pretty much chewed him out last time I saw him." He'd taken responsibility and laid out his feelings in a way that I knew from experience made you vulnerable and nauseous.

"Yeah, you know I'm not Grant's biggest fan, but that took balls." Jillian slowly took the iPad out of my hands—I didn't realize I'd been gripping it so hard—and set it on the coffee table.

Grant's letter. Phoebe's damn column. Whoever Brendan was seen with. Together, it was too much, burying me with doubts and fear and a healthy dose of anger. I felt the past pain of loving Grant and the current pain of loving Brendan.

And I did love Brendan—not just as a friend. I was *in* love with him. Like crazy, all-consuming, wanted-to-share-everything-with-him love.

Mom was wrong—now it seemed ridiculous that I'd ever worried about it, actually. How we loved didn't come from genetics. She and I might both fall in love quickly, but I'd never fallen out, not really. Sure, I had relationships that didn't work out, but it was why I got crushed at the end of every one I'd ever had, even if I'd been the one to end them. I cared. I fell. I loved.

I stood, not knowing where I was going, but knowing I needed to go somewhere. Do something. My life was getting away from me again, control slipping from me, one inch at a time. All the anger and emotions I'd ever repressed—even the ones I thought I'd gotten over—were coming back with a vengeance.

And I needed to get away from them before I broke down and screamed until my throat was as raw as my heart.

Chapter Twenty-Six

$\mathcal{I}$ wasn't sure how I'd ended up in a tattoo parlor, or even made the decision to go there. Brendan had called me once, and while I'd gone back and forth for several seconds over whether to answer it, my heart so tied up in knots it made it hard to breathe, I wasn't ready to talk to him. As I took in the art on the walls of the parlor, I wondered how many people had gotten tattoos here that they later regretted. How many were wasted at the time. Because seriously, not everything that happens in Vegas stays here.

I was sure plenty of people had come in for well-thought-out tattoos, or even spontaneous ones they loved. I highly doubted any of them had come for the reason I had, though. I strolled up to the front desk.

"Did you have an appointment?" the tattoo-covered girl behind it asked.

"Not exactly." I hated when people said that. Either you did or you didn't. Yet here I was saying it anyway. "I'm looking for Wild Bill. Is he in?"

She glanced toward a room with an open door. "He's in, and his last client just left. He can probably squeeze you in if you know what tattoo you want."

Just to see her reaction, I wanted to tell her that he was my anger management sponsor. It wasn't technically true, but if I was going to talk to someone about feeling so frustrated I could scream and never stop, Wild Bill seemed like the type to understand. "Can you just tell him that Dakota Halifax is here to see him?"

She started to stand, but Wild Bill stuck his head out. He did a double take and then a giant grin overtook his face. "Hey! You here for ink?"

"I was hoping to talk, actually."

He swept a hand toward his open door. "The doctor is in."

I sat in a chair in the corner, and within a few minutes I'd spilled my guts. Honestly, the reason I'd chosen him was because I thought all the built-up anger inside me might freak out Jillian, and I didn't have anyone else to talk to who I thought would truly understand. "Now it's like all the emotions I kept bottled up for years are coming out at once, and despite the tricks I learned from class, my life's totally out of control again. And I know I can't control everything, but I don't know how to deal anymore. It's gonna take more than redirecting thoughts and breathing, that's for damn sure. But at the same time, I don't want to slip again. Does that make sense?"

"I hear ya, girl," he said, then leaned in close, like he was about to divulge his greatest secret. "Wanna know what I do when I get that frustrated?"

I nodded.

Wild Bill stood. "Follow me."

It crossed my mind I should probably ask where we were going, but I didn't bother. There was a glint in Wild Bill's eye, and I knew he had a plan. It felt so nice to be focused on something else besides all the anxiety and frustration suffocating me that I went with it.

He pushed out the back of the tattoo studio and we crossed

through an alleyway. Total mugging territory, but if a guy chose to mug Wild Bill, I pitied him. He knocked on the back door of a run-down brick building, and I suddenly thought not asking had been a bad move. Add this situation to the list of things that were out of my control in my life. In fact, I was pretty sure Wild Bill was about to ply me with drugs. Maybe that was how he mellowed out, but I needed a more permanent solution.

The dude who answered the door was twice as wide as Wild Bill and looked like his face had been run into a wall repeatedly, until it was flat, his nose crooked to one side.

"Um, Bill?" I took a step back.

He clamped my hand in his massive one and pulled me into the room. There was a boxing ring in the middle, where two guys were sparring, and the rest of the room was filled with a variety of punching bags. The place smelled like a typical gym, a mix of leather, slightly stale air, and sweat.

"We need to get out a little aggression," Wild Bill said, and the flat-faced guy nodded.

"Take as long as you need," the owner or worker or whoever he was said, giving Wild Bill's back a hard pat.

Wild Bill grabbed a pair of boxing gloves out of a locker and led me over to a punching bag. "You ever hit one of these?"

In all the years of sports, from football to baseball to soccer, I'd never done any boxing—not unless I counted a few air punches thrown during circuit-training classes. I shook my head, and Wild Bill put the gloves on my fists. "When I need to get out anger, or I'm frustrated, or I just need a way to clear my head, this is what I do."

My gaze traveled over his muscular arms. It looked like he did this a lot.

Wild Bill demonstrated how to stand. "Now, pivot with your hips and punch the bag right in the middle. Keep your fist tight."

I swung, a loud, satisfying smack filling the air.

"Good," he said. "Who do you want to punch out?"

"No one."

Wild Bill raised a bushy eyebrow.

"Okay, Phoebe would be a good place to start."

Wild Bill gestured at the black, cracked-leather bag. "Swing away."

"But isn't it bad to imagine this? Aren't we supposed to not harbor damaging images?"

"What we're supposed to do is not act on them. This is the best way I've found to get it out of my head, though. Now, instead of getting into a fight at the bar, I step away, then come here and pummel the bag. Trust me, it'll feel like just what you need."

I hit it once, twice, three times.

Wild Bill grabbed the swinging bag and held it in place, stopping the creak of the chain securing it to the ceiling. "Who else? What about that guy who left you at the altar?"

"I'm okay with it. I've moved on, and he even wrote an apology in the paper." For everyone in the city to read.

"Bullshit. Think about all the anger and frustration you've ever had with him, and you punch it out. Keep hitting until you can't swing anymore."

I sucked in a deep breath and swung. Again and again. My arms burned and my lungs worked harder and harder with every hit. When I couldn't hit with my fists anymore, I kicked. I kicked away the hit to my self-esteem when Mom left. The frustration over the fact that my finally telling her how I felt only made her leave. The damage Grant had done to my heart. The image of Brendan with the woman from his work—the one who hadn't even known his name. I kicked and punched until I fell into a pile on the mat, breaths sawing in and out of my mouth, my chest heaving with the effort.

Wild Bill sat next to me. "Feel better?"

I wiped my forearm across my sweaty forehead. My anger was

indeed gone, and while not much had changed since I came in, I felt like I could take on anything. "Yeah."

"If you want a membership here, I could talk to Dan."

I glanced around at all the equipment, along with the guys using it. "I'd like that."

Wild Bill gave a sharp nod. I pushed myself to my knees and hugged him. "Thanks."

"Anytime, darlin'."

Hugging a grizzled tattoo artist I'd met in mandatory anger management class, exhausted to the point my lungs were on fire, I found what I needed. I felt in control—not of everything going on, 'cause whoa, my life was a total soap opera lately—but of myself.

More importantly, I was ready to tackle the issue that I'd been avoiding for way too long.

Brendan was in the kitchen when I got back to the house. "What the hell, Deej? I tell you I need to talk, and you just fall off the face of the earth. I was starting to get worried."

His voice made my heart hitch, and I tried not to think about how it'd shatter into a million little pieces if this all went wrong. "I am sorry about that. And I'm ready to talk." I took a deep breath, preparing for the hard stuff. "Did you know you've been in the social column this past week?"

"That's what I wanted to talk to you about."

I braced for his words, telling myself I could handle anything. I was strong. I'd been abandoned by my mom, left at the altar, and had my humiliation and love life printed for thousands to read, and I was still fighting.

Brendan moved around the counter, and his eyes bored into me. Despite how strong I was, the thought of losing him sent a sharp pang through my chest. If there were even an ounce of him that still wanted me, I'd fight like hell to keep him.

"Am I just 'the one for right now'? Is that how you really see me?" he asked.

I shook my head. "No. I did tell Phoebe that, though. She was crying and she asked about you and me, and I was trying to be civil—I have no idea why, because she obviously isn't. I realize it sounds like an insult to you, especially in print."

"Yeah, I'll admit it sucked to read that. I was surprised at how hard it hit me, actually."

"Is that why you were 'canoodling' with that woman from your work at Terra?"

Brendan's eyebrows drew together. "What?"

"That's what Phoebe's column said today. I assumed it was the girl who called you Brandon. I hope she at least knows your name now," I muttered and then bit my lip, forcing myself to meet his gaze. "Or was it someone else? Just tell me the truth so I can try to deal with it."

"I did meet Sheila at Terra—she called me and said she needed to talk. I tried to blow it off, but she insisted, and you were out with your mom, so…"

Lead filled my chest, leaving it heavy and cold. I gripped the counter for support, sure my knees were about to buckle.

"She showed me the paper. The part that said you thought I was the one for now. Said she thought I should know."

I pictured the raven-haired woman and the way she'd flirted with him. "I'm sure she did." As jealousy and anger rose up, I took a deep breath, focusing on what was important. "So you…took solace in her arms?"

He wrinkled his nose. "Of course not. She hugged me when she saw how upset I was and told me that I deserved better. I was so stunned at first, my mind going a hundred miles a minute as I tried to deal with feeling like I'd been punched in the gut. But when she hugged me tighter and suggested we go to her place, I pushed her away and told her I was still with you. I thought there had to be a good explanation, and I've been trying to figure out where we stand since. Last night you were clearly too out of it to talk when you came home, and then this morning you just left. I was starting to think you were gonna dump me—or that you already had and I just didn't know it yet."

A relieved laugh bubbled from my lips.

"D.J., you're kind of killing me here. You've been acting so strange lately, so if there's something you need to tell me…"

I flung my arms around him. It took him a moment to reciprocate, but all the pieces inside me that'd felt broken came together. There were still a few gaps, but they didn't hurt as badly anymore. "I'm sorry, I'm just so happy that it was all blown out of proportion." For a moment I hung on, but then I knew it was time to talk it out before anything else happened—no more being scared or having to wonder. Reluctantly, I pulled back. "Look, the reason I said what I did to Phoebe was because I didn't want to say anything that'd make you run. I know you're not crazy about serious relationships. And I know I made it sound like I wasn't either, and that I didn't even like weddings anymore, but I was in a bad place that night, and the fact of the matter is, I do care about those things."

"You think I don't know that?"

"But…"

Brendan swept my hair off my face and rested his hand on my neck. "Any time the topic comes up or you talk about the weddings you're planning, I see it. You've got the worst poker face ever, and I'm good at spotting tells." His thumb moved over my pulse point, making it beat even faster.

"Look, there's nothing wrong with just remaining friends. We could still pull it off now, but if we go much longer…" My heart pounded against my rib cage, like it was trying to escape my chest and run away before it had the chance to get hurt again. Then there was his thumb still pressed to my skin, making it hard to think about actually being only friends. "I don't want to ruin everything we already have. It'd kill me to lose you again."

"You won't ever lose me." His quiet but firm words caressed my skin and helped ease the fears battling it out inside of me. "I don't want to ruin our friendship, but I also don't want to regret not taking a chance on being with the most amazing woman I've ever met." He leaned in and softly kissed my lips.

I blinked through forming tears, wanting that to be enough, but needing to make sure I was 100 percent clear, no more having to wonder. "So you're okay with you and me being in a committed relationship, that someday in the future—but maybe not the way, *way* future—could head in an even more serious direction?"

He inhaled a breath and I held mine. Then he looked me in the eye. "I'm more than okay with that. I want you to know that I plan on sticking around. I'm not leaving Vegas again, and I'm not giving up on what we have, even if it gets rough. I'm all in."

"Me too." Hope rose up and my cheeks started to hurt from smiling. All the crappy stuff was almost out of the way. I wanted to ignore it, but I didn't want it to bite me later. "Um, speaking of rough, and in the spirit of full disclosure and all, Phoebe's column made it sound like I was single and carefree at the dance club, so the entire city pretty much thinks we're done already. Not a big deal, because it's clearly not true, but I wanted you to hear it from me this time. And then…well, Grant sorta wrote a letter to the editor to apologize for standing me up at the altar."

Brendan tensed, a muscle flicking in his jaw.

I put my hand on his chest. "Actually, it was nice—the closure we both needed, I suppose. The fact is, because of how things ended with him, I've been holding back. But I'm done being afraid. I don't want to scare you, but I also want to be honest with you. I like being in relationships, and I tend to fall in love fast." I shrugged, as if the statement didn't weigh a thousand pounds. "It's who I am."

"Well, I've never liked relationships much, and I don't fall fast," Brendan said.

I tried to swallow but couldn't.

He dragged his fingers down my neck and across my collarbone. "This time is different, though. I'm in love with you already, D.J."

My heart morphed into tingly butterflies, and comforting warmth filled me from the inside out. "I love you, too," I said.

Brendan drew me to him and crushed his lips over mine, placing kiss after kiss on them. As they grew in urgency and intensity, the heat building between us firing hotter and higher, I pulled back.

He made a pouty sort of groan noise that made me laugh. I wrapped my arms tightly around him to show I wasn't going anywhere and pressed a kiss to his neck. "I just have to tell you one more thing." I dragged my lips to his ear and gently bit at his lobe.

"Yes," he said, his voice husky. "Whatever you say, I agree."

I smiled against his skin, exhaling a hot breath over where I'd placed the kiss, and slipped my hands under the back of his shirt, grinning when his muscles twitched under my fingertips. It was like playing sex chicken again, but this time, we were both going to win. For a moment I forgot what was so important, but then it slowly came back to me. "I just want you to know that this time is different. Yes, I've loved other guys before, but it's never consumed me like this. I've never experienced this kind of passion and security, all rolled into one. And because of that, this time is different for me, too. So…yeah."

The seductive grin curved his lips, making heat pool low in my stomach. "Yeah."

One simple word, yet it wrapped around me and filled my heart with so much love I thought it'd burst. I wrapped my arms around him tighter, pressing my body flush against his. "Well, now that that's all out there, I should also mention that this afternoon I discovered how much physical exertion helps me stay sane."

His fingers dug into my skin. "I'm warning you, it would not be nice to tease me right now. My control is…" He recaptured my mouth, inhaling my startled breath and pressing me against the wall. I took a moment to soak in his weight pinning me down, the low groan that came from his lips.

"I'm done waiting," I whispered between labored breaths.

A squeal escaped my lips as he threw me over his shoulder, caveman-taking-his-woman style. In addition to being totally turned on, it gave me a pretty good view of his nice butt. He tossed me down on his bed and kissed me hard on the mouth. Then we made quick work of each other's clothes.

When we were both down to our underwear, my eyes devouring Brendan's athletic body and the trail of hair disappearing into his boxer briefs, he slowed down the tempo. He bit at my shoulder as he dragged his fingertips across my bare stomach, along the edge of my bra. Then he brushed the purple lace over the swell of my breast. Anticipation tingled across my skin, the heat building inside my core causing the most delicious, torturous mix. He hooked the strap with one finger, followed its line to the back, and undid the snap.

My heartbeats scattered in a hundred directions, throbbing and zipping as his calloused fingertips brushed me in the softest places. I tugged him closer so that his warm skin was against mine and kissed him, rolling my tongue with his. Last night when I was drunk, I'd apparently been bold enough to promise to make his wildest dreams come true. I wasn't sure if I could quite live up to that, but I planned on spending the whole night trying.

Part Five

LOW-KEY LIME - LOW

(ALL IS GOING ACCORDING TO PLAN. HITCHES ARE EASILY FIXED AND HANDLED FAIRLY EASILY. TEARS SHED ARE USUALLY HAPPY TEARS. IT'S EASY TO GET COMFORTABLE HERE, BUT NEARLY IMPOSSIBLE TO MAINTAIN FOR LONG PERIODS OF TIME.)

"Once in a while, right in the middle of an ordinary life, love gives us a fairy tale."

—ANONYMOUS

Chapter Twenty-Seven

GET READY TO WED by Dakota Halifax
Wardrobe Malfunctions

While Miss Jackson's um, slip, was seen by millions, yours would be seen by people you run into on a regular basis, making it even more awkward. So here's a little help to avoid wardrobe malfunctions on your special day. First off, choose a wedding dress that fits you well. Never assume you can diet yourself into a smaller size. (Your significant other likes you for you—he better, anyway.) If you do actually pull off the diet of the decade, the dress can always be taken in. Making it bigger is practically impossible. If you choose a strapless gown, make sure it fits you well and have fashion tape. Brides in strapless gowns often feel the need to hook their thumbs in the gowns and pull up. You don't want every picture to have your thumbs in your dress. Oh, and bridesmaids? When you help out your bride by fluffing out her train, remember it's not necessary to fluff too high. The back row might enjoy the show of the bride's something blue, but I doubt that's the memory she wants her guests to have.

Broken zippers equal big problems. Never yank on difficult zippers. Keep wax on hand. It's usually fairly easy to find a candle at a wedding if necessary, and lead from a pencil also works in a pinch.

Next on my list is keeping your dress in pristine condition. Don't drink any colored beverage until after the ceremony, and watch where you sit. Remember those M&M's you dropped in your car? You don't want to find them melted onto your white gown. Choose flowers that don't stain. Have the florist remove the stamen, especially in lilies. They make yellow messes everywhere and are an allergy sufferer's nightmare.

As for the guys, check your zippers, shine your shoes, and take a little extra time grooming yourself—this means the beard goes if the bride so demands. Why? Because she's the bride. And while everyone will mostly be looking at her, you might get a glance or two as well, so go ahead and put your best face forward. It's one day. I promise you can make it.

It'd been a long time since I'd been nervous for a wedding, but my stomach was churning and my pulse was pounding like I'd just done three rounds at the boxing gym. Valentina Maddox and Marcus Beecham were practically Vegas royalty, and their wedding was definitely fit for a queen and king.

The fairy-tale theme was starting to take shape. If it didn't shimmer or sparkle, it was covered in flowers. Some things managed both. There was a fountain centerpiece that was covered in flowers, each tier a different combination with long floral vines and lights draping down to look like sprays of water.

The centerpieces on the reception tables were just as complicated. Valentina had wanted red roses frozen in glass, à la *Beauty and the Beast*, but then she'd worried people would think she looked at Marcus as a beast, and then she also loved *all* the fairy tales. So, in a bout of genius or possibly insanity, I'd suggested incorporating them all. So there were silver and crystal Cinderella coaches with glass slippers, seashells with candles for *The Little Mermaid*, and gold and bejeweled *Sleeping Beauty* books modeled after the one in the beginning of the movie. Then there were all the bouquets on the tables as well. The aisle was covered in "orchid" and "cherry" petals, or pink and red to any dudes in the area. I'd lost count of how many flowers we'd ordered, but let's just say it'd rival the Tournament of Roses Parade.

"Where's this one go?" a girl asked me, lugging a bouquet so huge she nearly tipped with the weight.

"There's a matching one in the truck, right?"

She nodded and wobbled.

I gripped the other side. "Up front. One will be on each side of where the bride and groom stand." Walking backward, I made my way to the front of the aisle, where the couple would be saying their I dos.

I looked up at the guy hanging the sheer peach blush fabric over the top of the aisle. "That bouquet in the middle is slightly off-center. Move it like six inches to the right, please."

I'd never been in charge of such a large group of people, but a wedding of this size required hiring extra staff. So far they were doing remarkably well, and most importantly, following my directions to a T. Admittedly, it was pretty fun consulting my list and pointing and ordering. In a way, it reminded me of the way my dad coached. Just call me the wedding coach. Go team!

Of course if my team slipped, most of the city would see it.

Not to mention, Valentina and I had become friends through the planning, and I didn't want to disappoint her. And if that wasn't enough pressure, it'd be fully covered in the *Beacon*. Front-page stuff. I had no doubt my frenemy Phoebe would also be keeping a close eye on Brendan and me, eager to report the state of our relationship as she saw it.

Over the past three months, Brendan and I had fallen into an amazing groove of being best friends who were also dating and living together. We'd survived the busiest part of the wedding season, as well as Brendan's spending a week at the Aces Casino here and there when high-demand clients requested it. Through it all, there'd been a slew of mentions and speculations about our relationship in the social column.

Of course I'd kept tight-lipped on the subject, even though I wanted to shout our love from the rooftops—especially during that amazing lust phase in the beginning where we were in bed as often as possible, a giddy haze of sex and laughing and discovering every little thing about each other. Even when the deeper love took over, there was still a whole lot of lust going on. But the only statement I ever gave was that I didn't comment on my personal relationships anymore.

Any time Phoebe's columns got to me or life felt out of control and I could feel Code Tangerine or Fuchsia sneaking in, I hit the boxing gym. I'd also joined a soccer league. My business was providing me with a steady income and then some, and there was talk of my column being syndicated. The thought of it reaching the whole country was awesome, and only a tiny bit terrifying.

All in all, life was pretty much perfect. Sure, there were non-perfect days, but they didn't seem so bad when I came home to Cupid and Brendan.

I just have to get through tonight, and then I get to spend a few quiet days with my boys.

The final touches for the ceremony were in place just in time for Valentina to show up. I led her back to the room where she'd be getting ready.

"Can you believe I'm getting married today?" Valentina asked with a squeal.

"It's going to be the event of the year." *No pressure.* "I think the whole city's coming to see how amazing you look and to celebrate your and Marcus's union."

Again, no pressure. Oh, and I need to double-check on the fireworks and my firemen before I forget. Instead of waiting to call the fire department, I'd asked if they'd send over a few just in case. I didn't even know how Mr. Maddox had gotten the fireworks show approved, and I'm not sure I wanted to.

Naomi, one of the bridesmaids, pushed into the room, so hard the door crashed against the wall. "Sarah's appendix burst this morning! I just found out from her mom. Apparently she's not coming."

Apparently, I thought, but kept it in. My brain was already whirring, trying to come up with all the ways to console the bride if she freaked, which she probably was going to in three, two…

"What are we going to do?" Valentina ran a hand through her dark hair, her eyes wide. "It's gonna throw off the whole wedding! And how will we line up? We got it all down at practice and… How…? I…"

"Everyone remain calm," I said in my best we-can-survive-this voice. "We'll figure it out." I put my hand on Valentina's shoulder. "Would you rather have one less bridesmaid, or do you want to find an emergency fill-in?"

She blinked at me a few times. "I don't want it to look uneven. We need someone to fill in, I guess."

"Can you think of anyone?"

Valentina tapped a chin to her finger. She muttered something about if she asked that girl then another one would be angry. Then there was someone who didn't get along with the other girls.

She mentioned one name and Naomi pointed out that she'd just broken up with one of the groomsmen and decided she couldn't face him, so refused to come.

Then Valentina's gaze moved to me, and a prickly sense of foreboding crept up my spine. "You could do it."

"Oh no. I've got to run the wedding."

"You've got a whole staff to help with that. And what better way to watch for problems than to be *in* the wedding?" Valentina stepped closer, eyes shiny with hope. "I think the world of you and I've enjoyed working with you this past year—I never thought planning my wedding would be so fun. Had I known you before I'd already picked all of my bridesmaids, I would've totally asked you to be one."

My heart went a little mushy on me—all those weddings I'd attended, but never once as a bridesmaid. The happy vibes were quickly quashed with the truth, though. "Sarah's a toothpick. There's no way I'd fit in her dress."

Valentina crossed her arms and arched an eyebrow. "Are you saying you're giving up?"

She knew me too well, and she was using it to her advantage. Everything in me screamed this was a bad idea—that there had to be another way out of it.

But what the bride wants, the bride gets.

I couldn't breathe, much less move, and between the low-cut top and tightness of the dress, my girls were on display way more than I was comfortable with. I was pretty sure one would pop out if I moved too quickly, which was really inconvenient considering I needed to run around and make sure everything was good to go.

Brendan showed up about the time I was bossing the groomsmen around. His gaze moved to my chest and his eyes went wide, his mouth hanging open.

"I know. Don't ask."

He glanced from me to the girl sporting the identical cerulean dress, and his eyebrows knit together. "You're in the wedding? How did I miss that?"

"It *just* happened."

Mr. Maddox walked over and grinned. "Thanks for saving the day, Dakota. Sarah's appendix sure chose an inconvenient time to burst, didn't it?"

Under normal circumstances, I'd say it wasn't fair to blame someone for something out of their control, but since I was the one encased in a dress two sizes too small, I figured that gave me the freedom to blame anyone I wanted. Thank goodness for the boxing and soccer, or there would've been no chance in hell the zipper would be hanging on. It was circling the drain as it was. "Happy to help. Now, I've got to go check on the catering. If you guys will excuse me…"

Brendan caught my arm and pulled me back for a kiss, not seeming to care about the fact that there were several people nearby, including his boss. As I sank into his embrace, my frayed nerves relaxed a fraction—that night I'd confessed everything to him, I'd told myself that I would've been strong enough to get over him if he didn't want me. It was probably a bluff then, but now I wouldn't even pretend I could ever get over him. He calmed me when I needed calming, made me laugh when I started to get too serious, and I was completely at ease being myself with him. I was still a fixer—when he had a rough day, I cooked him dinner, rented an action flick, and made sure he knew he and I could take on anything together. We were a great team.

"Good luck," he whispered and I let out a sigh—well, half of one, what with the dress-not-letting-me-breathe thing. "Not only are you going to knock it out of the park, you look really hot. No one's even going to notice anything else."

I grinned, thinking he was a charmer who'd be rewarded later, even if I sincerely hoped people noticed pretty much everything but me. Then I got back to work doing last-minute checks, my head clear and the end goal in sight. Any time I gestured with my arms—which I was realizing I did a lot—I was sure my dress was going to bust open.

By the time the ceremony started, I was alternatively hot and cold and my heart had relocated to my throat. Holding a bouquet was suddenly giving me traumatic flashbacks even though it wasn't my wedding, and *omigosh* there were a lot of people. If I didn't calm myself down, *my* appendix might just burst.

I could see my team taking care of things on the fringes, though, and while it was odd not to be the one doing it, it was nice to see they had it handled. My gaze drifted to Brendan sitting in the crowd, and he shot me a smile, along with a covert thumbs-up.

"If anyone here objects to this union," the preacher said, "speak now or forever hold your peace."

My head jerked toward the preacher, all my muscles coiling. These days most people left out that part, but this guy was old-school—pretty sure he'd been marrying people since they had to run from saber-toothed tigers. I glanced out at the crowd, silently threatening anyone who dared object.

The I dos were exchanged, Valentina and Marcus were officially pronounced husband and wife, and the preacher told Marcus, "You may now kiss the bride."

As they kissed, the tingly love hope I'd missed for a while filled me, leaving me grinning from ear to ear. *Man, I love my job.*

Valentina's train snagged on a chair as she went to go down the aisle, and I automatically reached forward to fix it. I heard a rip from behind me, one of those noises you're afraid to move after. *Maybe it was just a tiny tear. Nothing to worry about.*

But then I felt a breeze against my back, the kind uninhibited by fabric. So when the rest of the wedding party followed after the couple, I walked backward, away from everyone else. I tried to glance over my shoulder to assess the damage, but I couldn't see anything. The fabric was obviously split, though. I wrenched my arm behind me and felt down the fabric. The zipper was still zipped, but the material next to it was gaping.

"Oh, holy crap." If it'd happened to anyone else, I'd be there to fix it. Only now *I* was the girl in the dress, and my sewing kit was buried somewhere in the bridal room, and I needed to make sure the reception was good to go.

I knew being in a wedding was a bad idea. Obviously I needed to stay *behind* the scenes from now on. No more walking down the aisle or standing up front. If only I'd known that before I'd squeezed myself into the dress.

I sent a few frantic texts to Jillian and the rest of my team. Jillian assured me everything was running smoothly in the tents, and that I had a few minutes until everyone started missing me. I was just about to head to the bridal room when Brendan called my name.

"Hey," he said as he moved closer. "What's wrong?"

"I'm having a dress emergency, and I need to get back out there." I spun to show him my current I'm-up-to-my-eyeballs situation. I waited for him to gasp or freak out, but then I realized he was a guy. What I didn't expect was for him to reach his hand into the gap and run his fingers across my bare skin. My pulse quickened and my mouth went dry.

"I don't see the problem," Brendan said, and his fingers dipped lower.

I glanced over my shoulder at him, my skin humming from his touch. The half smile on his face made it even harder to focus on the task at hand. "It might be convenient for *you*, but I'd rather not show the rest of the wedding party quite so much skin."

"What do you need?"

I thought of what I'd do if another bridesmaid were sporting the ripped-open dress. I had a ton of safety pins, but I didn't think

Valentina was going for the Goth look. But stitching it all would take too long—longer than I had. I'd just change back into the dress I brought for the wedding, but I worried Valentina would want more pictures, and I'd survived this long being a temporary bridesmaid. Which left one quick fix that might work. "I'm going to have to superglue myself into the dress—actually, you need to superglue me in. You think you can do that?"

"Sure." Brendan followed me to get my wedding kit and I handed over the superglue. Within a few minutes I was glued inside the dress—pretty sure some of the fabric was glued to my skin, too, but I'd worry about that later.

My phone suddenly erupted with texts—Valentina was looking for me, waiting because she needed me at the table so they could start the food.

"Thanks, babe," I said to Brendan, giving him a quick kiss on the cheek. "I don't know what I would do without you."

"Just keep that in mind for me, will you?"

Something about the way he said it made me pause and study him. "And why would I need to do that?"

"You'll see," he said, mischief flickering in his eyes. "Now go." He smacked me on the butt. "I'll catch up with you when it's all said and done."

Oh sure, like I could just go and not obsess about his cryptic words. But since I really couldn't spare any more time away from the reception, I charged out of the room, praying there'd be no more malfunctions.

Chapter Twenty-Eight

Fireworks lit the sky over the small lake on the grounds, their colorful bursts bright against the dark sky and reflecting on the water. A beautiful end to a beautiful reception. All the guests were turned toward the show, their smiling faces tipped up. The stress of the event leaked out of me with a long exhale, but despite being exhausted, a sense of accomplishment lifted me.

I did it. Pulled off an extravagant wedding, despite being a last-minute bridesmaid who's glued into her dress.

There'd even been a moment when the older Mrs. Maddox got mad at the photographer for bossing her around. She'd whacked him with her purse and everything.

Ah, grandmas, the ticking time bombs of weddings. But now she was happy, eating her cake and watching the show, too, her son next to her—it was nice to see such a big man so wrapped up in keeping his mother, wife, and daughter happy. Not always an easy combination, especially when a wedding was involved.

Footsteps caught my attention. A glance over my shoulder told me it was Brendan. He wrapped his arms around me, pulling my back to his chest, and rested his chin on my shoulder.

"It's beautiful, isn't it?" I asked.

Brendan pressed his lips against my neck and muttered, "Mm-hmm," the vibration of his deep voice against my skin sending a spike of heat through me. For a few moments, we watched the fireworks, and all seemed right in the world.

Then Brendan whispered my name, his breath against my ear sending a pleasant shiver down my spine. He ran his hands down my sides, gripped my hips, and turned me to face him. His eyebrows were drawn low and his mouth was set in a determined line.

He rubbed his fingers across his brow and then blew out a shaky breath. "I didn't expect to be so nervous." He glanced at the fireworks now exploding faster and faster, on their way to the big finale. "I'm glad I waited till right now, though."

Nervous? His nerves must be transferring to me, because my stomach was currently twisting itself into a tight ball.

Brendan cleared his throat. "When I first came to Vegas, I thought it'd be fun to see you again. I didn't expect you to be so beautiful, or to have as much fun as I did with you. I thought living with you would be an adventure…" He dragged a knuckle down my jawline, and all I could do was blink, blink, blink, trying to piece together where he was going with this. "I didn't expect to fall in love with you so fast.

"Dakota Jane Halifax"—Brendan dropped to a knee and held out his hand, revealing a roll of Life Savers—"I figured I'd let you pick the color and size it yourself this time."

My heart beat like it meant to leap out of my chest. Tears sprang to my eyes. "Are you saying…?"

Brendan took my hand. "Will you marry me?"

A lump lodged in my throat. I thought about what it'd be like to be Brendan West's wife, and how I wanted that more than anything. But then I thought about standing in a wedding dress, waiting for him to come…

And waiting.

And waiting.

Panic crept in, squeezing and digging up all my insecurities. I scratched at my chest, trying to get it to stop.

Brendan ran his thumb over my knuckles. "Do I need to remind you that this is really just a formality? You already said yes when you were nine, and I'm totally holding you to it." The teasing smile curving his lips faded. "D.J.?"

I tugged on the neckline of my dress, finding words impossible to get out for a couple of seconds. "I love you, and I want to, I do, but… After what happened last time, I don't know if I can."

I'd dealt with my anger and feeling out of control, but this was different. Everything inside me now tied standing in a wedding dress to crushing pain. "I guess if we maybe do one of those drive-through chapels. That way there's no escape and I'm not worried about you standing me up. Or like the courthouse, even." I pressed my lips together and gave a sharp nod. "Yeah, I could do that."

"Drive-through wedding? Courthouse? You don't really want that." His grip on my hand tightened. "Just like you never wanted to get married as part of a cruise. I know, because I know you. You want the big wedding, and you're getting it. And I'm not going to stand you up. I don't need time. I'm surer about this than anything I've ever been in my life. Marry me, D.J. Just say yes."

I stared at him, taking in his dirty-blond hair, his dark eyes, the slope of his nose, and the twist of his lips. I'd never loved anything so much in my life. Tears filled my eyes, blurring the world around us. I glanced from the Life Savers in my hand back to him. I wrapped my hand around the roll of candy and nodded. "Yes."

A slow smile spread across his face, and then he reached into his pocket and pulled out a glittering ring that was definitely not made of candy.

Chapter Twenty-Nine

GET READY TO WED by Dakota Halifax
A Little Advice for the Fellas

Today I'm breaking away from the usual and giving out advice to the grooms. Ladies, take this column to your significant other and tell him that if he cares about you, he'll read it. Guys, your girl just handed this to you. I just said that if you care, you'll read it. She's still staring at you, right? Yeah, you have no choice now. You might as well read on. Trust me, it's for the best. Really.

Don't take this the wrong way. I do want you to have a good time at your wedding. But are you the one sitting in my office week after week? Not usually, although some of you are, and more power to you. You might get more say than the others. I hate to break it to you, but the day is still mostly about the bride. As for the *Dumb and Dumber* suits that most of you would like to wear on your wedding day? Yes, they're hilarious. No, you can't wear them. Fine, if you think you can convince your fiancée, go ahead and ask. She said no, didn't she? Why don't you think of other things that you'd like at your wedding—things important to you that won't embarrass her when she goes to show off the wedding pictures to her friends. There's almost always a way to fit your personality into the wedding, too. A good wedding planner can help. (I'm not saying it has to be me, but I totally could find a way to bring it together. Just throwing it out there.)

Here's what else you need to do to make sure your wedding is the best possible experience for you and your bride. Be where you're supposed to be when you're supposed to be there, put your best face forward for pictures, and make sure your best man brings the rings. If your best man's memory is a little unreliable, enlist the help of your mom—just do whatever it takes to make sure those rings arrive. They're kind of a big part of the ceremony, and if you forget, your bride-to-be might think you did it on purpose.

Speaking of your fiancée, I know things are different. Most likely she's a little crazier and a lot more stressed out than you remember, but give her a break. She's been dreaming of this day all her life and she wants it to be perfect. She overlooks some of your bad habits, doesn't she? You love her, right? Good. Then cut her a little slack, let her know you appreciate her hard work, and get ready for a happy bride. When it's all said and done, she'll go back to her normal self and you'll be the lucky guy who snagged her.

Now that wasn't so hard, was it?

*Q*pushed my copy of the *Las Vegas Beacon* to the far corner of my desk, thinking I might check out the rest of the articles later. As for my column, I'd learned my lesson. Instead of writing a big bragging article about how I was going to get married—take two—I'd stuck with solid wedding advice. Not for Brendan, because if I were going to give him advice, it'd be for him to actually tell me what he wanted. Instead he told me to do whatever I wanted, from colors to food to dresses. Even the music. When one of my brides pushed her wedding date at the Sunset Gardens back a year—she found out she was pregnant and wanted at least six months after having the baby to make sure she fit into her wedding dress—I asked Brendan if he wanted the spot. It was my favorite place, and it was hard to book. He'd said he was ready, but I guess I was testing the waters to see how ready he actually was.

He'd said, "Hell yeah! Let's do it—the sooner, the better."

Which, in addition to making my heart pitter-patter, left me to plan a wedding in just over three months. Hey, if anyone could do it, I could. And I had. The caterer was set—Jillian, of course—and the venue, along with flowers, cake, and the music were all triple-checked and set to go.

On to the next item on my to-do list…

I scrolled to the number on my cell phone, my finger hovering over the call button as I stared at the number. I'd wanted to reach out for a while, but it was such a hard step to take. One I thought I shouldn't have to make. But I also knew that if I waited for my mom, I might wait forever. So I hit the button and listened to it ring, readying myself to leave a message.

"Dakota?"

Mom's real-life voice was unexpected enough that it took me a moment to form a response. "Hi, Mom. How are you?"

"I'm good. I like San Diego."

Her happiness sounded forced, and I wondered if she was ready to move on already.

"I was just calling to say…" I reached for my water bottle and took a sip. With how harsh she could be, I almost didn't want to tell her. I'd spent so long being happy about it, and I didn't want her telling me I was stupid to be trying again. Brendan was the one who kept insisting I'd regret it if I didn't at least ask. "I'm getting married, Mom. To Brendan. This weekend. And if you want…" Suddenly speaking in full sentences was such a challenge. "We're doing a big ceremony and a reception. And I know it's late notice, but I'd like you to be there. If you want to be. But if you can't get away, I completely understand."

I braced myself for disappointment—Brendan was already on high alert, ready to come to my office and take me out if this didn't go well.

"If you'll have me, I'd be honored," Mom said. "Dakota, you have to know that there's not a day that goes by that I haven't regretted the way we left things. I'm working on it, okay?"

The wall I'd put up around my heart to prepare for this conversation cracked, letting a soothing balm of relief in to take its place. I knew we'd never be completely okay, but I thought we might find a different kind of relationship now that both of our expectations had changed. She was my mom after all, and I'd miss her if she wasn't at my wedding. We made small talk for a little while, catching up on the months we'd missed. Apparently Frank had visited her there a few times, and they were talking again. Weird, but that was my mom and relationships.

She swore she'd be civil to Dad, too. Having them in the same room could very well be a disaster, but that often happened at weddings with split families, and I knew how to keep them separate if needed.

By the time I hung up, I felt pretty good about things. I checked off a few more last-minute items and smiled down at my list of todos, so many lines showing how much I'd done. My office door opened as I was closing down my computer for the day.

I blinked, thinking I must be seeing things. "Grant?"

He held up the same issue of the *Beacon* I'd been looking through earlier. "So it's true, then?"

"I'm sorry, but no girl actually wants *Dumb and Dumber* tuxes at her wedding."

"Not your column, Dakota. Phoebe's."

It'd been a while since I'd been in one of her columns, and since avoiding them helped keep my temper and ragey feelings toward her in check, I'd stopped reading them—it'd been good for me to stop caring what it said, and Jillian knew what to tell me and what to filter.

I sighed. "Do I want to know? Because I've been really working on my chi and—"

"The wedding of our very own Dakota Halifax and her fiancé, Brendan West, is scheduled for this weekend. I know we're all asking the same thing. Will this wedding stick? My guy told me the odds are 3 to 2. I haven't decided which side of the line I'm betting on."

I curled my hands around the arms of my office chair, squeezing as tightly as I could. "See, that's why I don't read it anymore. If you want to know the odds, you came to the wrong place."

"I mean the getting-married-this-weekend part."

It'd been ten months since Grant had jilted me at the altar. When it'd first happened, I never thought I'd be attempting to get married again so soon. But here we were, one failed romantic relationship and an uneasy friendship later. "I told you that he and I had gotten engaged." Funny enough, at a mutual acquaintance's wedding, one that I'd coordinated and he'd managed to attend. He'd been there with Amy, and while it was slightly awkward at first, enough time had passed for us to have a decent conversation—though Amy had clung to his arm pretty hard.

"No, your giant ring told me," he said, glancing at it now. After I'd told Brendan my ex had noticed the diamond before I'd even had a chance to break the news, he'd joked that it was worth every penny.

"Right. Well, the answer to your question is yes. Brendan and I are getting married this weekend."

"Let me guess. Sunset Gardens?"

Talking about wedding plans with Grant made all my nerve endings stand on end. All while I'd planned, I told myself that this wedding was happening, but I suppose a tiny part of me was preparing for if it didn't. Having to look at the guy who did stand me up was making that part double in size, and it was ugly with snarly teeth. I was going to need to hit the boxing gym tonight, I could feel it.

I tried to shake that off and focus on his question, wondering why he wanted to know. He'd seemed to have moved on with the mother of his son, and I was surprised at how glad I was to see him happy. So we were cool now. But if he was looking for an invite, he'd be looking forever. There was moving on, and then there was madness. "Yes, Sunset Gardens. An opening came up."

Grant glanced at the floor and then back up at me. "I should've known. You always talked about that place. It hit me after, you know... How I should've let you plan it your way. How selfish I'd been to even suggest that cruise, like another country would settle my cold feet."

"Grant, we've been over this already. Me in the paper. You in the paper. The whole city knows about it. Now if you'll excuse me..." I pushed out my chair. "I've got to close down the office."

"Dakota." Grant reached across for me, then seemed to think better of it and pulled back his hand. "Do you still hate me for standing you up?"

"I never hated you. Which was totally annoying." After the dust settled and I'd had time to reflect, I realized that everything between Grant and me had led me to Brendan, and for that, I was grateful, even though a less-painful path would've been nice.

"When I read you were getting married, it got me thinking, and I just... Amy and I already had a rough go our first time around. We're working on a relationship while trying to do what's best for our son. I want to do it right this time, but it scares me still. How'd you get over it?"

I thought of Brendan. While he didn't provide much input on what he wanted at our wedding, he did constantly ask me how it was going. When I talked nonstop about colors like champagne, blush, and merlot, he'd listen, even though he didn't care which tablecloths or placeholders or flowers I chose. And every morning, he'd hand me my coffee made up the way I liked, wrap his arms around me, and whisper in my ear how many days we had left until we were married.

"Not sure 'over it' is the right phrase. It's more like...hope. And faith."

"Well...congrats. And good luck. With everything." Grant held out his hand again, but this time for a handshake.

I took it, though it was an oddly formal gesture for everything we'd been through. "Good luck to you, too."

Grant and I stared at each other for a weird beat. Then he flashed me a smile and walked out, looking lighter than when he'd come in.

As the door closed behind him, it felt like a fresh new start was stretched out in front of me, shiny and full of endless happy possibilities.

Chapter Thirty

My veil fluttered in the breeze. I had on a strapless ivory dress with lace and ruffles and a merlot-colored sash, complete with matching heels that no one could see but I knew were there. Jillian was by my side dressed in a color the bridal shop referred to as blush, her sash the same color as mine—they really pulled the whole look I was going for together. The temperature was in the midseventies, perfect really. With my nerves and all the sweating they caused, I was glad for the breeze. The ceremony was inside, because March was a tricky month weather-wise, but I was outside because…well, because I was freaking the hell out.

"Take a deep breath," Jillian said, using the paper fan she'd made to blow more air onto my face. "Everything is going to be okay."

"Why did I let Brendan talk me into doing this? I wanted the wedding to be small. Like 'courtroom where no one knew us' small. I didn't want to deal with the guests."

"You say that, but you know you loved putting it all together." Jillian handed me a water bottle—I'd avoided it so I wouldn't need the bathroom five minutes in, but now that I couldn't breathe, needing to pee seemed like the least of my problems. "You don't want me to refer to you as the most difficult bride I've ever had to work with, do you?"

I shot her a dirty look. "I'm not difficult. Paranoid, sure, and for good reason, but not difficult." I took a healthy gulp of water, wishing it did a better job of calming me down.

"Think about it rationally. Brendan loves you. He's loved you since you were both little kids. It's, like, the most romantic story ever. Far better than what's his bucket." Jillian patted my shoulder. "There's no way he'd stand you up."

I sucked in a deep breath and let it out. "You're right. Of course he wouldn't do that to me." Still, I'd reluctantly left him at home that morning, wishing I could've cuffed him to me. I'd done the *no seeing each other all made up before the ceremony* thing, and it had done nothing for my luck.

Everything was different this time, yet I couldn't stop thinking of last time, despite the closure I'd had with Grant. Despite that my mom was here and she and my dad had been semi-civil to each other. Dad was all set to walk me down the aisle, too, and he'd given me a pep talk last night.

I hadn't even asked *the* question, though, mostly because I was scared to be wrong again. But it was like it wanted to be let out, and every time I'd looked at Jillian all morning I'd almost asked it. *Can you believe I'm getting married?*

Maybe I'd utter it in my head once Brendan and I were in the front of the room, the preacher about to pronounce us husband and wife—that "if anyone objects" part had been removed. I had enough things giving me heart palpitations already.

"Ready to go in?" Jillian asked.

I started toward the door, but the chime of her text stopped me. She frowned at her phone. Then she sent a text. Got one. She turned away and called someone, but whoever it was didn't appear to answer, because she slowly lowered the phone without saying anything. When she glanced at me, she shot me the fakest smile ever, a hint of worry flashing behind her eyes.

"What's going on?" I asked.

"Nothing."

I crossed my arms and squared off in front of her. "Jillian. I know when something's off at a wedding. It's what I've built my entire career on."

"Brendan's just…not…quite…here. Yet! But he will be! Any minute, so don't you worry!"

Of course my body did the opposite of what she told it to do, worry rising up, making my palms sweat and my throat go dry. It didn't help that she'd been overly enthusiastic about her reassurances, all exclamations. Rookie mistake, really. "Not here? Did you call him?"

The way she bit her lip told me all I needed to know. That was the call she'd made, and he hadn't answered.

My breaths came faster and faster, but no air filled my lungs. Dizziness set in; my knees wobbled. "This is feeling a little too déjà vu for me. You add a boatload of people dressed in obnoxious Hawaiian print staring at me, and I'm back in Jamaica."

"Yeah, but this is different," Jillian said. "Brendan's excited about the wedding, and I know he wouldn't hurt you. Plus, he's seen me wield a knife."

I pushed my hands into my hair, beyond caring if I messed it up. Tears blurred my eyes. The world around me spun.

"Give me just one sec." Jillian stepped off to the side, pulled out my cell—the one she'd confiscated so I didn't work my entire wedding—and dialed a number. Brendan's, no doubt. She hung up without speaking.

I stepped just through the open door and peeked inside the chapel. People filled the benches, all waiting for a ceremony. Phoebe was even in the back—I hadn't invited her, but apparently she was George from Classifieds' plus one. She was going to have a field day, and I wasn't sure if I should cry or start throwing stuff. At least Wild Bill was also here, because I had a feeling I might need him to do some skull crushing or anger managing—I wasn't sure which yet. Possibly both.

I turned to Jillian. "What time is it?"

"Traffic was so bad this morning, don't you think?"

I held out my hand for my phone and Jillian hesitantly dropped it into my hand. The display told me that we had five minutes until the ceremony was scheduled to start.

And my groom wasn't here and wasn't answering the phone. "Not again," I muttered, the words leaking out of me and taking all my energy. I sagged against the building. The seriousness of the situation was setting in; my doubts were turning to cold, hard facts. He wasn't here. Not answering his phone. Might not be coming at all. My internal organs shriveled up and started dying slow and painful deaths. Darkness crowded in, pushing out every happy emotion I'd ever had.

"Why don't we go back inside and wait in the air-conditioned room?" Jillian tugged me toward the door, but I pulled free.

If I were on the other side of me, I'd be thinking of a way to take things down from Code Fuchsia. Since I wasn't on the other side, though, I was about to see what was past that level. Rage Red? Apocalyptic Black?

Whatever color code I was, if Brendan didn't show up in five minutes, I was running away. I'd never write another column again. Wedding planning was out, too. There was no hope after this, just crushing depression that threatened to bury me deeper each day. Maybe I'd join the circus. Be the woman who made men commit and bolt last minute. People would pay to see that, right?

A guy in a tux came around the front of the building. Not my guy. Nope, his groomsman, Adam, who worked in the control room of the Aces Casino. He'd shown up. That sure was nice of him. He motioned Jillian over. She looked at me and I knew she was afraid to leave me alone.

If she told me not to worry one more time, I might just turn bridezilla on her. Difficult would look like a walk in the park. She hurried over to Adam. As they spoke, she swung her arms around, and I couldn't tell if it was angry or upset or clueless or breaking awful, horrible news.

My breaths tripped over each other, so fast my head started to spin. Which was no good. If I needed to flee, I needed to drive.

Then Jillian and Adam disappeared around the front of the church, and I wondered if they'd decided to get out while the getting was good.

An eternity later—or maybe a couple of minutes, it's hard to keep track of time when the ground is opening under you and you're dying inside, all while trying to hold back tears because waterproof mascara is a lie—Adam came back with Jillian. Her hands were out, the way one would approach a ravenous tiger, and alarm screeched through my veins. "Now, I want you to remain calm," she said.

"Calm?" My voice was so high I could hardly believe it was mine. "I'm getting stood up at the altar for the second time in less than a year and you want me to remain *calm*?"

"You're not getting stood up," Adam said. "Brendan was in a car accident."

I jerked my head toward him, my heart dropping like a lead weight in my gut. "What? Is he okay?" Talk about whiplash emotions. From crushed to being worried he was about to tell me something that'd crush me even worse than being stood up again.

Adam put his hand on my shoulder. "It was a minor accident— a fender bender, really. He's fine, but the cops arrived on the scene and wouldn't let him go until the paramedics checked him out. The passenger side got crunched, and his cell with it, so that's why he didn't call."

Jillian smiled, and I didn't get how she could right now. Was she not listening? And having the passenger side being smashed in didn't sound like a freaking fender bender. "Dakota, Brendan just got here. One of the officers gave him a ride, and he's here, and he wants to get married still."

All the air whooshed out of my lungs and I plunked down on the ground, too relieved to care if my dress got dirty. Brendan was okay. Brendan wanted to get married.

As if my brain needed to hear it again, I inwardly repeated it to myself over and over. *He's okay, he's okay, he's okay.*

He wants *to get married.*

Jillian squatted to be on my level. "He was going to come over and talk to you—I've never seen him so anxious. But I figure you guys have had enough bad luck, and letting him see you after surviving his morning seemed like tempting fate. So I told him to get into place like we practiced yesterday."

Blinking at the forming tears wasn't holding them back, so I waved my hand in front of my eyes. It wasn't exactly helping, either. Jillian handed me the tissues she'd tucked into her sash— the way I'd shown her to.

I dabbed at my eyes and inhaled a couple of heaving breaths.

Adam jabbed a finger over his shoulder. "I'm going to go inside and get into place. But I swore to Brendan I'd personally check you were okay, and that you understood. So..." He leaned in, his eyebrows all scrunched up. "Are you? Okay?"

I nodded, though I wasn't quite sure. Jillian helped me to my feet and brushed off my dress. Adam went around the front and Jillian ushered me in the back door. We lined up at the back corner as we'd rehearsed, and I managed to get my tears under control.

Jillian went to take a step, but I reached out and grabbed her arm. "Wait," I whispered, and she spun around. "Can you believe I'm getting married today?"

A smile curved her lips, and she threw her arms around me in a display of girliness that wasn't usually her style. "Yes, yes you are."

Dad stepped into place, extending his elbow to me. I hooked onto it and then leaned in and kissed his cheek. Mom and I were still working things out, but this guy had been there for me through everything, and the fact that he was here to give me away made gratitude warm me from the inside out. More tears tried to form and I quickly blinked them away. Dad covered my hand on his arm with his free one and gave it a quick squeeze.

The "Wedding March" started up, and although I'd instructed brides on what to do hundreds of times, I almost forgot what I was supposed to do. For one, my view was skewed. I felt like I was in the wrong place, and why was the aisle so damn long?

But then I saw Brendan at the front. Standing there, waiting for me. More tears formed, and I knew it'd be a miracle if I made it through the ceremony without my mascara relocating to my cheeks.

Dad kept me steady as we made our way down the aisle. Just before he handed me off to Brendan, he leaned in and whispered, "I'm proud of you, girl. Keep your eye on the prize and you'll be fine."

Brendan was definitely a nice-looking prize. There was a faint scratch on the side of his face, but other than that, there were no signs of injury. The tux made him look all debonair and yummy, and the grin he shot me made my heart soar.

"Are you okay?" I whispered.

He nodded. "And getting better by the second."

I flung my arms around him and smashed my lips to his. Because he was okay, and he was here, and I loved him so much I couldn't wait.

The preacher cleared his throat. "I'm not quite to that part yet. Why don't you guys get up here and I'll get you married?"

Brendan took my hand, lacing my fingers with his, and we made the final steps to the altar together. The preacher raised his voice and addressed the crowd. "We are gathered here today for the union of Brendan West and Dakota Halifax…"

I tried to pay attention as he continued to talk, but all I could focus on was Brendan's face and the feel of my hand in his. I couldn't think clearly until after he grinned at me and said, "I do." I, of course, did too.

And then the preacher said those magical words. "You may now kiss your bride."

Brendan wrapped his arm around me, holding me steady as he lowered his mouth to mine. We'd shared a lot of kisses, and while this wasn't our raciest—being in a chapel and all—it was different. Deeper. A celebration of our lives, officially merged together. I barely registered the people cheering for us.

"So." Brendan kept me tight against him, his eyes peering into mine. "What do you think, Mrs. Dakota Jane West?"

I smiled and slipped my hands into the jacket of his tux, hugging him tight. "I think I totally got married today."

Epilogue

GET READY TO WED by Dakota Halifax
Happily Ever After the Ceremony

I was scared to say anything about it before—you all know what a disaster my first attempt down the aisle turned out to be. But it's official. I'm a married woman. I'd like to thank my vendors, family, friends, and everyone else who made it all possible. I had my dream wedding, and it was the happiest day of my life. That said, it wasn't the wedding itself (even though it did rock) that made me so happy. It's been the after that has made it all worth it. I know I'm still reeling from that newlywed high, so you'll have to forgive me for going on and on, but my husband is amazing. It just keeps getting better and better. I have to pinch myself constantly to make sure that I'm not dreaming. I know there's going to be ups and downs. In fact, the very first day I met my husband he threw a stick at me and I punched him in the face. Of course, we were in second grade, and I'd like to think I've come a long way since then. Now we disagree on more grown-up things such as control of the remote, who's the better driver, and how to decorate our living room.

What I'm trying to say is this: Brides, you don't have to sweat the small stuff, because the reward of marrying the right guy is twenty times better than the perfect ceremony. If you're a control-freak perfectionist like me, then you still want it to go perfectly, despite knowing that. I understand, which is why I spend my days trying to make that happen for every bride. But trust me, when you think back, the mishaps will only make the memories more vivid. Having your family and friends there to watch you commit yourself to someone you love is much more important than any minor fiasco.

So my advice today is for both before and after the ceremony. Take some time to relax and enjoy each other. I had more fun on my honeymoon than I did the entire time at my wedding because it was completely stress-free. Put aside your ginormous to-do list, slow down, and be happy you found someone you love. I hope your weddings all go as planned, but more than that, I wish you the best of luck on your happily ever after.

Acknowledgments

Where to even start? This book has been quite the journey, and I was pretty sure it was trying to kill me there for a bit. Luckily, both it and I survived. I'd like to thank Amanda Price for being my enforcer when I needed help focusing, for helping me play "this line or that one" as I wrote, and for always being there when I need to chat or vent, as well as making me laugh. Best friend EVER! Big thanks to my editor, Stacy Abrams, for her mad editing skills. When I turned this book in, I told her I knew something was missing, and thank goodness she pinpointed what it was and helped make it so much better! Every book I'm so grateful to her, Alycia Tornetta, Liz Pelletier, and all of the people at Entangled Publishing for giving my books, and me, a home. I love writing for you all!

Thanks to Candace Havens for her input and enthusiasm for the story, to my publicity team, Katie Clapsadl and Heather Riccio, and to Libby Murphy, for designing the perfect cover. Big shout out to CKM, for all the emails and support. Rachel Harris, Tara Fuller, Melissa West, Lisa Burstein, Cole Gibsen, Rhonda Helms, Christina Lee, Stina Lindenblatt, Wendy Higgins, and Megan Erickson, what would I do without you? I'm so happy I could meet so many of you in person this year — we'll always have Coops, right? LOL. I heart you girls so hard!

My family and friends are always so great at cheering me on through all the writing stages. Thanks to my neighbor, Mare, who has taken my kids so I can write and edit, and to my awesome husband, Michael, who helps pick up the slack when the cleaning and cooking fall by the writing wayside. And to my kids, who get as excited about book releases as I do (probably because it means dinner out with soda and dessert). Thanks to my parents, siblings, and in-laws, who are always checking in on how the books are going. I feel so lucky to do something I love, and to have the people I love get that.

As usual, gotta say hi to my TZWNDU gals, who give me a place to chat, and to the Colorado Indie Authors for all the support and fun lunches. Extra hugs to Anne Eliot for always being there for me and for making me laugh until I cry, whether over the phone or while taking awesome selfies in hipster restaurants. Thanks to the countless bloggers who help me spread the word about my books and are always there when I need a favor. Even better, I now count you as friends, and just have to say you gals rock!

Big thanks to my readers! So many of you have sent me messages and tweets and I appreciate every single one of them and you. Thanks so much!

Looking for more strong heroines and to-die-for heroes?
Try these Entangled Select novels...

DYED AND GONE

by Beth Yarnall

When Dhane, a dynamic celebrity hairstylist, is found dead, Azalea March suspects foul play. Her friend Vivian confesses to the murder and is arrested, but Azalea knows there's no way she could have done it. Vivian's protecting someone. But who? Now Azalea and Alex, the sexy detective from her past, must comb through clues more twisted than a spiral perm. But the truth is stranger than anything found on the Las Vegas Strip, and proving Vivian's innocence turns out to be more difficult than transforming a brunette into a blonde.

SHOT OF RED

by Tracy March

When biotech company heiress Mia Moncure learns her ex-boyfriend, the company's PR Director, has died in a suspicious accident in Switzerland, Mia suspects murder. Determined to reveal a killer, she turns to sexy Gio Lorenzo, Communications Director for her mother, a high-ranking senator—and the recent one-night stand Mia has been desperate to escape. While negotiating their rocky relationship, they race to uncover a deadly scheme that could ruin her family's reputation. But millions of people are being vaccinated, and there's more than her family's legacy at stake.

DECONSTRUCTING LILA

by Shannon Leigh

Lila Gentry returns to her small Texas hometown to restore a famous whorehouse where her great-great grandmother was a madam in the 1880s. On her agenda is winning back Jake, the one that got away. But how do you rope a man who doesn't want to be wrangled? Jake lives by one creed: Keep it simple. His ex showing up in town, and rehashing old feelings complicates his life and makes him think about things he'd rather forget. Working together stirs up old feelings, but it will take some sweet-talking and finesse to bring these two together.

A DUKE'S WICKED KISS

by Kathleen Bittner Roth

The Duke of Ravenswood, secret head of the British Foreign Service, has no time for relationships. Miss Suri Thurston knows the pain of abandonment. When Suri appears in Delhi, the Duke's resolve is tested as he finds his heart forever bound to her by the one haunting kiss they shared once upon a time. With Suri's vengeful Indian family looking for her death, and insurgents intent on mutiny tearing their world apart, can their love rise above the scandal of the marriage they both desperately want?

HONOR RECLAIMED

by Tonya Burrows

An interview with a runaway Afghani child bride lands photojournalist Phoebe Leighton in the middle of an arms deal. Forming an unlikely alliance with a ragtag team of mercenaries, she meets Seth Harlan, a former Marine sniper with PTSD. He ignites passions within her she thought long dead, but she's hiding a secret that could destroy him. Racing against the clock, Seth, Phoebe, and the rest of HORNET struggle to stop a ruthless warlord bent on power, revenge…and death.

MALICIOUS MISCHIEF

by Marianne Harden

Twenty-four-year-old college dropout Rylie Keyes won't be able to stop the forced sale of her and her grandfather's home, a house that has been in the family for ages unless she keeps her job. But that means figuring out the truth about a senior citizen who was found murdered while in her care. She must align with a circus-bike-wheeling Samoan while juggling the attention of two very hot cops. As she trudges through this new realm of perseverance, she has no idea that she just might win, or lose, a little piece of her heart.